BLADE GUNNER

A <u>LIQUID COOL</u> CYBERPUNK DETECTIVE NOVEL

Book Two

AUSTIN DRAGON

Published by Well-Tailored Books, California

Blade Gunner
(Liquid Cool, Book 2)

978-1-946590-55-8 (paperback)
978-0-9967060-7-0 (ebook)

http://www.austindragon.com

Book cover design by Whendell Souza

Printed in the United States of America

CONTENTS

Introduction

"Men are canine and women are feline." I always remembered that phrase. In my high-tech, low-life world of crime, cases were also canine or feline. The canine ones required so much vigilance, because they were so damn dangerous. The danger was physical, extreme, right in front of you, and in your face—but you didn't only see it. You heard it and felt it—hopefully, not in the form of a laser blast between the eyes.

Feline cases were just as dangerous—deceptively so, even at their most calm and cerebral. Quiet one moment, and then the violence came at you in a flash. Then all was quiet again, like a wily cat sitting on a ledge, always watching you with one eye. Cuddly and soft, but razor-sharp claws right beneath that fluffy fur.

I was planning to present my next case of note—a feline case—to show off my suave intellectual skills, since so many people think private street detectives are all a bunch of doofuses. But there was a canine case so outrageous in its violence and frenzy, I don't know how the hell I survived. I did everything I could to avoid the violence, but somehow always found myself in the middle of it, as if I were some kind of cosmic magnet for the stuff.

The case was that of the ***Blade Gunner***.

I had a lot of favorite sayings, like "the grime and crime of Metropolis," but that case gave me another: "Sometimes, I don't know which is crazier—the criminal—or the client."

PART ONE

Space Girl

CHAPTER 1

Sarah C

Earth.

The universally recognized image of the planet—big, blue, and pristine—took up the entire digital screen of the space station's interior wall. An orange number "10" appeared in the center and silently counted down—finally 3, 2, 1. The screen disappeared and revealed the true view of the planet below through the massive view port—an Earth covered with colossal storm clouds, and encircled by millions of satellites in every shape and size. It was an orbiting, man-made, metallic sea of space junk.

The proceedings began again as the parties re-entered the cavernous courtroom. The Five Judges, each in flowing white robes with red, upturned, pointed collars, and red cuffs from the wrist to the forearm, looked on from their hoverbenches, hanging several feet from the floor. The twenty-something female defendant, Sarah C, was floated in effortlessly, in the weightless environment. She wore a simple white outfit, her wrists handcuffed in front of her, each arm held by one of two white-uniformed women with white police hats, all three of them standing on a hoverplatform. Three attorneys in dark suits flew in on another hoverplatform, a few feet off the ground, facing the Judges.

The bailiff's computer voice sounded over the system. "Case Number 102684 is back in session."

The Lead Judge in the center, the only one wearing a red judicial cap, stared at the defendant for a moment. Sarah C was smart enough to remove the smirk from her face, but a smirk briefly flashed on the female Lead Judge's face before she spoke.

"The Chamber has completed its deliberation, and you, Defendant 102684, have been found guilty of all charges. However, mere moments ago, a plea agreement was agreed upon, and entered into the official record, avoiding the prescribed sentence of execution by summary spacing. You will, instead, as part of the plea agreement, be sentenced to permanent exile. You will be taken from our paradise here up above, and sent to live your full and final days on the rock below, known as planet Earth.

"Additionally, the Chamber was informed that as part of your plea agreement, your sentence would be carried out a year from the final adjournment of today's proceedings, which this court sees for the ruse that it is. Undoubtedly, time to allow your cunning attorneys to find a way to circumvent your exile, as deftly as they circumvented your scheduled death sentence.

"That is the message from this scandalous case. For a blood member of a Founder, laws and consequences are mere annoyances to be defied after the fact—even high crimes against Utopia itself. This court, however, rejects that notion with all the contempt we can summon from the pits of our souls. The Chamber has no authority to change the commuted sentence, but it does retain the authority to decide when a sentence begins. Your family is not the only ones with power here above. The Chamber, hereby, unilaterally revokes the one-year stay, and your sentence will be carried out this very second—now!"

"No!" Sarah C yelled. Her three lawyers, a few feet away, looked at each other, not knowing what to do. They protested as the two police agents flew the struggling defendant out of the Z-gravity room.

The rain was heavy as the spaceship descended from the overcast sky. It didn't land, but hovered a few feet from the ground as an exit door opened.

A woman clad in a hooded, fitted, white coat was pushed out. She picked herself off the ground, and stood with her head down as the spaceship rose, the vapor smoke, and turbulence engulfing her. The ship was soon gone; the vapor cloud quickly dissipated. She finally looked up at the spaceship, craning her neck as far back as it could go. After moments of watching, she looked back down to the ground, then fainted.

Thirty years later.

She was clad in a black slicker, the hood fastened tight around her head. She sat on the monorail with a weary face pressed against the glass, watching, buildings and neon signs flashing by.

There were only two other people in the car—an elderly man sleeping with his head tilted back, snoring loudly, and a sidewalk johnny who seemed to have a permanent smile on his face and, every so often, burst out laughing for no apparent reason.

The monorail stopped, and Sarah C got up from her seat, with a long rectangular box marked "Roses" tucked under one arm. She exited onto the platform. It was sheltered, but the rain was so heavy that she still needed her umbrella, which popped open as she walked to the elevator capsules.

Sarah C stood under her umbrella. She was now wearing dark purple shades as the stranger lit her black cigarette for her. The streets were still dark despite the multitude of flashy neon signs, but Metropolis was always that way—neon and rain all day long.

"Who are the roses for?" the man asked. He had one of those everyman amiable faces, a lit cigarette in the corner of his mouth. He was wrapped in his trench coat slicker, and one hand held a hovercycle helmet.

"Friends," she answered. "Positive that's the building with the Liquid Cool Detective Agency?"

"Yeah. Across the street. Look at that." He pointed her attention to a rider on a flashing yellow hoverbike, descending to the ground. "Nice bike! I say, that's a nice bike!" he yelled out, and got an acknowledging thumbs-up from the rider.

"Hoverbiking for how long?" she asked, glancing to study the style of helmet in his hand.

"All my life. I used to do the craziest things on my hoverbike—but that was decades ago."

"A simpler time," Sarah C said. "A better time."

"A better time?" He grinned. "That's youth playing tricks on your eyes. We were miserable back then, too."

"No, it was better."

The man's mobile phone rang. It had an amusing ringtone. "I'll ignore it."

"Don't do that on my account."

"I can pick up a call in the rain any time. Running into someone like you is a different story."

"How long have you been waiting for me?"

"Waiting for someone like you?" He smiled again. "All my life."

"This detective. What's his name again?"

"Cruz. Not sure about the first name. I should actually know that."

"Yes, Cruz."

"He's quite the celebrity nowadays. Stealing all the high-profile business in the trade. Came out of nowhere. A guy like me has to be inventive. Maybe I can get the cases he doesn't want. Maybe I can get the cases that never quite make it to his front door. A man's gotta eat."

"That's why you're staked out in front of his building. You're a detective, too?"

"Better than him."

"How do you know?"

"I know all. I even have the business references to prove it."

"You haven't asked what kind of case I have."

"What kind of case do you have?"

"It's one of those cases that if I told you, then I'd have to kill you."

The man laughed. "Then Cruz is your detective."

"You give up too easily. You won't steal any cases from him like that."

"Why does your face seem so familiar to me?"

"It's one of those faces. Everyone says that to me."

"I feel we've met before. Maybe a long time ago."

"Where and when?"

"Not sure. I want to say, not of this world, but—"

"But what?"

The man took the cigarette from his mouth to hold it in his free hand. "Follower of the Five Principles. Does that mean anything to you?"

"Sorry, I don't do self-help or self-actualization courses. Never have—and five is definitely not one of my lucky numbers. I'll avoid anything to do with it, all the days of my life on this rock."

"Never mind. It was a proverbial stab in the dark."

"What does it mean? I take it you weren't referring to a self-help book."

"Not important. Only a follower would know."

"No, I'm not 'only a follower.' I was never a follower. I was always a leader." Sarah C's gaze drifted away from his. "I was a queen of the *transcendence*. Now, I'm a nameless wanderer, on a worthless planet, in a nothing city, with its delusions of greatness."

"Is it as bad as all that?"

"It is. You'll never know how bad it is for me, how bad it has been, hanging on by the thinnest thread. How did you find me?"

"What?" he asked.

"How did you find me?"

The man's smile disappeared. "'Find' implies looking. I may be a private detective in what you call a nothing city, but this is the supercity of Metropolis. The largest of them all. You bumped into me."

"Time has been much kinder to you than it has been to me. Why is it like that for men, but not women? If there is a God, maybe that's the proof he's a man." She dropped her cigarette to the ground. "He still has the contract out on me, doesn't he?"

"Who? I take it you're not referring to God."

"The one whose initial comes after S and before U. The initial I can never speak."

The man stared at her.

"After all these many years." She shook her head. "He never stops— but unfortunately, you will."

The man wore fancy wingtip dress shoes. She couldn't take her eyes off them as the rain ran down them, toes pointed to the dark sky. His gun hand was still locked onto the laser pistol lying to his side on the ground. She stepped away from the body, and toward her ultimate destination. However, "across the street," in a supercity with monolith skyscrapers, meant the steps to the building she wanted were by no means close, especially with the increasing downpour. She touched the side of her purple glasses to switch to binocular-view.

A yellow hovertaxi appeared above the entrance and descended. It touched down on the ground, and a passenger exited. Out stepped a finely-dressed woman—faux-fur coat, black mesh veil hat, pleated dress with black nylons, and neon-tipped heeled boots. High class. The woman slowly walked up the stairs, and into the building as Sarah C watched.

Sarah C held her box of *roses* tightly, waiting. She had it planned out in her head: Give the woman time to get to the elevator capsules, and off on her way. Then, she would make it to the *Liquid Cool* offices. There, she—Sarah C—would be this Cruz, the detective's final client of the day.

CHAPTER 2

The Trix Gang

"The 11:05 shuttle for Metropolis departs in five minutes," the automated male voice reverberated through the terminal.

Terrene Station was where movie stars, business moguls, political bosses, and the super-wealthy used to fly out of, in the bygone era when Metropolis was only a megacity, and there was nothing between the two points except empty sky lanes through marshy wetlands. Those former dead zones were now overrun by hundreds of monolith towers and thousands of super-skyscrapers (not as big, but still big). The historic Uptown had become an outer low-town, but it remained one of the largest air and space flight terminals in the world. Inside its connecting gray dome structures was a macrocosm of life not unlike any other city. There were the permanent "residents"—the lookout larrys, hustler harrys, and fast-finger freddies. "No ruffs, and no rough stuff allowed" was the code of these not-so-mean streets, because it was all about the continuous hustle to get the next buck or two. The city streets had their sidewalk johnnies; here, under the dome of Terrene

Station, they were called "domies." Everyone else was passing through, even Terrene Station employees.

Though it would never be raining underneath here, people still walked about with their hooded slickers and wet-wear—everyone with their colored shades. From an outside entrance, a fashionably dressed woman walked in. She wore a white slicker and a big, white, wide hat; her hands were in the jacket pockets. She was closely followed by her gang—six men, a variety of dress styles, hairstyles, heights, and ethnicities.

She stopped, and gestured with a wave of her chin. The henchmen walked past her to the elevators. A few orange-Mohawked domies on hoverskates glided towards her, all of them in black and red slickers. She pulled one hand slightly from her pocket, flashing a gun, without ever looking at them. The domies stopped, did a complete one-eighty, and glided away.

"The 11:05 shuttle for Metropolis has departed. The 11:10 shuttle for Metropolis departs in five minutes," the automated voice called out.

The woman turned, and strolled back out the entrance.

The gang walked in unison, each looking at his own mobile phone display. One of them acknowledged the information they needed with a nod, and soon they were all nodding. They stopped at the gigantic terminal map display hanging above them. A beam flashed on them.

"You are here," the robotic voice called out, showing their location on the map.

One man pointed to the elevators and they all jogged to them as a door opened. People had barely gotten out before the group filed in and the doors closed. The elevator took them up to the next level, where they ran out and across a moving walkway to another set of elevators. Again, they got in as people were getting out. They repeated their actions until they arrived at the world-famous Château.

All the sub-terminals eventually emptied into the Château—the largest of the Terrene Station dome terminals. As soon as they exited the elevator it was obvious they were in the high-class section. It was where the most luxurious, expensive domestic hovershuttles, and all off-world space flights, arrived and departed.

To see the Château was to be in awe. People from all over came to the terminal to stare at its splendor, as it was unlike anything in the world. Floors, walls, and ceilings of speckled golden marble, majestic Greek Ionic columns that stretched to the dome's ceiling, and then there were the statues: modern versions of gods from Ancient Greece and Rome—kings, queens, warriors, and beasts.

One of the gang pointed to the clear observation elevators at the side. From there, they would be able to see the shuttles docked, arriving and departing—the perfect bird's-eye view of the Château. They ran to another bank of elevators opening, filled with exiting travelers, and piled in.

The elevator door was about to close, when a hand popped through. The warning alarm sounded as the door opened. A clean-shaven man wearing a tan fedora and a tan coat slicker stepped in.

"Please do not put hands or feet in the closing door. Safety measures are in place to prevent injury, but measures do fail, and maimings and disfigurements have occurred. Terrene Station is a wholly owned subsidiary of the Metropolis Government, and is not liable for any injuries caused, directly or indirectly, by actions of human error. This elevator capsule is under twenty-four-hour surveillance, and recording at all times," the automated voice said.

The man in the tan fedora didn't turn around to face the door like most people did. He stood facing the gang members.

Tattoo wore blue-glowing black shades on his tattooed face. Ponytail's black ponytail reached past his waist. Werewolf's mouth was closed, but his oversized incisors pushed out the sides of his lip, and he had a strange feral look in his eyes. With dark shades over his eyes, Yellow was dressed in a yellow suit, matching yellow boots, and had black shoulder-length hair. Cool Asian was dressed in a black suit from head to toe, wearing dark shades. Big Black was the tallest and biggest of them all, wearing a gray leather vest over his black top and leather jeans; like Werewolf, he wore no colored shades.

They watched the man, who stared back with no emotion at all. He looked at one, then the next, and so on.

"Observation Deck," the robotic voice called out.

The man in the tan fedora stepped to the side. The gang watched him as they brushed past, exiting the elevator. The man stepped back to his spot, but this time turned around to face them. The gang stopped and stared at him.

"What's your name, fool?" Big Black asked. "So the next time we see you I can knock your head off."

"Cruz," the man answered, as the elevator doors closed.

The gang stood there a few moments, laughing to themselves.

"People are just askin' to get killed," Big Black said.

They moved to the railing for a clear view of the entire Château. There were four mega-statues at four corners of the ground floor of the terminal—Roman centurions in different poses, each with a different weapon: spear, trident, sword, and spiked shield.

Big Black pointed.

There were many entrances, but there was only one main (and historic) entrance. They all agreed, nodding.

Back to the elevator they ran, as the doors opened automatically from motion sensors. They half-expected to see the tan fedora man again, but that was wishful thinking.

Returning to the ground level, they jogged in unison to the historic steps, which were nearly one-story high, but seemed much taller, because they were so wide. Tattoo and Yellow left the others to wait, while they took two steps at a time to the top. They stopped, and instinctively reached into their jackets. Outside the tinted doors, they saw bouncing lights. The doors opened automatically.

A street kid on a neon pogo stick came through, then another, then one after another. They wore different-colored slickers, tops, and shades, but all of them had the same jeans and sideways-turned caps. The street kids were not kids, but punks of some gang, and this sub-terminal was their turf. They bounced down the steps, some sticking out a leg to do it one-leg-style.

The last punk was not skinny at all but a fat slob with silver and gold chains around his neck, along with colored beads, clear plastic shoelaces, and a few different ties. He bounced down using what could only be called a utility pogo-stick to hold his weight; rather than a steady glow, it flashed different colors.

Yellow and Tattoo watched him bounce down, and then they saw it—him. Strapped to the back of the fat punk was a midget with a full mustache and beard. He flashed a gang sign at them. Tattoo flashed a sign back at him, and the midget gave him a thumbs up.

When these last two gang members touched down onto ground level, their pogo sticks stopped, and rose from the ground. They flew to the front of the pack. The other gang members stopped bouncing to go into hovermode too, and flew after their leader in unison.

Tattoo and Yellow laughed as they exchanged words. Both disappeared out the doors for a few moments, then returned. They ran back down the steps to the others waiting.

With a few quick words, they decided. Big Black and Yellow ran off. Werewolf remained where he was, at one side of the majestic steps, and

Ponytail took a position at the opposite side. Tattoo and Cool Asian moved back several yards, until they were both behind one of the terminal Roman centurion mega-statues.

A woman came through the entrance doors with her mobile phone in one hand. In the other hand, she pushed a hoverstroller as she started down the steps. She spoke quietly as she smiled at her baby. Mother and child were in matching gray slickers, with stylish yellow hats underneath.

Coming around the bend at the bottom of the steps, an old man appeared, his back hunched, and his head drooped as he slowly shuffled along. He glanced back to notice a group of noisy Boy Scouts overtaking him, in their waterproof blue uniforms and hats. Amusingly, they all wore brass knuckles on each hand; they weren't going be assaulted by any Terrene Station punks.

Werewolf and Ponytail, at the bottom of the steps on either end, watched, but ignored them. They returned their attention to the main entrance doors at the top.

"Twelve noon shuttle for Metropolis departing in five minutes," the automated voice called out.

He arrived. There were those of the wealthy class who had only to be seen to announce their status. Was it an attitude? The way they moved? Certainly their dress told the tale. Mr. Looper strutted through the entrance, followed by six other men, and started down the steps. They were all dressed in slick trench coats and old-style hats. They wore black derbies, but he had donned an expensive tan homburg.

The Boy Scouts, talking and goofing around amongst themselves, started up the steps. The old man stepped past Werewolf, and started up the steps.

Ponytail moved from his spot, and walked to the center. He smiled. Mr. Looper, even from his distance, immediately noticed the man at the bottom of the steps, and then glanced at the other man at the bottom, near him—Werewolf.

Mr. Looper made a simple waving gesture with his arm. His six men quickly reached into their coats. One of the Boy Scouts walking up the steps noticed, and stopped.

Werewolf and Ponytail reached into their coats. The same Boy Scout, his head turned back, noticed them too—with an expression of sheer panic.

Mr. Looper didn't see it until it was too late. Laser pulses flew through the air from multiple directions. Tattoo and Cool Asian fired from behind the closest mega-statute, Big Black from behind another mega-statute. Five of Looper's men were hit instantly.

Werewolf shot wildly, hitting the sixth bodyguard, and two of the Boy Scouts. The rest of them dived for cover. The woman yelled as she fell back and her hoverbaby carriage continued automatically down the steps.

Mr. Looper pressed down as close to the steps as his body could manage, as the shots from Werewolf continued.

The man in the tan fedora hat appeared—Cruz.

He came from nowhere, flying past on a hoverboard before Tattoo and Cool Asian noticed him. The detective wasn't holding a weapon, but threw something at Werewolf to catch, which he did. The grenade— home security model—exploded in his hands, and sent the gang member into the air, crashing into one mega-statue, splitting it in half. Both pieces and the (dead) gang member crashed back to the ground.

Cruz leaped off his hoverboard to run up the stairs, spun around— now with weapon in hand—and shot at both Tattoo and Cool Asian. He missed them, but hit the statue. Both gang members took cover. Cruz heard the woman scream again, and turned. The hovercarriage with the baby was sliding wildly down the steps under its own power.

"Get that baby carriage!" Cruz yelled to one of the Boy Scouts.

One began to get up, and immediately got shot.

Cruz glanced back to see Ponytail aiming at him. Cruz ignored him, and dived for the baby carriage. One laser shot barely missed him, hitting the carriage, and the mother screamed. Cruz returned fire without looking, and grabbed for the hovercarriage.

Mr. Looper stood, and a retractable laser rifle extended from his hand. He shot at Ponytail once. The gang member was hit by a missile-like round; his body sailed back and away until both he and his yelling were gone. Lasers rounds blasted the weapon out of Looper's hand, exploding it to pieces as he grimaced and fell back to the steps.

Three gang members ran to him for the kill-shot, when suddenly the hoverbaby carriage flew in front of Mr. Looper, blocking the laser blasts as it hit the side of the wall.

Cruz took out Tattoo with a headshot in one move, and with another, ran back down the stairs with the gray-slickered, yellow-hat-wearing baby in the other arm. He sprayed laser rounds at the other two gang members—both Big Black and Cool Asian took cover.

Cruz hopped back on his hoverboard as Yellow appeared from behind the mega-statue with a Terminator-laser machine-gun.

"You're dead!" the Boy Scouts yelled out in unison, as they all fired at him with their concealed mini-laser pistols.

Yellow yelled as he was shot full of holes like Swiss cheese, dropping to the ground on top of his laser machine-gun.

Cool Asian shot Mr. Looper in the arm. Cruz shot him in the head, right between the eyes, shattering his shades, then shot Big Black in the head, too.

Big Black only fell to one knee, and started laughing as he looked up at Cruz.

"I told you when I saw you again, I'd knock your head off."

The cyborg stood up, his eyes shining red as he reached into one pocket and flipped his wrist. The weapon extended to its full menace—a two-foot silver mace. Razor-sharp spikes popped out.

Pop!

The blast from Cruz's pop-gun blew a hole in the cyborg's chest and he slowly, with a shocked expression on his face, fell back like a stiff board of plywood, crashing to the ground with a loud thud. Cruz's weapon retracted from his wrist and into his right jacket sleeve.

Cruz looked at the baby in his arm, who was quietly watching everything with wide-eyed amusement while sucking his thumb. Cruz then looked around the terminal.

The old man had frozen in place on the first step during the shootout. He was literally holding up his head with his hands, as if his neck were made of silly putty, looking all around.

Cruz looked at the Boy Scouts who were all—at least those not shot—frozen in place, still pointing their mini-laser pistols in the direction of the gang member they had shot dead.

Cruz looked at Mr. Looper.

"You all right?"

"I'm alive," he answered, holding his shoulder.

"My baby!" the woman yelled out, snapping out of her shock, She began running down the steps.

"Ma'am," Cruz yelled out. "Stay right where you are! The scene isn't secure."

Cruz whipped around, pulled his omega-gun from his jacket, and pointed.

The woman in white stood with one hand in the pocket of her slicker coat.

Cruz didn't flinch as he aimed. With this gun setting, he didn't have to squeeze the trigger. All he had to do was let go for its automatic firing to commence. The woman in white knew this.

The tell-tale flashing red and blue lights beamed through the dome roof port-windows of the Château.

"This is the Police! Drop your weapons! Put your hands up or be fired upon and killed!"

She looked at Cruz a final time, turned, and ran as fast as she could out of the terminal. The arrival of Metro Police often had that effect on criminals.

"Ga-ga, goo-goo!" the baby burst out, with the biggest grin.

"Yeah, it was fun for me, too," Cruz said. He frowned as his nostrils flared. "You could have waited to take a dump in your pants until *after* I handed you back to your mother." He frowned again. "Nasty!"

PART TWO

A.O.I.

CHAPTER 3

Bionic Betty

Well, if you didn't guess it, I was that guy in the tan fedora, flying around on the hoverboard, exchanging laser gunfire with hoodlums, and saving babies. My name's Cruz, and I was a private detective in the largest supercity in the world—Metropolis.

Don't bother asking my first name, because no one ever called me by that, not even my parents. "I'm Cruz."—a one-time classic hovercar restorer and racer, a former laborer, private investigator extraordinaire. It was the last bit that everyone—friends, enemies, and frenemies alike—cared about. Supposedly, I was famous, which I still didn't know how to take, since I hadn't been in the business for a full year yet.

Here I applied my new trade in the supercity of all supercities. More than fifty million people crammed into a neon jungle of concrete and steel, with hovercars buzzing around in the air, the gray-clad populace crawling around its grimy streets, and the ever-rain falling from the sky. This was certainly not the future any of our ancestors had counted on. This was Metropolis.

Being a detective was a state of being unlike anything else. According to Labor stats, being a police officer was undeniably *less* dangerous than my chosen occupation. Criminals were mean, but the police were meaner. They had to be. Metropolis demanded nothing less, because the criminal class was definitely no joke. The police had to be the most formidable pack animals in the universe. The difference between live criminals and dead criminals was, the latter had the misfortune of running into the police while committing their crimes. But even with a half-million police force, Metropolis was still a supercity of fifty million. The police couldn't be everywhere, even if they'd wanted to be. High-tech surveillance greatly extended their presence, but again, this was still a supercity with plenty of dark streets, corner hangouts, and back alleys. I'd learned that simple fact when I was a police intern in high school. Police *investigate* crime, but they rarely *prevent* it. That's how it's always been. It wasn't personal, it was just the way of life. Another factoid I kept to myself, and far, far away from the wife-to-be, was that being a full-blown criminal punk was only *slightly* more dangerous than being a private civilian detective.

Why did I do it, then? I had been a hovercar restorer of some note, living a simple legacy-baby life, getting ready to marry a great gal in China Doll—despite her homicidal parents (more on that latter). Why upset the apple cart of life? Because I wanted "more." I wasn't like all the other Average Joes and Janes in this rainy, gray world. Wake up, exist, eat, sleep, repeat. I wanted more, because I was more, even if it was the dangerous world of being a private detective. I had to admit, I was good at it. A patchwork of unrelated hard skills, behavioral idiosyncrasies, and anti-authoritarian attitudes made me a natural. Who knew borderline obsessive-compulsive disorder and video game mastery could be so handy? That, incidentally, is how I'd mastered my latest skill: hoverboarding.

The one thing I never did was complain that I was bored. You never knew what was going to happen next. Was your client going to give you an electric bag of cash or shoot you? Was the criminal gang member going to give you some street intel, or shoot you? Yeah, I had a thing about being shot.

People not in-the-know—the masses—thought being a detective was cool. Those in-the-know—people with brains—knew it was a sign of insanity. What else could it be, when you knowingly went into a legal business in which you had to deal with crazy maniacs for a living? If it were illegal, you could at least get somewhat properly compensated before you were killed. Detectives, police, and soldiers—we were all crazy to do what we did, but we loved it anyway. I took pride in being an honest detective, since there were so few of us. It fit nicely with my contrarian personality. Most detectives were corrupt gutter rats, so that meant I had to be the Honest Abe in the bunch, to singlehandedly uplift the profession.

This case was the perfect example. I was hired by a "businessman," a former crook who claimed to have left the crime biz many decades ago, to keep an eye on another "businessman," a former crook who was also supposedly out of the crime biz, but not too long ago. It didn't take me long to figure out that the guy he wanted me to "keep an eye on" had a contract hit on him.

Why did I take the case? Why didn't I walk away? Honestly, because I needed the cash. I had no other cases at the time, despite my supposed fame, and running a detective business was not cheap. Why did I even talk with him to begin with? I liked his hat. That was my latest thing. I was becoming more cultured. I wore my own trademark tan fedora, but didn't know much about hats in general, so I was becoming a genuine hat aficionado.

This guy had worn a stately homburg. At our first meeting, we spent more time talking about classic hats, than we did about the case. We missed the good ol' days when people wore real hats, and not plastic hoodies all the time. Every generation talks about the "good ol' days." Funny, how when we were actually in the "good ol' days" we called it every word in the dictionary of profanity, but "good" and couldn't wait to get to the "future." Then we got to the "future" and reminisced about that past.

From Mr. Looper's standpoint, he was making me one of his pals. You couldn't say "No" to a pal. You had to help your pal. From my standpoint, he was a crook, no matter how legitimate everyone said he was, and how genuinely likable he was, but I'd been in a dry spell for months; all my daily shoe-leather solicitation for new cases was not proving fruitful. I was a new "celebrity" among the detective class, but I hadn't gotten a solid case in over a month. All I was getting was the daily nonsense—people who I knew couldn't pay me. It had been the same when I was in the hovercar restoration business. You don't deal with people who can't pay. So, I'd work the dangerous case because at least I'd get paid. That was the only news my bank account was interested in, not to mention my one spoiled employee.

What the heck! I was on Circuit Circle, which encircled all of Buzz Town and where my Liquid Cool Detective Agency office was located. As I pulled out of the sky traffic and drove my vehicle into the parking garage, I replayed the events of my Château shootout. What did I think I was doing? Flying around on hoverboards, holding babies, shooting multiple bad guys. Just because I had cool weapons didn't mean I was immune from getting shot. What was wrong with me? I wasn't sure where this recent cockiness was coming from. It wasn't as if I had successfully completed any recent cases. It couldn't be my upcoming wedding—that was the opposite of giddy, especially when my mind went to images of my homicidal parents-in-law-to-be. I had gotten back my gun permit, combined with my bona fide detective license (which still had its new car smell), and concealed weapons permit, a while ago, so it couldn't be that. Regardless of the reason, I needed to get rid of this Rambo-like sense of invincibility fast.

Then I realized my "pal" Mr. Looper, that lying, pseudo-criminal client of mine, had sent me into a contract hit by a gang of assassins. I never took bodyguard jobs. You were really rolling the dice with your life on such gigs. But that's exactly what I'd done, or what he'd had me do. "Oh, no, Cruz. I've got my own bodyguards, mean sons-of-bitches with big guns. They protect me fine. I need someone else to scope around the place, someone new; someone no one knows. My extra set of eyes and ears. That's what I'll be paying you for. Easy cash for an hour of easy work." Easy money? Mean bodyguards with big guns? No, not easy! The Boy Scouts took out more bad guys than his useless bodyguards. I was the one who saved my "pal" Mr. Looper—while carrying a baby! At least he was a paying client, and he'd added a big bonus, without my having to suggest it. I also got a nice media write-up for saving that baby. And, I didn't get shot.

I strolled out the elevator on the 100th floor, and headed to my office. My Liquid Cool offices were located in the business tower on Circuit Circle, which some people referred to as the Circuit; others, the Circle. To this day, I had no idea who my secret benefactor was who had given me the office space for free, and springboarded my detective career. It was that single gesture that had started me on my path of being a detective in the first place, even more so than my first unofficial case. Business cards and an official office—Now you were the real deal.

After a few incidents of people shooting at me in my own office (once, when the future wife was present), I turned my office into a secret police-style command post to prevent any future attacks. The entire hallway on this floor, the elevator, the parking lot, and main entrances were monitored by secret video cameras. If any sucker shooter came for me, I was going to see them long before they bolted into my office.

It was becoming a ritual: reaching my office door, staring at the words LIQUID COOL in bright neon blue letters on the wall, I said with a smile, "Mine." I swung the main door open.

There was my secretary, Punch Judy, at her desk, with her silly French punk music playing in the background. She always kept the music low, so I guess I couldn't complain too much. She had short crimson hair, a simulated mole, a dot, above her lips, and pink lipstick. She always wore sleeveless tops inside, as she loved to show off her buff-looking bionic arms. If not for their hard edges, they'd look real, with their flesh-colored paint.

My ex-felon cyborg secretary's name was Punch Judy, but I called her PJ, and she never said "Good morning."

The office was empty, so I could be free with my commentary. "How's my ex-posh French gangster doing today?"

"I was never a gangster," she said, standing from her desk. She was in black leggings and heeled boots. "Posh gangs had class—but that was then. I am chief office manager of Liquid Cool now."

"Are we, now? As long as it still says 'secretary' on your business cards, I don't care what you call yourself. Weren't you 'office manager' just last week?"

"That was months ago."

PJ did rule the reception-waiting area, which she had turned into a hipster, scenester space, with psychedelic posters on the wall around her work area, behind a silver barrier. Behind that, was her glass desk with see-through glass drawers. The source of her French music (now the office music) was a boom box on top of the desk, along with her own mobile computer.

My "kingdom" was the private office with a smaller version of the LIQUID COOL neon blue letters on the wall.

"When do I get paid again?" PJ asked, as I walked to my office.

I stopped. "Why?"

"Why? Because I haven't been paid in three months."

"Neither have I."

"You're a famous detective now. You need to get the paying clients in here."

"You need to keep the non-paying clients off my video-phone."

"People want to talk to you. You're famous."

"I wish I weren't famous, because all we get is lots of clients, but only one in a million can pay. This is a detective agency, not a charity. I'm not working for free."

"You better not. You need to take more criminal clients."

"No. If that becomes my only clientele, soon I won't know who the good guys are, and who the bad guys are." I shook my head. "Life becomes too confusing. I want simple."

"Then government and corporate clients it is."

I frowned. "I want Average Joe and Jane cases."

"Average Joe and Jane can't pay. You need big cases. Big pay days. So, government, corporate, and criminals. That's your clientele. Why do I have to tell you the same thing every day?"

"Why can't I get the cases I want? I'm supposed to be famous."

"Every case you get is not going to be some grandiose, end-of-the-world, remarkable case."

"Even when you speak English, you're speaking French, do you know that?"

"I knew that first case was going to mess up your mind. That should have been your last case, not your first. You judge everything by that case, now."

"No, I don't. I want cases where I don't get shot at, or I don't need to take a super-shower afterward, because I'm dealing with morally or physically nasty people, or where clients won't put me to sleep because they're so boring."

PJ started laughing. "The impossible dream," she began singing.

"Okay, once the French singing starts, I go to my office."

I wasn't going to tell her that I had been paid with a fat wad of money (the common street expression, since we didn't use wads of money anymore, fat or otherwise) in my pocket. I marched into my office. On the desk, as always, were the messages arranged in the order PJ considered priority. In other words, those quickest to pay. The type of client, type of case, and danger level were all irrelevant to her, but very relevant to me. I was the one out there.

"Where's my hoverboard?" I heard her yell.

"It's in the Pony."

She appeared at the door. "What am I going to do with it there? Did you damage it?"

"What does an ex-posh gang member need with a hoverboard?"

"Never you mind. I want my hoverboard undamaged. I still want to know why you needed it. You hate skaters."

"You don't need to be a skater to use a hoverboard."

"Where did you learn to hoverboard, anyway? I thought you were only a hovercar man."

"Everyone knows how to hoverboard. We did that as kids. Once you learn, you never forget. Besides, I'm a man of many talents."

PJ started laughing, and was about to say something snarky, but there was a beep from outside at her desk. Someone was coming.

I heard the front door open, and people talking, but I stood at my desk looking at the messages. When I looked up, all I saw was PJ's back to me, at the entrance to my office. She stepped backwards, and then I saw the woman in front of her.

"Ma'am, you need an appointment," PJ said to her.

The woman was finely dressed in a faux-fur coat, with a black mesh veil hat. She was all in black—dress, nylons, and heeled boots, with white glowing tips. She lifted the veil on her hat.

Her eyes were locked on mine. I quickly tried to size her up, to see if I needed to grab my office weapon from underneath my desk.

"You're him," the woman said, and smiled.

She moved past PJ and walked to me. Her smiling face did not make me feel any better. I still had a knot in my stomach that something was off about this situation.

"You look exactly like your T-shirt."

That comment made me dislike her. Before I had been only indifferent toward her. I'm sure from PJ's viewpoint the woman was on the "good list." How many detectives, serious ones, were being franchised around the city by their secretary and associates with stupid Liquid Cool T-shirts, with my face on them? It cheapened me and cheapened my business. PJ told me it was a legitimate revenue stream for the business, and that I shouldn't complain.

"I need you to help me," the woman said.

Now I was concerned. She had that wide-eyed, "yes-I'm-crazy-and-off-my-meds" look.

"Maybe we can set up a good time for you to come back," I said. "I have to go out to my next appointment."

"Oh, no, Mr. Cruz. That won't do. That won't do at all." Her eyes drifted to my desk, and then back to me. "I look so pale. My limbs are so pale. They wouldn't be so pale if they were real."

"Ma'am, all your limbs are bionic?"

My question was more of a code to PJ to get ready.

The woman laughed. "I'm not that bionic." Her laughing stopped, and her smile disappeared. "You're scared of me now."

"Ma'am, I'm not a cyborg at all," I said.

"That's an offensive term, cyborg. What does that even mean? It's offensive."

"It means cybernetic organism," PJ said.

"I'm a woman, not an organism. Germs are organisms. Why aren't you offended by such a word?"

"I'm not offended," PJ answered.

The woman smiled. "Your boss is scared of me, but not you. That means you're like me."

"You need to leave now," PJ said in a bossy tone.

"You need to make me."

I was about to say something. I didn't know what, but something. It was already too late. The woman extended one arm, and knocked PJ across my office into the wall. I could see the anger rise in PJ's face as she clenched her teeth, jumped up, and rushed the woman.

PJ had two fully bionic arms. I was the one responsible for her getting them—though at the time, it was to save her life, which I did. There was a reason for Punch Judy's name. She loved to punch people, she was good at it, and she'd had a fair amount of trouble with law enforcement over it. But here in my office the woman blocked every one of PJ's punches effortlessly. The woman dropped her purse to the ground and I instinctively knew things were going to go from bad to worse. The woman lifted her arms in a boxing stance,throwing an array of punches not at PJ, but at PJ's bionic arms, with tremendous force and speed.

"Oww!" I had never heard PJ get hit in her bionic arms before and cry out, "Oww!" No one had ever out-boxed PJ.

PJ dropped her arms. I couldn't believe it!

"PJ, don't—!" The woman punched PJ in the head and my secretary crashed to the ground like a bag of old bricks, unconscious.

"Why did you have to do that?" I asked, pointing my electric rifle—my office weapon from underneath my desk—at her. "You shouldn't have done that. That's my employee you just knocked out."

"I'm sorry. My mind isn't functioning properly."

I shot her point-blank in the chest. I wasn't going to fall for the "stall for time" trick.

She stood there looking at me. "I think I'm more cybernetic than organism at this stage of my life."

This was just what I needed. PJ aside, I continued to have serious problems with cyborgs in my office. Was I going to have to shoot her in the head? Or did she have bionic legs too, and was she about to kick me out of my own 100-story window?

Then we were blinded by science.

Metropolis was always either dark, or overcast, so it was as if someone had turned on the sun outside my office window. It was the science of photonic stun technology—the act of shining a big, bright light on an Earther made them freeze, because they were so unaccustomed to it. These lights were ultra-bright and both of us were blinded; neither closing our eyes, nor shielding them with our hands would be of any use. I knew what was coming next.

"This is the police!" The second time in a day I'd heard that foreboding announcement from above. The police hovercruisers were right outside my 100-story office window.

"Unauthorized cyborg!" That voice came from right inside my office!

There was a gushing sound and I watched as the woman became frozen in place. Her entire body was enveloped in a powdered ice substance. The spotlights cut off from outside my window. The aftereffect of their stun-lights kept me blind for a few moments, but then I began to make out their shapes. There were several police officers in my office. They'd gotten to use two "toys" from the many non-lethal weapons in their arsenal. A couple of them walked up to the incapacitated "iced" woman, picked her up like a mannequin, and carried her out.

Why did she have to be crazy? Based on her style of dress, she could have been a potential client who actually could have paid to hire me.

I recognized two of the officers in the room. Ebony and Ivory. My police "friends," Officers Break and Caps in their silver-and-black body-armored uniforms.

"Mr. Cruz," Office Break said. "You can't seem to stay away from trouble or the police."

"I try real hard to, Officer Break. I promise I do. But we need to get my secretary to the hospital, pronto."

"Yes, and then we—" he said pointing to himself, his partner, then me "—will go down to the station, shall we?"

CHAPTER 4

Officers Break and Caps

I was still massaging my eyes as I sat in the back of their police hovercruiser.

"Why did you use so much power?" I asked. "I'm still seeing spots."

"Why are you complaining?" Officer Caps muttered from the passenger seat. "Your client was blinded and flash-frozen. You should be thankful."

"I'll be thankful as soon as I can see two fingers in front of my face again—and she was not my client. We didn't get that established yet."

"She was beating up that cyborg gang member in your employ," Officer Caps continued.

"PJ isn't a gang member."

"Beating up your cyborg ex-gang member—"

"Don't you know the city of Metropolis encourages employers to hire ex-felons as part of the government's Anti-Recidivism Initiative?"

Officer Break, in the driver's seat, began to laugh.

"It's the surest path to a life of rehabilitation, and returning the individual to the community of productive citizens." I recited the quote as best I could remember.

"As I was saying," Officer Caps continued, "assaulting your ex-gang member, model-citizen-to-be employee, and you were pointing a rifle at her. Is that the definition of a client to you? I wonder if she knows you blew someone out of that window there in your office. Another cyborg, I believe."

"That was self-defense, but an accident. It was all instinct."

"What is it with you and cyborgs?" Officer Caps asked.

"What do you mean?"

"You're always shooting cyborgs, getting shot at by cyborgs, having a cyborg work for you, and you're marrying one."

"Dot isn't a cyborg. She just has a cybernetic neck."

The officers started laughing again.

"I believe that's called a cyborg," Officer Caps said as he looked back at me.

"Oh, I understand now," I said. "You're trying to get me to invite you to the wedding. I'm not falling for your Jedi mind tricks." They laughed again.

"Knowing you as we do," Officer Break said, "someone there, or near there, will end up calling the police for some disturbance or another. You're the only person I know who's getting fitted for a tux, and body armor, at the same time."

"Wait," I said. "How did you know I was getting a fitted bullet-proof vest for the wedding? That was supposed to be a secret. Don't tell anyone. I'm using a bunch of wedding money for it, but they think I'm using it for extra finger food. You should have seen the food budget from the parents-in-law. How much finger food can people eat? It's one wedding, not the city of Metropolis."

I was a never-ending source of amusement for Ebony and Ivory. But actually, they were right: I *was* going to be wearing my vest, and maybe it would be wise to invite as many cops as possible. All I had to say was "free food," and they'd be there. Police were never truly off-duty, so they'd be carrying all kinds of concealed weapons. With my rep, and already-growing unpopularity among the criminal class, I was genuinely concerned that some crazy maniac would show up, and cause some trouble. For me, there was no place as blissfully safe as a room filled with armed street police. I was about to get a humpback-whale-sized dose of bliss; we were heading to Downtown Metropolis to Police One—the central police headquarters for the supercity's half-million strong police force.

I was an anomaly in every sense when it came to the police. High-end private investigation mega-firms felt any contact with the police was beneath them. The less-than-savory detective outfits out there had the same view of police as the criminals did—the "enemy."

It was a completely different story with me, even aside from the successful wrap-up of my Watch Conspiracy Case, and one of my biggest police allies being none other than the president of the Metropolis Police Union. I knew many of the rank-and-file police, they all knew me by sight, and more importantly, they liked me. I was the guy who had saved the City, and fingered a cop-killer conspirator within the government itself. I had a "get-out-of-jail card" from them, to use whenever I needed it for life. I had no intention of ever being in such a situation, but I had learned the hard way that the year was young and life was long.

PJ had been flown to City General, still unconscious. Whatever that "anti-personnel" ice was, that they had used on the cyborg woman, had burnt a hole in my office floor carpet, which meant I had another set of expenses waiting for me when I got back. The business was closed, with my being chauffeured to Police Central, and my secretary-office manager being carted off to the hospital. Yes, this was how it always was in the city. One moment you were saving clients and babies, the next, this.

"I never saw her before," I said to them.

Officer Break and Officer Caps were unique themselves. They had given up on moving up the management ladder to stay on the streets, which made them highly respected by both the beat cops, and office brass.

"Why do you have so many people trying to hurt you?" Officer Break asked.

"The hat," I answered. "They're envious of the hat."

Officer Break glanced at me in the rear-view mirror, and Officer Caps turned around to look at me.

"This isn't a laughing matter," Officer Caps said to me. "She was an escaped mental patient. We got on her trail when we learned she had substantially, and illegally, upgraded her bionic parts."

"You think she did that to get me?"

"You tell us."

I shook my head. "No. I think she came up there as a client, that's it— but like you said, she's crazy. I'll go talk to her, and find out what she wanted, when they get her back on her meds. When someone wants to off you, they don't spend time talking to you, or picking a fight with your secretary. They just do it—or try to."

"Didn't she beat up your own secretary who's a cyborg too, or did you forget that?" Officer Caps asked.

"She out-punched your Punch Judy," Officer Break added.

"I didn't say she wasn't dangerous."

"No, you said she wasn't there to off you. I wonder what would have happened to you if we hadn't shown up."

"I would have shot her, of course."

"You know why we used the ice?"

"I need to get me some of that," I said.

"She took a considerable amount of laser fire from a half dozen security guards when she escaped. Apparently, she's not too bothered by it, so your little Junior G-man electric rifle wouldn't have helped you too much back there."

"I still don't think she came to hurt me."

"When they're not shooting at you, you're shooting at them." Officer Caps turned back around. "I'm surprised the building puts up with you."

"It's funny you say that," I said as I looked out the windows at the sky traffic through the rain. "At my apartment building, some of my friendly co-tenants are circulating a petition to have me evicted. They say I'm a 'menace to society.'" Both officers began to laugh. "I thought you two would appreciate their sense of humor."

Metropolis Police Central was at the opposite end of the street from City Hall, and looked like a cubical fortress. It was said to be the deepest building in the world, burrowing endless levels into the ground—a holdover of dark days, when nuclear annihilation and civil unrest of a Biblical proportion were the daily fears of government bureaucrats. All that was long before the supercities of today, and the rain.

To think, not too long ago, there was practically a civil war between the rank-and-file police officers versus the police brass, the mayor, City Hall, and Up-Top—the latter sending spaceships to hover and protect the mayor from the cops. It was the police who were rioting in the streets, not the people. Insanity.

Walking through the place, it was as if none of it had ever happened, business as usual. At the end of the day, humans were like all other animals; they wanted order, the routine of life, no matter how miserable it was.

Officers Break and Caps had me wait near their cubicle area as they chatted with none other than Detective "Do-Little," or actually, Detective Monitor. He wasn't particularly well liked by the street police class for the simple reason that he had never been a street cop or, because of his politically connected family, had been one for no more than five minutes before he was promoted. "His daddy knew people" was the rumor. Some time in the future, because of his family connections, he could be the police chief if that's what he wanted. He was one of those guys. Life was already planned and set; the world was just going through the motions.

The three of them walked up to me.

"Looks like we came to your aid in the nick of time," Detective Monitor said.

"Why?" I asked.

"We found a body near your offices. Deceased male. Registered detective like you. Looks like she killed him before going up to do the same to you."

I looked away. Maybe I was wrong about her. She had killed some guy near my office? "Maybe you did get to me in time. I'm supposed to be getting married, so I can't get dead. The fiancée would kill me."

We all stood around the video monitor display at an empty desk, and watched five officers carrying my supposed client-to-be bionic woman, strapped to a hoverbed, no arms, no legs, to Booking. She was completely helpless. I felt sorry for her. The "ice" they had incapacitated her with was melting off, but her body still had a thin film of the stuff. The residue on her eyebrows and eyes made her look like an albino.

Anyone with any kind of bionic part or implant had to be registered in the police database along with their specific part or implant; all modifications had to approved and registered. If someone was classified as an unauthorized cyborg, they could be legally stripped of every last part from their body and the government was not obligated to give them anything to replace it. As a practice they did, but always some cheap plastic replacement, which was often worse than having nothing at all.

However, criminals made all kinds of illegal modifications, and didn't care about the law. That's why they were called criminals.

"I can't believe she killed someone before coming up to my office," I said.

"She did," Monitor said.

The police had said it, but I still didn't quite believe it. I had no reason to disbelieve them, though. I didn't know her, and had never seen her before. For all I knew, she was a multiple murdering maniac. But still, my gut said otherwise. I just didn't see it in her eyes. I'm sure I was being stupid. People got killed all the time in this city, and they surely didn't see the murderous intention in their assailants' eyes before the act.

"Can I talk to her?"

Officers Break and Caps grinned. Monitor wasn't amused.

"Why?" he asked.

"Just to talk."

"You think she'll confess to you, rather than to us?"

"Yeah," I answered. "She has one of my Liquid Cool T-shirts."

The officers burst out laughing. "Get out of here," Monitor said, dismissing me with a hand gesture, and walking away.

To be truthful, it was quite depressing. T-shirts of me floating around in the Metropolis economy. I was thankful for the rain, because you couldn't see who or what was on a T-shirt in the rain, and under a zipped-up slicker.

I decided I was going to talk to the bionic woman, but it would have to be another day. She wasn't going anywhere, especially now that they thought she had killed someone. I'd wait until she was transferred to the Metro Jail, pending trial. I'd see her then. I wanted to at least know why she'd planned to kill me, if that was her intention. Well, at least she didn't shoot me.

CHAPTER 5

Chief Hub

The black-market bionics business was huge. The only thing worse was the black-market virtual reality business (more on that in my next case). But I had to get my mind focused on all the errands I had to do for the day, and, of course, stop by the hospital to see PJ.

"Are you Mr. Cruz?" a voice said.

I had learned the hard way that anyone asking that question who was out of my line of sight was cause for concern—but I was in Metro Police headquarters. Everyone was packing a gun, but they were police. I wasn't going to get shot here. That's why I had enjoyed being a police intern here, when I was a kid. I was in a place away from the streets, where no trouble could find me. What could possibly go wrong here?

I turned and saw the man. He was a senior police management type.

"Yes?"

The man hesitated, and seemed to be arguing with himself as to whether he should continue. "Please wait here." He turned around, and disappeared down a hallway.

I stood there, looking around. What was going on?

The man returned with the chief of police himself. Chief Hub and I stared at one another for a while. We had quite a roller-coaster of history, going back to my last big case. He had hated me when he'd first met me, but after the crisis of the last case (during which he and his seven sons had acted as bodyguards to protect me from a street hit from the *entire* Animal Farm Crime Syndicate), I had returned the favor. I had hated him too, but the same crisis had showed me he wasn't a complete sewer slug. I supposed we both had a more neutral view of each other these days.

He was a six-foot-tall, musclebound veteran officer. Dark hair, thick mustache, and dark green eyes squinting at me.

"Mr. Cruz," he started. "Compstat Connie."

The Crime Information Center (CIC) of the Metropolis Police Department was run by Compstat Connie, the entire multi-hundreds-of-millions-of-dollars division. Compstat (Computer Statistics) was all the crime data collected in the city and drove everything that the police did—deployment, budgets, resources, and personnel.

"Yeah. What about Compstat Connie? Did something happen to her?" I was concerned.

"Nothing happened to her. She's out sick," he replied.

"Okay."

"I was on the phone with C.C. and she's coughing and wheezing badly. I told her that it was a priority that we have a designated replacement for her in our meeting, happening now. Imagine my surprise when she named you, a civilian, to replace her."

"What? What are you talking about? I'm not a policeman or police employee."

"She named you."

"Why would Compstat Connie do that?" I stood there with a stunned look.

"It's not the normal kind of meeting."

I should have run out of the police station right then and there. "What does 'not normal' mean?"

"I have only one question for you. Can you do that thing she does?"

"What thing?"

"If you know CC, you should know."

"No one can do what Compstat Connie can do. She's the original non-cyborg human computer. She knows everything. I wish I could do a fraction of what she can do."

"But can you do a fraction of what she can do?"

"I guess. Maybe."

"That's good enough. A fraction of something is better than nothing of nothing. Come with us."

Hub gestured, and I reluctantly followed. He stopped and turned back.

"You're very popular with the rank-and-file, but that's not the case with the brass. Please remember that and behave accordingly. The meeting is a strategic one. No rank-and-file. None of your fans or groupies will be there."

"Management and above."

Hub gave me a smirk. "And Feds."

"Oh, wonderful. Let me upchuck my breakfast now, before we walk in."

Hub pointed at me. "Behave. You're representing me. You're representing CC. Don't embarrass Compstat Connie. She *will* come after you."

I nodded. "Yeah, she will."

Hub saw my expression change, and knew I had decided to keep my low opinions of police brass to myself. We started down the hall again.

It was a sea of navy, white, and black. Uniformed brass with rank insignia on their shoulders glared at me as soon as they saw me behind Chief Hub and his aide.

They didn't like me. I didn't like them. So, there were no hurt feelings.

"What is that civilian doing here?" one of the navy-uniformed officers asked.

"This is the person C.C. said should take her place," Hub answered.

"You can't be serious," another police brass said. "He's a civilian. He's not even law enforcement."

I bit my lip to keep from saying something. Behaving myself was going to be hard in that room.

"Why would the head of CIC offer an outside civilian to be her in-meeting replacement? Hub, what kind of department are you running here?"

"I run an exceptional department, I'll have you know. C.C. said him, but if you don't want him, we can ask him to leave. C.C. is sick as a dog. He's who she named to replace her to analyze the data everyone said had to be analyzed now in this meeting. So, what does everyone want to do? Decide now."

He looked around the room, but all of them, frowning men and women, remained quiet, staring at me.

"Cruz, is it?" one of them asked me. "Why would Compstat Connie, the head of CIC, ask you to come into a top-secret meeting to act as her proxy?"

Top-secret? Hub hadn't told me that.

Hub gave me a look.

"Back in the day, I interned here at Police One—"

A few of them looked at each other. "Intern? The department has interns?" one of them asked.

"It was a program we had back then. The police internship program with the local Metro high schools," Hub said. "You remember it. It was discontinued over 15 years ago."

I continued. "When I was interning, I reported to Compstat Connie. Then, because of my last big case, that—" I bit my lip to contain the snark—"I consulted with her, and I remembered I'd learned so much working in CIC, so I started volunteering. I helped her with extra work projects, and I'd be like an—apprentice."

"Apprentice to learn what?" another officer asked.

"The complete criminal database of the Metropolis CIC," I answered. "Every arrestee, felon, and person of interest."

It was as if I had dropped a bomb in the room. The men and women looked at each other. Hub squinted as he looked at me, thinking.

"Are you saying what I think you're saying?" Hub asked. "You're memorizing the mug shots of all criminals in Metropolis."

"That's not possible. I told you. No one can do what Compstat Connie can do. She's the original human memory computer. I'm not memorizing it. I'm—becoming familiar with it."

"Does he have clearance for that?" another officer asked.

"Mugshots are in the public record," I snapped back.

Hub now had his hands on his hips, still thinking. "Why would you attempt to do something like that?" he asked.

"I'm tired of getting shot at by strangers," I replied. "I want to know who's shooting at me."

Hub held back a grin. "I know that's not the truth, but I'll let it go."

A man in black stepped up to us. "This is all very fascinating, but as has been mentioned, this is a top-secret meeting. He's a civilian, and that means he's unauthorized. Chief Hub, get someone else to replace your CIC director, and show the 'private defective' to the street."

I was pissed. "You have no reason—"

Hub held up his hand to stop my coming rant. He turned to the Fed. "We can have him leave without being rude."

"Mr. Cruz, sorry, but you have to go," Hub said to me.

"No, he's not. The P.I. stays," a voice said.

Everyone turned. It was Wilford G., Jr., the head of the powerful Metro Police Union, standing at the door.

When I became a detective, I read every book I could find on the subject, but my favorite was *How to be a Great Detective with 100 Rules.* It was written by a Wilford G., who had been a Metropolis private detective for over 70 years, until his death at the age of 92. Wilford G., Jr. was his son, and, as Hub put it, one of my police fans on the street.

"This is not a union matter, Wil. Why are you here?" a captain asked.

"Based on all the people in this room, it is a police matter. Why was I not invited?"

"This is a strategic meeting of leadership, so you can take the P.I. with you as you both leave," another said.

"I'm curious, can you even remember how long it's been since you were a real cop?" he snapped.

Oh, that did it. The police captain marched toward Wilford G., Jr. The two men were held away from each other, as the insults and curses flew.

This was better than reality TV. Then Chief Hub tapped me. I looked. In his hand was a digital notepad with a list of names. I took the pad, and actually recognized some of the names. Hub noticed the slightly concerned expression on my face.

In the corner of the room was a mobile computer deadbolted to the desk. I walked to it, sat down, and started typing, with Hub and his aide looking over my shoulder.

I stopped. "Are you saying these people are in the city?"

"Why?"

"Are they here?"

"Maybe."

I typed more, to quickly crosscheck other databases. I realized why Compstat Connie had fingered me as her proxy. All I could do was sit back and sigh when I was finished.

"What?" Hub asked. "What is it?"

"How do you project this display onto the main projection screen?" I asked.

The aide stepped up to the keyboard and hit some keys. The large screen at the front of the room started to lower. The shouts and pushing stopped, as everyone looked at the screen, then at the three of us in the corner.

I dragged the mobile computer and desk to the center of room, walked back to grab my chair, and walked back to the desk to sit down.

"This is Neck Muncher. I'm giving you their street names. He's supposedly a cannibal. This is Crossbow. This is Church Lady. This is Pipsqueak." I rattled off about a half dozen other names as each of their mugshots appeared on the screen.

I sat back in the chair with my arms folded.

"They're not just contract killers. They're the best contract killers from Up-Top, which means they're better than the ones here on Earth."

The room looked at the mugshots on the screen, and then back at me.

"Why are the highest-paid, most dangerous contract killers in the universe all in Metropolis? One of them alone could rack up a serious body count, including street police—but all of them? And, since none of them have been found dead, we can surmise they're all working together—on the same job. What kind of contract kill job brings the highest-paid assassins in the universe to Metropolis?"

CHAPTER 6

Punch Judy

That's when they kicked me out of the room.

Even my pal Wilford G., Jr. left me to be pushed out, with the door slamming inches from my nose. The commotion in that briefing room was so loud, that officers in their cubicles were all standing, looking at me and the door, assuming I was the cause.

Before becoming a detective, I had become a known player in the hovercar restoration business because I had learned everything there was to know about hovercars. I was only a kid but knew as much as the godfathers of the industry, who had acquired their knowledge over decades. I planned to do the same with the criminal class of Metropolis. Know every one of them, what they did, and what they could be up to, so I could figure out how to get myself a case. Hustle, hustle, hustle was what it was all about. Find the clients, find the criminals, find the cases. Generate income.

Despite my boast of a newfound "hobby" of reviewing every criminal low-life file there was, becoming the successor to Compstat Connie was not the motive. Hub was right. My motives were far less altruistic. I was looking for someone. In my last big case, I had learned that the psycho cyborg Red Rabbit, with his "lightning" rifle, had put out a contract hit on me, and hired no fewer than three guys to carry it out. The first one missed me in front of my place, the Concrete Mama; the second was thrown through a door by PJ, and shot out the 100th floor by me; but the third had disappeared. Luckily for Police One, I was memorizing every contract killer there was. I knew what he looked like, and what his nickname was, which is why I was also studying criminal nicknames.

The crime world was fascinating. I learned there were contract killers, and then there were assassins—the contract killer elites. It seemed no matter where you went, you couldn't escape the distinctions of class—the regular folk and the elite. Contractors were killers. Assassins were a whole higher level of death and destruction. These weren't POIs—persons of interest; they were AOIs (my term)— assassins of interest, and they were here. Those on Hub's list were "no joke." Meaning, if they were on one planet, you'd want to be on another.

I suddenly had an uncontrollable urge to find my girlfriend, and suggest that we take a "spontaneous" vacation *far, far away* from Metropolis for a little while—but first things first.

I caught a hovercab to Metro General. The city's main hospital was only at the end of the street, but in a supercity like Metropolis, that meant it was many miles away, and I was not in the mood to walk in the rain.

All I had to say was that I was Punch Judy's employer, and they practically rolled out the red carpet for me. When I reached her room on the 116th floor, there she was in a silver hospital gown, in her bed, one arm holding her forehead. I noticed an orderly at her bedside, looking at her bio-bed vitals display.

"Why are you holding your forehead like that?" I asked.

"That woman damaged my face!"

"Don't touch it then, or it won't heal."

"No, it looks bad. I don't want anyone to see it."

"It's really not that bad, Miss," the orderly said to her.

"Get me bandages!" she yelled at him.

"Don't get her bandages," I said. "Get her some kind of that spray-on skin."

"Oh yes. Good thinking. Bandages are ugly. It must match, though," she directed the orderly.

"Miss, we don't have anything like that. This is not a salon, and even if we did have, that would not be hospital standard issue."

"Hospital standard issue is ugly!" PJ yelled. "If I'm dead, I wouldn't want hospital clothes. Look at this ugly hospital gown. Where are my clothes?"

"You have no one but yourself to blame for being here," I interrupted, "and don't yell at the orderly. He didn't throw you into a wall."

"That stupid woman. Who fights like that? Who hits you in your arms? What kind of fighting is that?"

"It worked, didn't it?"

"My shoulders are sore. My trapezius muscles are sore. That stupid woman—!"

"Why did you drop your arms?" I yelled at her. "What kind of street fighter are you? You're supposed to be an ex-gang member. You're Punch Judy. You forgot how to punch?"

"She tried to knock my arms out of my shoulder sockets, the stupid woman! If it had been a man, I wouldn't have allowed that to happen. You show a sister some solidarity, and that's what a woman does to you. Never again! Man or woman, I'm going to pound them into the ground—or just shoot them with my rifle."

I could see the orderly was getting more uncomfortable as our conversation, if you can call it that, went on.

"Why do you have such crazy people come into your office?"

"I thought she was okay. You said she had a Liquid Cool T-shirt."

"She did—but she was crazy."

"Miss, the soreness of your injuries will disappear in a few days," the orderly said.

"I want drugs!"

"Miss, I'll give you some standard aspirin for the pain and inflammation."

PJ made a gagging sound. "Standard issue again."

"Miss, how did you lose your arms?"

She pointed at me with the hand not covering her forehead. "He cut them off."

The look on the orderly's face was one of pure shock. He stared at me with a deer-in-the-headlights expression, then stepped back from PJ's hospital bed.

"I'll step away from the door so you can run," I said to him.

I did, and that orderly flew out of the room as if he were wearing a jetpack. I looked at PJ. One hand was on her forehead, the other over her mouth, to hold back her laughter.

"Why do you do that? Why do you tell people that?"

"Well, it's true."

"At least tell them the whole story."

PJ glanced at the door, smiling. I turned to see three big orderlies, one hospital police officer, and the original orderly standing behind them.

"She said he cut off her arms. That's why she has the cybernetic ones."

"She's my employee, you idiot," I said. "Can't you tell when someone's joking with you?"

The hulking orderlies looked at PJ. The police officer looked at PJ. They saw PJ laughing, and then turned to glare at the orderly in unison.

"You're an idiot," one of the big orderlies said. They all disappeared down the hall.

The orderly pointed at PJ. "No aspirin or pain killers for you!" He disappeared. PJ was still laughing.

"You won't be laughing when the pain really kicks in—and stop touching your forehead. Hands, organic or bionic, have all kinds of germs. Just put the spray-on skin over it, and no one will notice anything."

"They don't have any, and they won't get me any."

"He told you already. This is a hospital, not the store at the local beauty salon."

"Get me some."

"Me? Where?"

"What do you mean, where?"

"Eye Candy is too far away for me to go and come back."

"It's not far at all."

"I have one of Dot's sheer neck scarves in the Pony. I'll get that; you can wrap it around your forehead, and that's it. You can take yourself to the salon yourself. I cut off your arms, not your legs, so use them."

PJ had been in a terrible hovercar accident. In the crash, it had flipped and landed on her. Her arms had been crushed and pinned; the hovercar had caught on fire. She was going to get burnt alive, or the hovercar would blow up from the leaking fuel. I had to act—fast. No ambulance or fire crew was there to help. So, I used the laser cutter in my vehicle—used for hovercar restoration gigs—to do what needed to be done. Her arms were gone anyway, and it was either them, or her life. I saved her life.

The first time PJ had said that to Officers Break and Caps—before we were all such "good friends"—they were seriously about to shoot me, thinking I was some kind of arm-choppin' psycho. I made PJ promise to keep the circumstances of her cyborgism to herself, especially in front of law enforcement and medical personnel—but she still did it to get a laugh.

Another hovercab took me back to my place at the Concrete Mama in Rabbit City. Finally, I could get my own vehicle. I was in my Ford Pony, in the fast lane of sky traffic. It was a bright red, muscle hovercar classic— high-performance, super-charged, advanced nitro-acceleration hydrogen engine. Hovertraffic was packed, but it was moving. I had errands to run, and I was determined to get them all done.

The music in my Pony was rarely on. Real drivers like me focused on the driving—watching the sky lane traffic, anticipating the movements of other hovercars, glancing at my vehicle's displays. Defensive driving theory wasn't some class you watched on the mobile computer; it was a state of mind. With the music off, I could also think. Was I free and clear, or would another series of unrelated events connect to drop me into the center of another mess? I had to pray that the police brass would leave me out of whatever was going on. Compstat Connie wouldn't be sick forever. She'd be back to handle the chief and his merry men. All I wanted was to be left alone to do my pre-wedding errands in peace.

However, I would still look at possible travel destinations to get far, far away from Metropolis with my fiancée. I'd keep the details about a gang of homicidal assassins descending upon Metropolis to myself. All I needed to say was that we needed a nice little getaway to mark the end of our bachelor-bachelorette life.

I smiled at my prevaricating prowess with the wife-to-be. A must for any successful, self-respecting private detective in the city, who didn't want to find himself banished from the residence, and sleeping in his own red Pony.

PART THREE

The Martian Chronicle

CHAPTER 7

The Sandman

"Lunar shuttle 107, you are cleared for descent," Metro International Control announced.

"Control, acknowledged. Landing vector plotted and submitted," the captain responded.

The large triple-decker passenger space cruiser glided through the first orbital ring—the man-made construct, one of five, dwarfed the size of the approaching space shuttle. Each successive ring floated at lower and lower orbits above the storm clouds covering Earth. With all the orbiting space traffic, it looked as if the planet were spitting out a steady stream of debris into the atmosphere—a debris of thousands of spacecraft, all in their separate zones, going to their separate destinations, spiraling from close to ground, into the stratosphere, into space, to the moon and beyond. Above Earth, all spacecraft, construction craft, and stations were white, as if there were some unwritten law that no other color was allowed, save for sensor, directional, and beacon lights.

The shuttle continued its descent, a brief burn through the atmosphere, and then through the clouds. At night, with every hover, air, and space vehicle lit up, the view of Metro International and Interspace Airport looked as if extraterrestrial aliens had landed, and were flying out for their next planetary conquest.

With the craft successfully landing, passengers immediately disembarked for the arrival gates. First class and priority passengers came first and were waved through by customs agents, without a second look. Everyone else was individually scrutinized.

"First time to Earth?" the black-uniformed customs agent asked.

"Yes, officer," replied the large woman in yellow.

"Do you have anything to declare?"

"No, officer."

"Anyone give you anything to bring to Earth?"

"No, officer."

"How long will you be on Earth, ma'am."

"Two weeks."

The agent watched her. For a second, he thought he saw her face twitch.

"You have a good trip, ma'am. Welcome to Earth."

"Thank you, officer."

The woman shuffled along and the agent motioned to the next passenger he wanted to spot check.

She had gotten her luggage—ten suitcases in all, piled high on a hoverdolley—and stood outside the ground-floor terminal doors under cover. The rain was pouring. A hovertaxi swooped down from nowhere to hang right across from her.

"Taxi, ma'am?" the turban-wearing driver asked.

She smiled and nodded. The driver put the last of her luggage in his trunk, and the large woman in yellow showed him the address on her mobile card phone display. The taxi driver double-checked it with what he had on the display screen of his own mobile phone. "Got it! You're not coming, ma'am?"

"I have to wait for my colleagues on the next plane, but I can't lug around all these bags everywhere. I'm not as nimble as in my youth."

"Okay."

"I'll pay up front, and you can check them in at the hotel for me. I'll pay you extra for that." The woman waved her mobile card phone.

The taxi driver smiled. "No problem, ma'am. I can do all that. You really live on the moon?"

"Sidonia Colony."

"Oh, very high-class."

"High-class all the way."

The taxi driver took her mobile card phone for payment. In moments, he was finished, and flew off, leaving the woman behind as she waved goodbye.

She turned and started walking, not back into the terminal, but along the sidewalk outside its doors. Through arriving passengers, departing ones, luggage check-in people and domies, she walked.

After a couple of miles she turned a corner into a tight alleyway that she barely fit into, and continued. No people, no surveillance. She pulled her body through to the end.

When she emerged from the alleyway, five miles later, soaking wet, and her yellow pantsuit caked with black grime, she stopped. Her eyes turned black. Her body began to shake violently. It expanded, and opened into pieces to reveal a Black man inside, dressed in a silver suit. He stepped out of the android suit and into the pouring rain, looking up. His eyes closed. He stood a while as the rain washed over him. He tilted his head back down, as his eyes opened. He pulled out a silver pair of shades from his jacket. Once on, he ran, and disappeared into the night rain.

CHAPTER 8

Theo

Wharf City cargo workers watched the commercial cargo hovercruisers slowly descend, as massive cube containers were lowered to the loading docks. Dozens of workers, some on foot, others on hoverlifts, situated themselves to receive the containers.

"When were these ships cleared?" a dock supervisor asked.

"I found out the same time you did," the manager answered.

"Where are they from?"

"I don't know. The moon, Mars, who cares?"

"Did they even go through bio-contamination?"

"Of course."

"As long as they've irradiated everything."

"There's nothing biological or organic in these containers. Let's get 'em loaded, and get out of here before we get washed away by all this damn rain."

On the 10th floor of the 20-story cargo container, in the center section, a light powered up on one of the many metal boxes. It opened, and a "coma-bed" extended. More indicator lights turned on, some flashing. The outside front panel slid down and through the window of the inner covering, a Caucasian man slept—scraggly black hair, a full mustache and beard, wearing a skintight black suit.

His eyes opened.

Cargo workers swarmed around the massive cube containers, as others flew by on hovercargo lifts. A crew marched to the latest one to be dropped down.

"Wait up," a worker yelled out, rushing to catch up.

"Catch up," the crew leader yelled back.

The trailing crew member ran past the shadow between the cube containers, when he noticed a flash, as if someone had taken his picture.

"What?" He stopped. "Who's there?" He walked a bit to the shadow, then immediately started backing away. Someone was coming out.

"Hey, what's taking you so long?" the crew leader yelled back at him.

The man turned and ran to his crew, but still watched behind him. The shadow of the person was gone.

CHAPTER 9

The Martian

A shuttle pod slowed its approach, and docked with the arrival hub of the Praetoria Interpol Space Station. From a distance, it looked like an upside-down lava lamp with two Saturn-like rings, one near the top, and one dead-center. Circling the bright white structure near the center ring were several large flying saucer spaceships.

A man dressed in a brownish-red suit, and carrying a silver briefcase, came through the arrival hallway. Two officers in black uniforms waited; one extended a hand to the arriving agent.

"How was your trip, sir?"

They shook hands. "Like all space travel—quiet. I slept most of the trip."

"I've never been to Mars myself."

"You're not missing anything. It's a city with all the vices as any other. It's just red. Do I have time to settle in?"

"They want to see you right away."

The agent was now sitting in a plush white chair, rereading the display of a tablet. He looked up, his eyes squinted.

"How many know about this?"

The man sitting across from him was in a casual white uniform. "As of now—two," Seraff answered.

"I don't like what you're suggesting."

"I don't like having to suggest it."

"You reassigned me from Mars to do what, then?"

"To find out for certain."

"Do I get staff?"

"Of course."

"Do you believe the report?"

Seraff hesitated a moment. "I don't get paid to guess. You're here to ensure that I have the facts for Command."

"Why aren't you doing this, then?"

"There are other—confidential matters I can't disclose, that require my presence here. Therefore, the field work must be delegated to others, for the present time."

"How high up in Command?"

"For you or me?"

"You. Based on the suspicions of this report, with the obvious sensitivities and security concerns, it's inconceivable you'd delegate this to anyone outside of yourself."

"Unfortunately, I cannot say. I need it handled by someone I trust, and who has a flawless record of discretion. Everything you need is in the report."

"I don't believe the report. Earth security is a joke, but Interpol? How could these men get past us—undetected? The top crime lords of off-world—Impossible."

Seraff leaned forward in his chair. "As I said, your task is to find out for sure."

"That means I have to go to Earth. I hate Earth."

"I have full confidence in you—even if you're a Martian."

"Thank you, spaceman. I feel the same about you." He turned off the tablet. "You want me to leave tomorrow."

"The rumor is true. Martians *are* mind readers."

Carter managed a smirk. "Questions. If I need help, someone I can trust, who do you have?"

"I'll have a list of names for you, law enforcement and civilian."

Carter's eyebrow raised. "Civilian? I don't think I'll get as desperate as that—but that does lead me to my next question."

"Your weapons are already waiting for you on the planet—and a few illegal, but necessary ones, for insurance."

"Which city on the depressing blue rock below us are you sending me to?"

"Metropolis."

PART FOUR

Blade Gunner!

CHAPTER 10

China Doll

Despite Ebony and Ivory's assessment of my inner circle, my girlfriend-fiancée was not a cyborg. Her neck, traps, breast bone, and that section of her spinal column were bionic—all courtesy of a freak childhood accident where my Dot literally lost her head. Though she had retired from the child hover-go-cart scene, and still suffered from a debilitating phobia of passing under bridges, she had more than moved past all that to become one of the most sought after fashionistas of Metropolis. She worked at the top full-service salon in the city—Eye Candy. She was not a cyborg. She was a fashionista extraordinaire.

The only cyborg in my life was my secretary PJ, who had to spend one more day at Metro General. I'd told her to call me when they discharged her, so I could pick her up and drive her home, which in our case was the same mega-apartment complex—the Concrete Mama. Knowing PJ as I did, she'd probably figure out some way to get the doctors to discharge her early to get rid of her, so I kept an ear out for that ring on my mobile. Some months back she had programmed my phone with the musical theme to some old movie (Jaws) to be her special ring tone. With her bionic fingers, she did so in, like, two seconds. I'd had the mobile for years and I still didn't know how to program ring tones, but she did, and got a good laugh, dialing me from the office phone to hear her handiwork.

Unlike most Metropolitans, I loved the rain but this was crazy. As I drove my Pony, I had my wipers on full-speed, but I could still barely see anything. My worry was the sky traffic around me. People couldn't drive in the rain, and every hovercar near me was nothing but a battering ram, waiting to attack my vintage Ford Pony. I was not having any of that, and drove in the slow lane, the bottommost sky lane where the geezers drove. Slow was good, in this mess. Slow meant no accidents. Everyone loved to be in a hurry, until they smashed into a hovertruck; then vehicles and bodies "returned to the surface" from twenty stories up. People always seemed to forget that hovercars were not anti-gravity cars. The former was science, the latter fantasy. Sadly, many people found that out the hard way every day.

The rain was so hard, because it was the rainy season of winter. It was quite amusing, since it always rained, but it was funny that climatologists still managed to figure out a way to come up with seasons. Winter and spring were the worst. This was not the right time for this kind of rain. I had a million errands to run in preparation for the wedding. My last big case, I had joked with Dot that we should just elope to New Vegas, to get it done in an hour by a certified Elvis priest, but now both of us were seriously considering it. The whole wedding thing was for the benefit of the parents on both sides, and an army of freeloader friends who would show up just to stuff their faces with food we had bought. It was going to be banquet-style, so that meant I would not be eating anything. Dot had her bridge-o-phobia; I had my germophobia. Food freeloaders! The more I thought about them, the madder I got. I had the wicked thought of lacing all the food with a diarrhetic, but they would know I was the evildoer as soon as I broke into laughter; our wedding would turn into a Wide, Wide World War of Mixed-Martial-Arts free-for-all with everyone after me.

Well, I couldn't lace any food if I really planned to invite all my new police friends, too.

"I want New Vegas!" I yelled at my mobile phone.

I had pulled off the sky lane, and landed on a roof parking lot. It was the slow lane, so it wasn't as if I were moving at any kind of discernible speed, anyway. She was at work, but I dialed up Dot just the same.

She laughed from my mobile's tiny display screen. Only her parents and I called her by her real name, Dot. She was known as China Doll; female friends called her China; men called her Doll.

Her hair was tied back, with the ponytail resting carefully on one shoulder, and her makeup was always perfect. She always wore a colored neck scarf, and today it was electric blue. Dot was forever the consummate fashionista, with every piece of clothing, every accessory, every piece of jewelry being the trendiest and most stylish.

"Tell me about it," she said. "This is not a wedding. This is like planning to build the first lunar colony. The work never ends."

"I thought your mother was helping you."

"She is."

"Oh."

"Oh? What did that 'Oh' mean?"

"It meant 'Oh.' Oh, she's helping you. She's helping you the way my Pops is helping me."

She started laughing again. "She's actually helping me, and not talking about helping me."

"If you say so. My vote is for New Vegas. We'd be there, married, and back before anyone got wise. That's a mountain of money we'd save. If only there were a way we could get the money, and ditch the big wedding. Now, that would be a wedding gift I'd wholeheartedly support."

"Cruz, as tempting as it is, there will be no New Vegas getaway. It's one of those rituals of life you can't escape."

"Rituals of life. It feels like a ritual of death. How many people are on the guest list now?"

"Cruz, stop obsessing over the guest list. They're family friends."

"Food free-loaders!"

"Weddings have food, Cruz."

"Give them water. We could just direct to them to walk outside, look up at the sky in the rain, and open their mouths. Water. That's all you get, you food free-loaders."

"Okay, I'm hanging up now. You're getting silly."

"Dog man!"

"Who's that?"

"He's the hoverfood truck guy by my place. The best hot dogs in Metropolis. He could cater—"

"Good night, Cruz. Back to work. Love and kisses. Bye."

With that, my impromptu video-call ended.

I don't know why she didn't like any of my ideas. I thought they were all stunningly stupendous.

Back to the slow lane, and geezers in the rain.

CHAPTER 11

Punch Judy

I wished there were someone I could have bet, because I would have won. A nurse called from Metro General and told me the floor doctor had "requested" that PJ "continue her convalescence at home."

"When I was there, the doctor was adamant that she stay the extra day," I said.

The stern-sounding nurse said, "The doctor has changed his mind."

"She was that good of a patient?"

"If by 'good' you mean she's a hyperactive, nonstop talking, chain-smoking, which is illegal anywhere in the hospital, by the way, wild woman, then yes."

"She's a character."

"Did you really cut off her arms?"

"Why did she tell you that? Why does she keep telling people that?"

"You can ask her when you come get her—and I mean—now."

"It's going to take me a little bit. I wasn't planning on driving there until tomorrow, and have you seen this rain?"

"We'll bundle her up for you, and have her waiting in the first-floor lobby. Take as long as you like."

She hung up the video-call on me.

I shook my head. "My secretary: making friends wherever she goes."

Maybe they didn't like her French accent.

I had all these errands to do, but was on chauffeur duty. There was PJ sitting in the main reception lobby, packed with the real dregs of human society—coughing, hack coughing, sneezing, sniffling, then swallowing their own mucous. It was the last place any germophobe would be caught in. I entered the main door, but my legs refused to move any farther.

PJ sat in a hoverwheelchair, which she had strategically placed back against the wall, and facing the entrance. She had seen me before I saw her, and leapt up from the chair. I could see from her expression that she wasn't happy.

"I hate this place," she said, as she walked past me, and out the door.

I followed as she marched to the elevators. "Why couldn't you behave yourself?"

"I wanted them to discharge me, but that didn't mean to put me down here with those people."

The elevator capsule arrived, and a few people got off before we stepped in.

"The food was terrible. The service was terrible. It was cold. They wouldn't keep the curtains closed. I don't want any hovercar drivers snapping pictures of me, half-naked in their stupid gown, and putting that on the Net. I should sue them."

I knew to keep quiet as I led her to my vehicle.

"Oh, and that man—that doctor! He was rude and stupid. I should have punched him, but I know that's what they wanted. They wanted to take off my arms." PJ looked at her left bionic arm as she flexed it, then the other. "Jealous."

I almost laughed, as I got into the Pony. She opened the passenger door, and got in too.

"Why is your car so clean?" she asked, as she looked around—the dashboard, my area, the top, and in the back.

"The Pony is not a car. The Pony is a classic hovervehicle. I drive a vehicle, not a hovercar. You drive a hovercar."

We coasted out of the parking lot. I stopped behind three hovercars ahead of us at a stop sign.

"It's too clean. It's as if you'd just bought it. It has no character."

"PJ, it's exactly how I like it."

"You collectors are all the same. You collect stuff, but don't use it."

"I drive my Pony every day."

"No one would know that by sitting in here."

"Good! I like clean. Clean is good. Clean is character. Would you prefer grimy and nasty?"

She sat back in her seat and smiled. "It won't last for long." She began to laugh.

"What does that mean? What won't last for long?"

"Aren't you getting married?"

"Yeah. Dot sits in the Pony all the time, and she believes in clean, too."

PJ laughed again. "You must be terrible at chess. What's going to happen when you have a baby in the car? Cruz, Junior, or Cruzalina?"

A wave of nausea came over me, and I began to look around my own vehicle.

"That baby will be flipping spit, throwing pacifiers and baby toys, all over the place." She began laughing again. "You and Dot better make sure that diaper is secure. Swoosh! Contents out, and all over your fancy leather! Your precious Pony will be one biohazard zone!"

I was sorely tempted to push PJ out of the vehicle right then and there, as she made fun of me. However, her reminder of the harsh reality of a not-too-distant future had my mind racing. How does one make a vintage hovervehicle baby-proof?

"And no, PJ, if it's a girl, her name will *not* be Cruzalina!"

CHAPTER 12

Phishy

Home, sweet home. The Concrete Mama.

The Concrete Mama was like a chunk of granite set down on Earth from space. It was a no-frills monolith tower of legacy housing. If there were ever a planetary shockwave from a nuclear blast, or an asteroid crash, you could bet the Concrete Mama would still be standing. It was ugly, but it would be here until the end of time in its ugliness. It had also been my home for fifteen years. For PJ, about a decade.

My legacy apartment had been willed to me by maternal grandparents. The residents who lived in the Concrete Mama were not rich and we weren't the traditional working class. We were just legacy babies—laborers. We had free housing for life, made a meager living to cover any other incidentals, and nothing more—but it was home, in Rabbit City.

It was here—within 15 minutes of your own place—that most vehicular accidents happened. Top of the list were parking lots. Here was where carelessness ruled. Any time I left or arrived at my own parking lot, I was on heightened alert.

PJ was still laughing and giggling, this time with various impersonations of what my future son or daughter would sound like in a baby voice. I focused on the parking lot and flew into my spot.

I slammed on the brakes! A figure jumped out at me with arms waving. Phishy! That crazy slider!

I rolled down my driver's side window a crack. "Are you crazy, Phishy?"

Phishy, with a smile from ear to ear, strutted over to me. He wore only colored shirts with fishes on them. Today's color was orange.

"Cruz, that's no way to greet your second best man."

"I have a best man already. There's no such thing as a *second* best man. Get out of my way, and get away from my vehicle."

Phishy was already peering inside the Pony to see who was in the passenger's seat. "Is that Dot with you?"

"No, it's PJ."

"Hi, Punch!"

All I heard from PJ, under her breath, was "It's stupid man." She had the seat reclined so far back that she was almost lying down, but adjusted it back up. "I'm getting out of here," she said to me.

I didn't even have time to answer before she had the passenger open, and had hopped out.

"Don't slam—"

Too late—my cyborg secretary slammed the passenger door shut. I felt my blood pressure rise a few points.

"Never slam a classic hovervehicle door! It's not a hovertruck or a piece of flying junk. Close, don't slam!" But PJ was already gone.

I noticed movement at my left side. Oh, no.

Phishy was spinning around, doing his "chicken dance." That was how he greeted me and, as always, I had to wait until he tired himself out with his dance jig.

"Are you done?"

Phishy stood up smiling.

"I'm going to leave you here, and do what I was doing before you jumped in front of a moving hovervehicle."

"Cruz, I got something for you."

"Sure you do. You wait. I'll park."

The Concrete Mama's residential parking was all subterranean, for those of us not blessed to live in the upper half of the tower. In heavy rain, the parking lot would leak virtually everywhere—the ceilings, the walls; many parts of the floor would flood—but it was my lucky day. My parking stall wasn't a mini-lake this time.

In my new detective profession, this was my inner circle of associates: PJ, the secretary-office manager-office bouncer, and Phishy, the street informer-personal gun dealer.

I walked back to him from the Pony; he was already stationed at the elevator to the main lobby. For those of us unlucky enough to live below the 101th floor, that's how it was: down to the main lobby, exit, walk to another set of elevators, then back up to your floor. I was doubly unlucky, as my apartment was on the 100th floor.

"What do you want, Phishy?"

"I have a job for you."

"No."

"But I'm your second best man."

"There's no such thing as a second best man. I've got a best man already."

"Run-Time won't mind at all, and I already got you some wedding presents."

I sighed, and didn't even want to think about what he might have purchased.

"It'd better be legal."

He laughed. "Of course."

"Seriously, Phishy. I've invited police too, as guests. The wedding will be packed with them."

"Yeah, the presents are legal. You and Dot will be speechless."

"That's what I'm afraid of."

"I'm hiring you."

"How much?"

He grinned. "You're still paying off the gun; that, we won't mention, so I'll just deduct it from your bill."

Unbelievable. I had to admit that Phishy had supplied me with not just the best weapons, but weapons that no other detective in Metropolis had—probably not even on the planet—my pop-gun and the omega-gun. I loved them. They had more than proven their value in saving my life, and putting down bad guys. But there was always something. The omega-gun was clearly not an Earth weapon, meaning it was from Up-Top, meaning it was probably super-illegal, meaning none of my police friends could know about it, meaning it was also super-expensive, which was why Phishy could run his payment scam on me. What he was charging me, in convenient and affordable monthly installments, was far, far less than what the weapons cost retail, or would cost on the black market.

"What's the job?"

"Bodyguard work."

"I don't do bodyguard work," I said—a lie.

"It's for me."

"Why do you need a bodyguard? What are you up to?"

We exited the elevator capsule, and I beheld the menagerie known as the main lobby. Sidewalk johnnies everywhere, watching me, more than a few with Liquid Cool T-shirts, and wearing fedoras.

If that weren't depressing enough, a lone man in a trench coat slicker and bellman's hat stood there, waiting for me.

CHAPTER 13

The Doorman

Of course, Phishy knew most of the sidewalk johnnies hanging out in the lobby as they always did. The crowd was larger than normal, because with the kind of rain that was pouring outside, even the most hardcore outdoors types were running for cover.

However, I wasn't focused on that. I let Phishy do his glad-handing greetings with his street associates. It was the doorman—his eyes. There was something I didn't like about them. They reminded me of shark eyes. I had never seen a live shark, let alone a shark's eyes, but I watched movies.

He was always friendly. Everyone at the Concrete Mama loved our new doorman—always neatly dressed, with accompanying doorman's cap, slicked-back black hair, and manicured nails. He was especially friendly towards me. I knew what the score was, though. Tenants had been asking for the building council to hire a full-time doorman for ages. Now they had one, but I had heard through the grapevine that it wasn't to provide Concrete Mama residents with an on-site concierge or to open the front door for little old lady tenants; it was because of me. Despite my detective "fame," the building council had deemed me a "menace." The doorman's other duties included watching me with those cold eyes of his. However, more than that, my gut felt he had another agenda besides the one he had been given.

There was nothing the building council could do to make me move. One hundred percent of the residents of this building were in legacy housing. Most were legacy babies like I used to be, which meant they really didn't work at all. I'm sure the events of my debut major case probably made more than a few of them pee their pants. They were probably hiding in their apartments, in their closets, or under their beds, wondering whether the city's police were coming for me, or city gangsters or if Up-Top flying saucers would laser beam our building from orbit. I actually didn't blame them; if the tables were turned, I would have thought the same.

"Good afternoon, Mr. Cruz, sir," the doorman said to me.

"Hello," I replied. I never did learn his name, because "Mr. Doorman" was what everyone in the Concrete Mama called him. I should have called him "Mr. Shark Eyes, sir."

"Cruz, we should wait here."

I had no intention of taking Phishy up to my place, but I wasn't going to hang out in the lobby, either.

"Why?"

"I told you."

"You've told me nothing."

"He's going to pick us up right out front."

Phishy and I were having a conversation, but we noticed that a crowd had formed, circling us—sidewalk johnnies, and the doorman. They were listening intently to every word out of our mouths.

"Don't you have something to do?" I asked all of them.

"Yeah. We're hanging in the lobby," one of the sidewalk johnnies said.

"Got another hot case, Mr. Cruz?" another asked.

"Sorry to intrude, Mr. Cruz, sir," the doorman said. "It's so fascinating to work every day in the building of a famous detective."

"I'm just a regular guy."

"So modest, too."

I watched him. His shark eyes didn't reveal anything, but that didn't silence my gut from telling me that he was nothing but bad news, despite his ever-friendly demeanor.

I turned to Phishy, and pointed at him. "Follow me."

We marched through everyone and out the front entrance, into a torrent of rain.

"Phishy, if you don't tell me what this is all about, I'll be leaving you right here. I have a warm, dry apartment waiting for me."

"I need you to go with me on a job, as my bodyguard—to make sure everything stays proper."

"I'm not doing a bodyguard job."

"Don't worry. It's not dangerous at all. You take us there, and wait in the car; we'll go in to get our stuff, then we'll come back out. You don't even have to use your vehicle."

"That's not a bodyguard job. That's a lookout job for criminal activity."

Phishy laughed. "I'm not criminal, Cruz. I'm as straight as you are. Oh, he's here!"

A large red hovercar descended to the ground. It looked like an old hoverfiretruck, though only half the length.

"Phishy, I'm not going anywhere."

"Ten bills," he yelled at me, and looked back up, waving to the hovertruck.

Ten bills. Hmm? That would make a big dent in the balance of my omega-gun.

"Cruz, my man!"

A look of shock gripped my face, and my mouth hung open. Before me was a dark mustached, bearded stick of a man, wearing a red slicker jacket and Christmas hat, both covered with flashing indicator lights. He had his arms outstretched, as if he expected me to run into them for a hug.

Blinky!

CHAPTER 14

Blinky

What's the one thing that any classic hovercar collector or restorer fears above all? Your vehicle getting stolen! It was a delicate balance of keeping your precious vehicle in mint condition, and deciding to fill it to the brim with the latest anti-theft technology on the market. There was no right answer. It often came down to where you lived, and if you had access to a private garage. I never did, but I had all kinds of secrets in protecting my Pony. I pretended not to care about hovercar security at all, when I was actually as obsessive about it as I was about my vehicle not getting scratched.

However, there was one time in a classic hovervehicle's life when it was completely vulnerable—at hovercar shows!

There I was, as a kid, entering my Ford Pony into one vintage hovercar show after another. That's how you built your rep, especially if you wanted to get into the classic hovercar restoring business. If you couldn't restore your own vehicle, no one was going to hire you to touch theirs. Right from the start, I impressed the OG "original gangsters" of classic hovercars. The old-timers inspected my vehicle from top to bottom, sat in the driver's seat, revved the engine. They looked at each other and nodded. Getting their thumbs-up seal of approval meant to everyone who was anything in the classic hovercar biz that I was legit, and operating at the top of the craft.

At a hovercar show, your vehicle was there for people to see. The doors were open, the keys were in the ignition, and the engines were purring. No one stole at a show. People had gotten executed for less. Well, that's what I'd thought.

One fateful day, I was chatting it up with the OGs about their vehicles, each centuries-old model worth millions, with hulky bodyguards standing next to them at all times. Then I heard it. Every classic hovercar driver knows the sound of their own vehicle's engine. We dream about it. I turned around to see a laughing guy in a Santa suit slam my doors shut from within the vehicle!

By the time I bolted to my Pony, it was in the air. However, the guy was not driving it away. He was doing a complete aerial donut. The spinning didn't stop and now everyone at the car show was watching, some laughing, some surprised, others in shock as I was. Then he stopped, and the hovercar dropped. People dived for cover, thinking it was crashing to the ground, but the man braked inches above the ground. The door opened, and all I heard was laughter, as the man got out. He was thin, but much taller than me.

I was on fire and it didn't matter whether he was five times my size. I was going to kill him. He saw my face, and took off like a gazelle. I ran after him.

"You're dead!" I yelled.

The man in the Santa suit never stopped running. He never looked back, and never slipped on the wet ground (I slipped several times). Thirty minutes of running through the city streets became an hour. I swore with every OCD fiber of my being that I was never going to stop until I caught him, and beat him ugly.

Two hours later, my legs simply gave out, and I collapsed to the ground. I wasn't out of energy, but my legs had their own mind. I sat on the ground, watching the Santa man disappear into the distance and the rain.

I was no less enraged, but I literally couldn't walk anymore. Luckily for me, more than one attendee from the hovercar show had followed me while I was chasing the Santa man. They got me into a hovertaxi, and back to the show, where the OGs had loaned me a couple of their bodyguards to watch my Pony.

"Does anyone know that thief's name?" I angrily asked.

"Yeah," said a guy with long, flowing white hair. "His name is Blinky. He's a small-time hustler in the city."

I looked for him, but never caught up with him again. I heard about him from time to time. No other fool wore a blinking Santa suit all year round—but that was a long time ago. I had been a kid in high school. As you get older and move on with life, you forget about all that silliness. But I never did forget his name.

I gave Phishy a dirty look, gave Blinky a disgusted look, and spun around to go back into my building.

"No, Cruz, we need you." Phishy ran after me.

"Why are you with him?" I pointed at Santa man.

"Blinky? He's an associate. He brought me the job."

"What job? I still don't know what any of this is about."

"I'll tell you all about it, man," Blinky interjected.

"Man? I'm not talking to you."

"Man, where's all this hostility coming from? Why you hatin' on Santa?"

"You are not Santa!"

"What'd I do to you, man?"

"You don't remember, do you?"

"Remember what, man?"

"A younger Blinky jumps into a classic red Ford Pony, at a major classic hovercar show, and does endless donuts with said vehicle."

Blinky started giggling. "I remember that. Man, that was, like, fifty years ago."

"Try not even twenty years ago."

"Man, some kid chased me. Was that your kid?"

"No, man, that was me."

Blinky burst out laughing, and then Phishy started laughing with him.

"That was you, man? Where was your hat? You weren't wearing your hat."

"My hat came later."

"Phishy, man. This cat chased me for hours. If I didn't have my stimulants, he would have caught me for sure. He was going to run the entire length of Metropolis to get me, but his legs must have given out on him." He looked at me, laughing. "You were that kid, man. Glad to see you've bulked up a bit. A wet kitten had more mass than you did back then."

"Drugs. I should have guessed it." I said to Phishy, "You and your man, Blinky, can do this job without me."

"We need you, Cruz."

"Phishy, the man asked a legit question." Blinky moved closer to me. I should have punched him. "Cruz, my man, Phishy and I are picking up an item for resale. That's it. You get to drive my vehicle. You can even do some donuts, if that makes you feel good. We pick up the item, while you wait in the truck. When we come out, you drive away."

"Yeah, Cruz," added Phishy.

"Why do you need a getaway driver?"

They laughed.

"Getaway driver, man? It's nothing like that."

"Phishy, you said something about a bodyguard."

"Yeah, a car bodyguard."

"What's the item?"

"Cruz, we'll pick it up and show it to you," Phishy said. "You know I don't do any crimes above misdemeanors, and this one is not even that. There's nothing to worry about. Your second best man wouldn't do that to you."

"You're getting married, man?" Blinky asked.

"No, you can't come to my wedding," I said. "We don't believe in Santa."

"I can't believe you're holding a grudge about something from fifty years ago, man. I'd never have remembered it, myself."

"Cruz," Phishy said to me. "Ten bills."

Phishy normally couldn't convince me to do anything, but with a limited cash flow, I could surely stand to shrink my debt.

"Where are you two picking up this item?"

"Now, Cruz," Phishy prepared me. "Don't panic. I know you've had some issues with the place, so you'll be able to understand why I need you on this one."

"Phishy, where?"

"Mad City."

Mad Heights was its real name, but its street name was Mad City and I'd almost died there in my last major case—multiple times, all on the same day. I'd sworn I would never go near that city again, but here I was flying to it.

The quest for money made people do very stupid things. There was no way I was going to drive his red firetruck into that place. I had my driver's gloves on as I raced down the fast lane in the Pony. Phishy was in the passenger seat, and Blinky was in the back seat.

"This is one sweet ride, man," Blinky said.

"Yeah, you would know. You were in it before. It's the same vehicle."

"I can't remember all that from that far back, man. I can barely remember what I did last week."

"That I can believe."

"Oh, Phishy, you remember the Mistress?"

"Oh, yeah. What happened?"

"Oh, man, Phishy. They found him stuffed in a dumpster over in Free City."

It was exactly what I was not interested in hearing. Two sliders in my vehicle chatting about their pseudo-criminal activities. Phishy was genuinely as averse to the hardcore criminal world as I was, but he did keep his finger on the pulse of the streets. Phishy knew everything and anything worth knowing or not knowing. If he didn't, he'd know who to go to, to find out.

Well, at least they were their own entertainment. I imagined they could go hours on end, chatting and giggling amongst themselves. It allowed me to focus on driving and watching my surroundings. The sky lanes to Mad City were as dangerous as any in the city. I was ready for anything.

Yet nothing did happen. We arrived without incident. Even the rain tapered down a bit.

"We'll go in, get it, and be right back," Phishy said to me.

I still didn't know what "it" was, but nodded as they ran off into some alleyway. I immediately closed the door, and took the Pony back up to about ten feet in the air in a blind spot between the ground lights. I tilted down the front of the car at an angle. My vehicle was backed up, almost touching the wall of the building, with the front pointing down, a maneuver called the "spider man." I could hang here, and easily watch everything around me.

People were scattered on the ground, walking to wherever. The occasional hovercar passed above. It was one in the morning, but Metropolis was a supercity that never slept, especially in the rainy season, when day and night looked the same. Thank goodness for clocks. Most of the legitimate world was fast asleep, but not the hustlers, or the detectives unfortunate enough to not have a good case at the present time to pay the bills.

I saw two figures dart out of the same alleyway—one in a bright red Santa suit. I had the Pony down and in front of them in seconds.

"Keep those feet on the floor, and away from the leather upholstery!" I yelled as they piled in.

When they were in, and the door closed, we were in the air. I couldn't get to the main sky lane quick enough to get away from there. I had noticed that Phishy was carrying a blocky briefcase.

"Well?" I asked.

"Smooth, man," Blinky answered. "No problems. I know these guys. They do good business. The people in the neighborhood are another matter."

I had been watching the rear-view mirror. Then I glanced at the rear-view monitor on my dashboard display.

Phishy noticed too. "Are we being followed?"

"I don't know. Let's find out."

My Ford Pony was one of the most powerful muscle hovercars ever. I gunned the engine, and we were at greater than 200 mph in seconds. As I climbed into the fast lane and left every hovervehicle in the dust, I flipped a switch under the dashboard.

"What did you do?" Phishy asked.

I didn't answer. I slowed the Pony, returning to normal speed, and one of the middle lanes.

"What did the switch do?" Phishy asked.

"Phishy, the man's car has super powers," Blinky said. "We mere mortals will never know, but if we were being followed, they were left behind in the last time zone, based on how fast this thing took off."

Phishy leaned a bit over to my driver's side, and then ducked his head.

"Leave the Pony alone," I said.

"I want to know what that secret switch does."

"Phishy, focus. What contraband do you have in that case?"

He laughed.

"There's no contraband here, man." Blinky annoyed me something fierce.

"Here, let me show you." Phishy rested the case on his lap, and opened it. "Can I turn on the inside light?"

"No!" I yelled, as I opened the glove box, and took out a pen light for him.

"Do you know what it is?" Phishy asked, as soon as he turned off his pen light inspection of the device.

"What is it?"

"It's a retriever."

I did a big no-no, and took my eyes off the sky lane to look at him. I quickly recovered, though.

"Phishy, man, he knows what it is."

Of course I knew what it was. I was a hovercar guy, and had used them before—but for vehicles. The retriever in the case was for people!

"Phishy. Those are illegal."

"No, they're not illegal. Cranial storage units are illegal, but their retrievers are not."

I was not happy. I felt sick. It was technology from the past, a very sick past. Criminals back then were so paranoid about government or corporate theft of their data, that they avoided the Net completely. That had given rise to data couriers; and that, to biological data storage devices. The sickest of all were cranial storage units—couriers turning sections of their skulls into data storage units. Retrievers could then jack-in to upload or download data. Yes, they were criminals, but electric lobotomies were not what the doctor ordered. So many died, or slowly died, from conditions that never should have existed. Installing a computer next to your brain inside your skull was so insane that even before the technology was outlawed by Earth and off-world, criminals cartels and corporations stopped using them. That was more than a century ago.

What made me sick was, if someone wanted to buy this retriever off Phishy and his new associate in the Santa suit, there was at least one poor slob out there who had some kind of data storage in his or her body.

"Phishy—"

"You don't have to say it, Cruz." Phishy had his sad face on. "You can just drop us off at the Concrete Mama, and Blinky and I will take it from there in his truck."

"Thanks, Cruz, man." Blinky leaned forward from the back seat. "You got us there and back. That's more than we could ask. I knew you hadn't given up on Santa and his helpers."

Phishy glanced back at him with a smile.

"Hey, man, I got a secret switch, too." With that, Blinky reached down to something on his belt, and the flashing indicator lights on his Santa suit went from mere points of illumination to a full, blinding light show of red, white, blue, and green. "Blinky says: *Cruz is the man!*" He repeated his announcement as he gyrated around on my back seat. The police should have used Blinky instead of photo-bombs to stun suspects, and save the city some money—just as effective.

I was being blinded by science in my own Pony, with the sound of Phishy's crazy laughter. How quickly could I get these two out of my vehicle?

CHAPTER 15

Swordplaya and the Killer Robot

When I returned to the Concrete Mama, it was late enough, or early enough, for there to be only a couple of sidewalk johnnies in the lobby. They were sleeping, sprawled out on lobby chairs. I got up to my apartment, showered, and got to bed as quickly as possible. I knew I'd get only a few hours of sleep before having to get "back on the road."

The wedding was not until next year, but we both felt so rushed in getting things ready. I remember when Dot's parents had told us that a year away was barely enough time, and we'd balked. We'd wanted it over and done in six months, until we learned the waiting list for any decent venue in the city was at least a year! That's what you get for living in a city with 50 million people.

Every day, it seemed, there was another piece of wedding preparation I had to do. Today I planned to swing by Let It Ride Enterprises in Peacock Hills to see my best man, Run-Time. I needed some of his infectious optimism on life. All this wedding stuff was wearing me out. I also had to focus on getting some paying clients. A famous detective with few paying clients wouldn't be famous for long.

I was in Harry's Haberdashery in Woodstock Falls. It's where I bought my own fedoras, and I'd decided I'd get a nice all-white one for the wedding, to match my suit, which I was having custom-made.

"That's a nice one," Harry said to me.

I stared through the display case at the hat. "Yeah, I think I'll take it."

"The wedding's around the corner."

"Yeah. Next year, but it sure feels like it's around the corner."

Harry turned around to grab a box and packing supplies from the shelf. "Mr. Cruz, look at it this way. If you don't do it right this time, you can always do it again—or as many times as it takes."

I smiled at him, shaking my head. "Mr. Harry, this is a one-time event in my life. I couldn't ever go through all this again. How long have you and the missus been together?"

"Thirty-two years."

"Yes, that's what I want. One-time. Go through the headaches and chaos once."

Harry created the box, lined it with plush felt wrapping, and reached down to remove the white fedora from the case. He handed it to me.

"This is one nice hat," I said.

"You're making a good purchase—but then you always do, Mr. Cruz."

I handed it to him to finish packing. Of course, I spent at least an hour in there talking about hats and life. I had to continue my training in becoming a hat connoisseur.

My mobile phone began ringing, and that was my cue to bid Harry goodbye until next time. As I grabbed the string handle of my hat box, I glanced at the caller ID.

"Phishy, why are you calling me? I thought we'd agreed to limit my exposure to you to no more than once a day."

I strolled out the door as I pushed it open.

"Phishy?"

The video screen was on, but there was no Phishy. I heard faint voices in the background. "Phishy?"

"Cruz—help me."

I stopped in my tracks. I had known Phishy for a while. I had heard him in every mood under the sun, except one. He sounded scared.

"Cruz, you've got to help me."

I still didn't see his face on the screen.

"What's going on, Phishy? Why can't I see you?"

"You gotta come help me, Cruz. I'm in trouble."

"Phishy, tell me what's going on."

"I think they're going to kill me."

"Who's going to kill you?" Now I was worried. "Where are you?"

I heard him speak again, but it was inaudible. Then the call disconnected. I looked at the phone. All my attempts to call him back went straight to voice mail. Then I got an email. I stared at the sender field. It was from Phishy.

The email didn't say a thing. It was a set of numbers—map coordinates. To be doing what I was doing, driving to some strange coordinates, was crazy, but I was doing it.

As I approached that section of the city, I realized where I was going. Being part of the hovercar race scene had familiarized me with practically every nook and cranny Metropolis had to hide. Wharf City had good parts and shady ones; of course, for me, it was the latter. It seemed too good to be true that there was a secure parking lot next to the coordinates. I didn't trust it, despite the visible guards and cameras. I found another lot two miles away, and landed my vehicle in one of the covered pods of the structure. I didn't mind walking in the rain. I did it all the time.

There was no need to rush, because I didn't know what I was rushing to.

I stopped for a moment and looked around for a long time. The coordinates were the entrance to a section of underground city tunnels. There was actually an amateur (and illegal) hovercar race that took place in the tunnels—I'd participated one year, and came in third. I didn't like being in underground tunnels then and I didn't like them now.

All the tunnels had to do with water drainage, and most were large enough to fly a hovertruck through with ease. Some were much larger than that, and if you found yourself in one of that size, you needed to get out of there as rapidly as possible. A flash flood of water would come through those large tunnels so quickly that not only would you not have time to react, they would also never find your body. The smaller tunnels were for supplemental drainage; they were okay.

No, they were not okay. Underground tunnels were not for sightseeing. But there I was, looking for Phishy.

I stopped.

The voices were barely audible, but I heard them. That was the direction I walked in, keeping to a minimum the sloshing of water that reached to my knees.

"Phishy, I think you're stalling for time."

"No, Swordplaya, he'll be here. I swear it."

There was Phishy. Even from my distance, hiding in the shadows, watching from around a corner, I could see he was shaking with fear. Surrounding him were a bunch of punks, all wearing bottom-half masks. The "cute" image on the masks were razor sharp white teeth. Street gangs always had to have some gimmick.

The obvious leader of the crew was the man Phishy was talking to. He was a bald guy in a suit. I could see a sheathed samurai sword hanging from his side—another wannabe samurai. The man turned his head in my direction. Besides the thin mustache, one of his eyes was a glowing red, and that part of his face was metal. I had too many cyborgs in my life.

"Shouldn't we join my master?"

The voice came from behind me in the dark, and before I could reach for my gun, both my wrists were grabbed by something powerful. My arms were lifted above my head, and I grimaced. There was nothing I could do as I was pushed into the view of the tunnel lights. It was a seven-foot humanoid robot, with the same razor-sharp white teeth images spray-painted where a mouth should be. It had multi-lens eyes in a circle configuration, and a blue armor-plated exterior.

Such robots were so illegal, that on sight police could blast them. Their builders or owners got mandatory prison sentences when caught, but that's why they were called criminals. They didn't follow the laws.

"Is this the guy?" Swordplaya asked Phishy.

Phishy nodded, and answered only when the gangster boss flashed him an angry look. "Yeah. Yes."

The robot had me suspended off my feet in the water, and pulled me to his boss. There, a couple of his punks frisked me, and took charge of the two guns in my shoulder holster, under my jacket. Then they frisked me again, a bit too thoroughly.

"Hey," I said. "There's frisking, and then there's manhandling my groin area more than is appropriate."

Their boss walked up to me with a smirk. "Sneaking up on Swordplaya is an impossible thing to do when the robot is watching my back, Mr. Blinky."

Blinky?

"Tell me what you want, so Phishy and I can get out of here," I said with no trace of fear in my voice.

"What makes you think either one of you are leaving this tunnel alive?"

"This is your associate, Mr. Blinky?" the gangster boss asked. "Where's your Santa costume? I hear you always wear a silly Santa get-up with flashy lights."

"Are we here to conclude business, or discuss fashion like a bunch of girls?"

He wasn't amused, and I could see a thought flash across his face as he slowly drew the sword from its sheath. I didn't like how the light reflected off its blade.

"Phishy, what's going on?" I asked. I had to get some insight into the scam Phishy was running to save his life.

"He said I double-crossed him by getting him a fake retriever. I told him I'd get him another, but he won't let me leave."

I looked at Swordplaya. "Why can't we get you another one?"

"Because this is a one-time event. My client demands secrecy. One retriever from the black market is one thing, but two? Too many questions will be asked."

"Oh, stop being stupid," I said, annoyed. "Why didn't you say so before? Tell your robot to let me go, give me the retriever, and I'll fix it. It's hardware from, like, a century ago. What do you expect?"

Swordplaya watched me, thinking.

"You know, Swordplayer—"

"Swordplaya," he corrected.

"You know, Swordplaya, I actually do have other business to do today. Maybe you and your kindergarten crew hang out in flooded tunnels, splashing water on each other for your twisted Kamasutra water games, but the rest of us have to work. Tell your robot to let me go! Then get the retriever!"

Swordplaya was pissed. He gestured to one of his punks. "Release him," he said to the robot.

"Did he pay us?" I asked Phishy.

"Not yet."

A punk appeared from the shadows with that boxy suitcase. I snatched it from him, and turned to the robot.

"Hold the case while I inspect it," I said to it.

The robot did as I commanded, and I opened the case. I hadn't wanted to see this piece of ancient hardware ever again, but here I was. As a germophobe, I always carried a pair of surgical gloves on my person for emergencies. I pulled them from a jacket pocket.

I picked up the device, and slowly scanned every inch of it with my eyes. "Anyone have tools?" I asked aloud.

"Swiss Army knife?" a punk asked.

"That'll do," I said.

I took apart the outer casing, so I could see the inner parts.

"It's fried," I said, looking up at Swordplaya.

"What do you mean, it's fried?"

"Just what I said. Wait." I looked at Phishy. "Was it working when you picked it up yesterday?"

"It was fine," he stuttered.

I pointed at Swordplaya. "You damaged it! I know exactly what you did."

You had to yell a lot when dealing with criminals who were more powerful than you. Make them think you were as tough as they were.

"I didn't damage it."

"Okay. Then tell me what you did. Step by step, when Phishy gave it to you."

Swordplaya looked around, then looked at one punk in particular, who looked away.

"That's what I thought," I said. "You tried to power up a piece of technology you had no idea how to use, and you fried it. Then you hold Phishy and me hostage for something you did. Pay us!"

"I'm not paying you!"

"We delivered as promised. Pay us! If you broke it, that's on you."

Swordplaya's mobile phone rang. I saw his face immediately change from menace to apprehension when he looked at the number. He answered it. "Yes." He listened a few moments, then returned the mobile to his pocket. "Double your money if you can fix it."

I looked at him. Phishy had told them I was Blinky because I was the only person he knew who could get him out of here alive, but I was so good at my act, that I realized there was a strong possibility that not only would we get out of here, but with a fat wad of cash each.

"Okay," I said. "Pay us, and I'll get started. Let's get out of this tunnel to someplace dry. I'll need real electronic tools, though."

"How long?" he asked.

I waited until one of the punks handed Phishy a duffel bag. My gaze turned to their boss. He smiled and gestured to another. The punk walked over to the bag, and opened it to peek inside.

"A few hours, to play it safe," I answered.

"No!" The yell from the shadows startled us all.

A man ran at us, and was immediately restrained. He was dressed like the other punks, but his face was a pasty white, and he had bags under his eyes as if he hadn't slept in weeks. The hair on the left side of his head was missing.

I knew immediately what I was seeing. "Oh, no," I said.

"You have to get that data out of his head, now," Swordplaya said.

"Why would you do this? Have you never heard of a simple data disk?"

"He's dead anyway. He knew the risks, and his family was richly compensated for his sacrifice. Your choice is simple, Mr. Blinky. Get the data out of his head before he dies. Or he dies, and we kill you both."

I pushed past all of them, and returned to the robot holding the case. "Are you programmed for mechanical repair functions?"

"I'm programmed for all advanced mechanical repair functions."

"Repair the damaged circuits of this device. I'll hold the case."

Criminals. Most of them were dumber than a rock, and these were no different. Swordplaya and company didn't need Phishy or me to repair the retriever. They had a robot that probably could have built one from scratch, if fed the proper specifications.

The robot fixed the device in less than a minute. Then I screwed the outer coverings back. I handed it to Swordplaya. "Here—and don't burn it out again. You need an external power source for it to work. In language that you can understand, that means connect it to that external power source before you turn it on."

The gangster wouldn't take it. "You do it."

"I am not downloading data from someone's skull."

"We paid you double. Finish the job."

"Please, get it out of my head," the man yelled.

"What were you going to use for an external power source?" I asked.

"We didn't know we needed one."

I shook my head. "Robot, plug into the device, to provide the necessary power for it to function." As the robot pulled a line from its chest plate, I said to the gangster, "Maybe *I* should take the robot home, since you don't know how to use it properly."

"It captured you, didn't it?"

"Yeah, but it can do a lot more than kill all kinds of people for you."

"Task complete," the robot said.

This was the part I was dreading. Where was the access point in the man's skull?

The man broke free from his comrades holding him. He pulled down a skin flap on the side of his head. "Here," he said.

I wanted to gag. A metallic access node protruded through the skin. "I sure hope they paid you a hell of a lot of money to do this to your body."

He smiled. "More."

I was about to insert the retriever, then stopped. I realized the very act of retrieving the data from the man would probably kill him.

"It's okay," he said. "I've already wrapped up all my affairs. I'm ready to go."

Wrapped up all his affairs. What a haunting concept. I felt so sorry for the man, for what I was about to do. I knew what to do, but had never done it. I had done so with hovercars, but not with people's skulls.

As soon as I inserted the retriever into his cranial node, his eyes started fluttering wildly, and his body shook. The others held him down as I looked at the retriever console. It didn't show how much data was being retrieved, only what percentage had been retrieved. The man's body shook more violently. By the time it was 75 percent done, he was shaking so violently that the robot had to hold him. Then it was done.

I pulled out the retriever from the cranial access node. The man's head flopped down. The whites of his eyes were browned, his mouth hung open, and there was an odor of burning flesh. The man was dead.

I covered my closed eyes with my hand, overcome by emotion.

"Here." I put the retriever in Swordplaya's hand. "Phishy and I are out of here."

"Thank you, Mr. Blinky," he said with a smile.

He obviously couldn't care less about the dead man, his man. Now I was faced with the prospect that the gangster could still kill Phishy and me.

I grabbed a frightened Phishy by the shirt, and I watched them all as we walked away into the tunnel. Swordplaya watched us like a hawk, and so did his punks, waiting for any command to gun us down.

"Swordplaya, don't even think of doing a double-cross," I yelled.

"I could use that money I paid you with," he said, "and I don't particularly need this retriever anymore. It's not even worth the effort to donate it to a museum."

"I don't really care what you do with it," I said. It was clear to me that Swordplaya planned to kill us anyway. "You're not very smart, are you?"

"That's a funny thing for you to say, Mr. Blinky, since you're the ones about to join my brain-fried former employee here."

"Hey, rockhead. How do you plan to retrieve the data from the retriever? You might want to consult with your robot before you do something stupid."

Swordplaya grabbed the retriever to look at the display. His mobile began ringing again. "Yes. We have it."

They didn't notice that Phishy and I were running away from them so fast, that if we went any faster, we'd achieve light speed.

CHAPTER 16

The Client

"We have to find the bigger tunnels," I said, as we ran deeper into the underground network.

"Bigger?" Phishy said, still shaken. "But the main outwash comes from those tunnels."

"Phishy, if they send the robot after us, we're through."

I finished my sentence, and we both heard fast-approaching sloshing behind us. They were closing in on us—fast. The decision I made then would determine whether we'd live another day, or if our bodies would disappear forever. No one knew we were there.

Swordplaya stood shining the light from his cyborg eye all around the tunnel, sword in hand. His robot stood next to him; its entire face was a spotlight, and scanned everything in sight. His gang stood behind him, waiting, each with machine guns.

"We know you're here," he yelled out.

We were shoved into upper crawl tunnels like rodents. I jumped up seven feet to an opening as if I were slam-ducking a basketball. I pulled myself in, reached down, and then pulled in Phishy, who had half scurried up the wall, he was so scared.

There we were, two of us, lying in the muck and mire of a crawl tunnel made for one, in a foot of water. No weapons. No water-proofing. We didn't dare move. The dark, tiny tunnel could have been infested with rats, or worse. Suddenly, I became terrified about the prospect of some isopod swimming into my face and latching on, but there was not a damn thing I could do about it. We were both the epitome of trapped helplessness.

The only thing saving us was the voluminous number of crawl tunnels in the section. Manually jumping up and looking inside each one would take forever. I wasn't going to take the chance that the robot didn't have air motion or vibration sensors. We were lucky that it didn't have advanced infrared, but even so, the heat from the walls would have nullified that ability. We had to lie as if we were dead, or we would be.

"Come out, Blinky and Phishy. Come out, wherever you are. We'll find you if we have to stand here all day and night."

I couldn't help but to look at Phishy—he was only about six inches from me. The outside tunnel lights did give us some illumination. He was so scared, fighting to keep from shaking, and pale as a ghost. I had never seen him like this. In fact, I couldn't remember a time when Phishy wasn't smiling or laughing. He didn't want to die today. That's why he had told them I was Blinky and called me. In his mind, I was the only person on the Earth who could keep him from dying today. The bad part was, if he were wrong, I'd be dead too—but I couldn't be angry with him.

We heard the gangster's mobile ring again.

"Yes," he answered. "We have them cornered, one of the smaller tunnels high up. How many are there? I don't know."

"There are 219 auxiliary tunnels that they could have gone into from the time their movement stopped," the robot said.

"219," he said into the mobile. "Thank you? What do you mean, 'Thank you?' Where do you want me to deliver the data and device? How? You're here. What do you mean, you're here?"

All we heard was a scream. The tunnel erupted in machine-gunfire and major laser gunfire that I assumed were from the robot. There were strange whizzing sounds, and then more human screams. Next was an explosion. Metal showered the tunnel. One hot fragment hit our crawl tunnel and landed right on my chin. I turned my head, and let it slide into the water.

My eyes widened in horror. Phishy had one hand holding his mobile in video-recording mode outside our tunnel. I slowly raised an arm out of the freezing water to tap him, but he saw my expression, and slowly lowered his hand away from the tunnel opening.

Literally seconds after his hand disappeared from the opening a light beam flashed by. My heart sank into my stomach. Whoever it was would have seen Phishy's hand and mobile for sure, if I hadn't acted.

We remained still, listening for any sound at all. Phishy started to get restless, but I raised an arm out of the water again, and grabbed his face. I slowly shook my head. He watched me as I lay back down and closed my eyes. We had to stay where we were.

I knew I had fallen asleep a couple of times. I considered this a stakeout, which many would admit I was better at than anyone else. Phishy and I would remain here playing dead for hours, days, if needed. I knew *he* was out there, waiting. I didn't know who he was, but he had killed Swordplaya, his robot, his men, and was waiting in the dark to kill us. Still I was betting on the fact that he had no desire to sit in the darkness, cold, and water forever. All things considered, Phishy and I were comfortable. The water was warm in this crawl tunnel, though I didn't want to guess why it was warm. I could have my germophobic attack *after* we escaped.

A noise. "You win, you lucky bastards."

What? I turned my head slowly to look at Phishy. He was looking at me too, with a perplexed look. Had we actually heard a voice say those words? Were we dreaming? I'd fallen asleep so many times in the many hours we had lain there in the muck and mire.

We heard sloshing around again, footsteps in the water. They were real. They came closer, stopped, started again, then disappeared in the distance. After a time, we didn't even hear their echoes.

PART FIVE

The Orochi Corporation

CHAPTER 17

Jabba the Butt

It was said that bad things always happened more frequently during rainy season. I had to agree, since Phishy and I could still find ourselves deader than dead. Phishy had been reduced to a traumatized puppy as we made our escape to the surface. I thought about folks, friends, and life—all normal things humans did when faced with their own mortality.

I had been peeking out of the crawl tunnel for the last hour, into the main tunnel. First to allow my eyes to adjust to the near-darkness, then to watch and listen for anything. Despite all the signs, I didn't think the client of the human formerly-known-as-Swordplaya had left us behind. I was certain he was waiting somewhere for us.

Most of the tunnel lights had been shot out, or at least that's what I assumed, because they were gone. The only illumination was from lights much farther away, in other sections of the tunnel. But there was something else. That was what I was trying to get a better look at as I slowly jutted out my head farther from our hiding place.

In my last case, I had tangled with a psycho cyborg criminal known as Red Rabbit, whose weapon of choice was what could only be called a lightning rifle. Who knew how many unlucky slobs he'd fried to death with that rifle? He'd tried to blast me, too.

The damage from the weapon this client had used was so powerful, that if Metro Police had known it existed, the entire supercity would have been on lockdown until they'd found it. There were dark chunks in the water which could only be what was left of bodies or body parts. I couldn't tell. Swordplaya's robot was a heavy-duty wrecker model, but even its impressive weaponry and shielding were no match at all. The damage from the weapon had blasted holes through solid rock, and possibly our way to freedom.

We would have to run for it, but having been prone for so long, soaking in the water, our muscles would probably cramp up. We had to get our circulation moving normally, before we made our break for it. I sat up a bit, and first started rigorously rubbing each arm, shaking my hands, then my thighs, all without making any noise. Phishy copied everything I did.

I was ready. Only time would tell if I were readying us for escape, or for death.

I took one more quick look all around, then I pulled my head back into the crawl tunnel, spun myself around to my original position, and slid back out, feet first.

What's that?

I couldn't pull myself back into the crawl tunnel fast enough. I realized what the rumbling sound approaching us was—the outwash!

We were either going to be lucky, and the water would flow past us, never quite reaching as high as we were, or we were about to be drowned.

"Hold your breath!" I yelled. "It's coming."

In a city where it always rained, Metropolis Water Works had to pump all that water somewhere. The tunnels took it out of the city and all the way to the ocean; otherwise Metropolis would be named Atlantis.

The water didn't reach as high as we were, but flowed right under the bottom edge of our tiny tunnel. We humans could build our supercities and space colonies, but all combined, it was still insignificant when it came to the power of Mother Nature. The water roared past us. I knew we'd be there a while. I also knew no one would ever see the bodies of the late Swordplaya, his punks, or his robot ever again. All evidence of this client's super-weapon would be erased, too. But then again, Phishy had recorded it all on his mobile.

The water was gone, and I didn't waste a second more. I jumped from the crawl tunnel and helped Phishy down. I led the way as we ran, and though I wanted to stop, I didn't. All inspections had to be done as we ran.

As we turned a corner into a lit section of the tunnels, we both almost screamed—dirt! The water hadn't done that. The client's super-weapon had blasted through solid rock and past it to expose the dirt of the Earth—ancient dirt. No average Metropolitan had seen real dirt in centuries. Ancient dirt meant ancient germs, fungus, insects, or flesh-eating ticks. The thought of it made Phishy and me run twice as fast. We were not going to be cocooned or injected with egg sacks, to have armies of bugs hatch inside us, to devour us from the inside out. Next we'd see real-life plants. Nasty!

It was a no-name sleazy bar-restaurant on the outskirts of Wharf City, but in our present mental state and physical condition, it was the same as Heaven. I was sure that to everyone who noticed us as we came through the front door, we looked as if we had walked off some kind of battlefield. My tan fedora and coat were long gone; I had dumped them in the outwash. Besides Phishy, everyone who knew I had been in that tunnel was dead, and I planned to keep it that way.

I wasn't clean and neat because I was a germophobe. I was that way because I had class. I was that way because I was a human being who didn't walk on all fours and wasn't born in a barn. Phishy and I walked in covered in grime and slime, soaking wet, but sat at one of the booths in the tiny restaurant part of the bar, yet it was a non-event to everyone inside—the bartender serving drinks, the barflies on stools slinging back their glasses of hard liquor, the patrons at booths or tables stuffing their faces with slop. In fact, none of them looked much cleaner than we did. Clearly, no health inspector had ever set foot in this joint.

"Give me your mobile."

Phishy handed it to me without a word.

"I'll get it back to you."

He nodded, trying to smile. Phishy was still shell-shocked.

"For the next few days, I want you to lay low," I said. "Do you have someplace safe to stay?"

He nodded again.

"I don't want to take any chances."

"He knows my name." Phishy lost it, and his eyes teared up.

He was right. Swordplaya and company were gone forever, but the person who killed them probably did know Phishy's name.

"Phishy."

It took him a bit to collect himself.

"We're going to take care of it. I promise. Leave right now, and stay with one of your friends you can trust, safe. Get rested up. Get yourself together. Send word to me, by one of your sidewalk johnny buddies, secretly, when you're settled. In fact, it's better I have your phone." I grabbed the phone and quickly ripped out its disk. "See. It's off. So, if he has it, or gets it, he'll think we were washed away too."

Phishy sniffled, and nodded.

"Call a taxi," I said.

"No, I'll walk. I need to be outside for a bit, to think and calm down."

"Yeah," I said. "I hear you—but don't take chances."

"I won't."

We stood, and Phishy looked at me for a moment. "Thanks for saving my life, Cruz. I shouldn't have done what I did, but only you could have saved me. I didn't want to die. I don't do real crime. I'm Phishy. All I do is hustle."

"Just get yourself to someplace safe and rest up. Think of it as vacation time."

"Yeah." He flashed a Phishy smile at me.

As he left the bar, I could see he was already started to return to normal. I was starting to return to normal again, because now I was having random thoughts of—wedding plans!

"Could I have some napkins?" I asked the bartender.

He glanced up at me for a second, then returned to pouring himself a drink. Was he really going to blatantly ignore me? I watched him with squinted eyes. I stepped to the bar, directly opposite him, and crossed my arms.

"Napkins."

"Are you going to pay for them?"

"Do you expect me to pay for napkins?"

"I don't get them for free."

"What kind of place is this? No one charges customers for napkins."

"You're not a customer. You haven't bought any booze, or food. My establishment isn't here for your personal hygiene needs, bub."

"Bub?"

"Yeah, bub. Napkins are for paying customers only."

"You're not a 'bub,' you're a bum. I want some napkins to wipe the grime off my face."

"What grime? You look fine to me."

Was he serious? I was a walking dirt mop.

"You know what, bub? Get your napkins from the restroom and get out of here." He pointed to the back of the bar.

A wave of panic came over me—public restroom?

I never ever, ever, ever used public restrooms. I didn't care how clean they were supposed to be. I had a routine in life, and made sure I stuck it, so I was close to home for any "pit stops." Public restrooms? I'd rather die.

"There or no napkins for you, bub."

I had to get this gunk off of me. I felt as if my skin were crawling. I had to chance it.

I gave the bartender a dirty look as I marched to the restrooms. My girlfriend Dot had been counseling me. She'd said I had to get over my phobia of public restrooms, especially if we wanted to travel, and with my new detective job, that could take me far away from the Concrete Mama. She told me she'd tackle her phobia of bridges, if I handled my phobia of public restrooms. Besides, she told me, that's where people go to wash their hands. Yes, I agreed with her that that was a very "pro-germophobic" activity, and we would slay our phobias together.

"MEN." I stopped at the door. All my will power would need to be summoned. I didn't even have gloves to wear. I pushed the door open with my foot, and stepped in, preparing myself for what I might see—or hear.

What I walked into was nothing short of a *house of horrors*. Immediately, I saw him—the man was more than 500 pounds, his back to me, straddling with one fat leg on the lip of the wall urinal, and his two hands, palms out, braced against the wall. It seemed that he was nothing but fat, and all his butt fat was flowing out of his pants to moon me.

It wasn't a restroom. My vehicle was larger, and the man took up half the room—literally; next to the urinal was a toilet with no partition whatsoever. Across was a sink with an empty towel dispenser.

"Who dat?" he said. The man's jelly dough head began to turn to look at me. An explosion of bodily functions.

"Ahh!"

I ran from that restroom so fast, I'm surprised I hadn't reached the necessary velocity for time travel. I was out the door and into the streets; if it had been the desert, there would have been a trailing dust cloud.

CHAPTER 18

Fraggy

What do you think were the chances I would ever set foot near a public restroom after that Restroom of Horror with Jabba the Butt?

There was no nice way to say it. I was having a full-blown panic attack due to my germophobia. This was actually very serious. The doctors had once told my parents that if I didn't grow out of the condition, I could have to be committed to a hermetically sealed Bubble Colony for those suffering from the same psychosis.

My Pops wasn't having any of that. "He has a phobia, not a psychosis; you're not sending our boy to the moon," he told them and that was that. No more doctors for me, only counselors—completely useless, the lot of them. My Gramps was the only counselor I'd needed. I'd asked him how he'd quit chain-smoking two packs of cigarettes a day 50 years ago, and he said, "I woke up one day, and said 'I'm not smoking anymore.'—and did it." That's what I did. I said "No" to my germophobia, so it couldn't prevent me from living my life.

Well, I was partially successful. I did live my life, but I had to avoid nastiness. If I found myself in nastiness, there was a chance of my having the attack I was having at the moment—but there was a quick cure that I had availed myself of only a few times before.

The Centers for Disease Control had a base in every major supercity in the world. Command post, research labs, vaccination storage, and, my personal favorite, Decon.

Metro Disease Control hated me. They had threatened to hire extra guards to keep me out the next time. Well, this was "the next time." Thanks to the heavy rain, they wouldn't know it was me until I was inside. I scaled the outer fence like a human centipede.

"Hey, this is restricted property!" I heard someone yell as I bolted across the parking lot.

I saw one, and then two other guards giving chase, but I was too fast for them. I outran them and leaped up the steps. I could see a guard at the reception desk notice my face. He turned around to press the button but—

"Ha!" I yelled. I was in before he could lock the doors, and sprinted down the hallway.

He clumsily came out from behind the counter. The other three guards ran in, already out of breath.

"Intruder alert!" sounded over the overhead.

I whipped around the corner, but glanced back for a second. There were about a dozen of them chasing me now. I knew they'd try to block my path, and already I heard feet running to me from around the corner ahead. I stopped and leaned against the wall. Three more guards barreled around, saw me, but couldn't stop in time. I was gone!

At this point, there were guards, scientists, and I think the main janitor and the housekeeping lady were chasing me now, too. I was in

Decon! There it was! I picked up speed and dived over the railing into the pool.

As my body sank slowly into the pool of decontamination gel, I stripped off as much of my clothing as possible, and threw the items as far away from me as I could. I flipped over, and saw a full audience watching me from the railing.

"Cruz, you're done!" one of the hulky bodyguards angrily yelled at me.

I simply smiled. My body submerged into the wonderful, beautiful, magnificent gel with its magical decontamination properties to erase all the filth, visible and microscopic, from my body. I would emerge better than a newborn baby after a morning bath. I would emerge as clean as was possible for a living human being.

The head of the Metropolitan Disease Control Center was a man by the name of Fraggioti. How a diminutive, spectacled scientist with Scandinavian lineage got an Italian name, I did not know. It didn't matter, because I called him Fraggy, and I had absolutely no respect for him.

I stood in his office wearing a biodegradable white paper top, pants, and booties. On either side were four guards. They were not happy.

"Mr. Cruz," Fraggy began, "the last time you breached this facility's security, I told you we would hire the necessary personnel to prevent you, and those like you, from trespassing."

I smiled. "Looks like you need more guards."

"Mr. Cruz, again, Metro Disease Control is not your personal residence, and the gel pool is not for your personal use. This is a multi-billion-dollar facility for the benefit of the people of Metropolis, not for a lone, infrequent, casual patient."

"Can I buy gel?"

"What? What are you asking, Mr. Cruz?"

"Can civilians buy gel to create their own home gel pools?"

"Mr. Cruz!" Fraggy calmed himself. "No, Mr. Cruz, neither you, nor the public, can buy gel for personal use."

"Why?"

"Why? Because it's for disease control use."

"Fraggy, here's the thing. You won't give me the gel. You won't sell me gel. So, until you give it to me, or sell it to me, I'm going to come here and swim in the gel pool."

"Mr. Cruz, I'm ready for you this time. I'm going to call the police. I'm going to have you arrested and jailed for trespass—"

"Hold on, Fraggy—"

"Mr. Cruz, my name is not Fraggy. I am Dr. Fraggioti."

"Fraggy, you've outlined a lot there. Let's just start with the police."

Fraggy's face was redder than red. He went to his desk and pressed a button on his vid-phone. "Elle, did you already call the police as I instructed?"

"I did, sir."

"And?"

"They're not coming."

"What do you mean, they're not coming?"

"They said they're not coming, and not to call them again about this."

Fraggy picked up the receiver and talked in a more hushed tone, but we still heard him.

"Elle, that is completely unacceptable, and I want you to contact the Director. You did. What did she say? Mr. Cruz has authority to use the gel pool? Who gave him that authority? The police chief of Metropolis. Thank you, Eleanor."

Fraggy slowly hung up the receiver.

"I'll see you next time, Fraggy," I said, waving.

CHAPTER 19

Run-Time

I had a ton of things to do, and they needed to get done quietly, secretly, and quickly. But when I got back to my apartment, it was into bed. I fell asleep instantly, and slept straight through the day. The gel pool might have invigorated me physically, but psychologically, my near-death experience had left me wasted. My body wasn't going to let me back into the waking world until I was fully re-powered.

When I called PJ at the office, I got an earful. A lot of people were looking for me, including Dot, who was about to call the police to find me. Even PJ was worried.

"You disappeared! You disappear around your birthday, but that was over months ago. Where did you go?" PJ asked.

"It was a case that went a bit sideways, but I'm fine. I need a new mobile, though. Have one for me when I get to the office."

"When will you be here? You have a lot of calls to make. Important calls. Paying clients. You need to get here right away."

"I'm on my way."

"Wait. Call Run-Time before you come in. He needs to talk to you right away."

"So, should I call Dot or Run-Time first?"

PJ laughed from my home phone's video monitor. "You're a grown man. Let's see if you can use your detective skills to figure that one out for yourself."

"Oh, and have some of our sidewalk johnny people waiting for me."

"Who the heck are sidewalk johnny people?"

"You know. The ones Phishy has do work for us. The ones wearing those stupid Liquid Cool T-shirts."

"Those T-shirts are not stupid. Phishy is stupid. I designed those T-shirts, and they're a good revenue stream for the office, especially if you're not bringing in paying clients."

"If you say so."

It was good to hear Dot's voice, and see her face, even if it was on a small screen. It took me almost half an hour to convince her that my cover story (also known as lying) about my disappearance yesterday was no big deal. There was no possible way I could tell her what'd really happened. I told her I'd make it up to her, and see her after her shift at Eye Candy for dinner.

Fortunately, my call to my best friend (and designated best man for the wedding) was much shorter. He wanted to see me at his offices. Run-Time had given me my first case, which had launched my career, and it seemed as if he was about to send another high-profile case my way.

All this time, my Pony was still parked in that Wharf City lot. Logically speaking, it would have been completely safe to have a hovercab drop me off to get it, but I was superstitious, and was not about to tempt fate. No, I didn't expect the killer of Swordplaya and Company to be waiting for me—he didn't even know who I was—but again, I was going nowhere near that city for as long as humanly possible.

This was a job for Flash. Run-Time's business empire was Let It Ride Enterprises. In Metropolis, he owned all the top car washes, hovercar body shops, hovercar rental shops, hovercycle rental shops, and hovertaxicab, hoverlimousine, and hovercar security services in the city.

Flash was the guy I always hired to provide hovercar security when I needed it. He was professional and reliable; I had used him almost exclusively for years. I had him stop by the Concrete Mama to get my extra set of keys, then left it to him to pick up the Pony and get it back home. There were very few people in this world I would let drive my vehicle; he was one of the select few, and he'd get it done without a hitch. I also didn't have to worry about Flash's safety. Run-Time's vehicle security people were all as well-armed as the police, and had military tactical training, too.

I'd been using the hovertaxi service more times in these past two days than I had in the entire past year. Despite the heavy rain and the traffic, the yellow hovercab made good time to Peacock Hills. It was a wealthy, "new money" business district of Metropolis—trendy and fresh, no silver-haired CEOs here. All the mega-multi-millionaire founders and presidents here were not even 40.

The Let It Ride Enterprises monolith building was on Electric Boulevard. Run-Time had three executive VPs in his company. As I left the elevator capsule, I was greeted by the female Lebanese one, in a yellow suit. I waved hello and called out to the three Let It Ride receptionists.

"Good morning, Mr. Cruz," they all greeted me.

I loved visiting, because the company's positive energy was so palpable and infectious. No matter who you were, whatever walk of life, here, you were treated like a celebrity. This was the empire that Founder, President, CEO, and COO, Run-Time had built—and quite an empire it was.

I was escorted up to the main offices, and there was the man himself. He was in a shiny, dark tan, slim-fit business suit, and a slim white tie. He wore his trademark Kangol hat. He greeted me as he always did, with a handshake and a hug. Every time, it was always as though it were the first time he'd met you. We'd been best friends since elementary school, but were all grown up now. He was a Who's Who of the Metropolis business elite.

"How's my best man doing?" I asked.

"How am I doing? What about you? Your fiancée was about to call the police to find you yesterday."

"It was nothing."

"Well, it was probably much more than that, but I won't pry."

He led me to his huge ivory desk for us to take a seat.

"Are you working on anything major?"

"Not at the moment. What's up?"

"I was told that you were at Police One the other day, and identified a list of newly arrived contract killers to our fair city."

Run-Time was connected to every part of the city's political and business elite.

"They told me the meeting was confidential."

"It was. But I have a possible client for you. Are you familiar with the royal family of Lux?"

"I think so. I might have seen them in the news at some point."

"Well, they're presently in the city. With this kind of a threat, police notify all high-profile visitors in the city as a courtesy—especially when law enforcement hasn't determined who the targets are."

"Do they think they're the targets? Why would any criminals want to harm them?"

"They're not taking any chances. They were quite intrigued when they learned that you, a civilian detective, was the one who ultimately identified the killers."

"I can't imagine the police would let that fact get out into the public."

"Not the public—but high-profile people have their ways of finding out what's really happening behind the scenes. They'd like to meet you."

"Meet me?"

"Yes."

"Okay." I shrugged. "If you recommend them, sure."

"They may want to hire you, or they may only want to be able to say they met a famous detective in Metropolis."

I laughed. "Famous? I don't feel famous. It's just me. Sure. When?"

"It may be as early as this afternoon or tomorrow morning."

"Okay, let me know and I'll be there."

"Good. We've gotten the business out of the way. Now let's talk about—"

"I know. Wedding preparations. You know, I've almost convinced Dot that we should just elope to New Vegas. What do you think? Could you help us out? We'd need bodyguard protection from her parents and mine because they'd come after us."

Run-Time laughed.

CHAPTER 20

The Sidewalk Johnny Brigade

Bless that Flash. I came out of my meeting with Run-Time and Flash had the Pony waiting for me in the Let It Ride valet parking. He had the receptionists let me know, as soon as I appeared. That's the kind of client service that separates exceptional companies from the rest. Flash anticipated my needs and saved me precious time. No hovercab back to the Concrete Mama.

I had already arrived in Buzz Town in the Pony, and was on Circuit Circle making my descent out of sky traffic, and into the Liquid Cool building. Funny that PJ had me calling it that now, even though all we had was one office in the monolith tower.

"There you are!" PJ jumped up from her desk, and put her hands on her hips as soon as I came through the door.

I was surprised to see that our lobby waiting area was filled with people waiting. That was a first. What grabbed my attention was two sidewalk johnnies sitting together wearing fedoras and Liquid Cool T-shirts. I hated those T-shirts with a passion, but PJ and Phishy had them all over town by now.

PJ followed me into my office. As I went to my desk, which had more messages on it than I had ever seen, she closed the door behind me.

"What the heck is going on here? I was gone for only one day, and look at all this business."

"Why do you think I was trying to call you?"

"Oh, do you have my new mobile?"

"Yes, right there." She pointed to a small box at the corner of my desk.

I opened the box to make sure PJ hadn't been cute and gotten me one that was hot pink or studded with faux diamonds. "Good, black and plain. A manly man's mobile!"

"At least 20 of the messages are from me. At least 30 will be from your girlfriend."

It didn't take long to activate my mobile phone and link to the Net to start downloading my video messages. "How can I have a 100 messages, and it's still downloading? I was only gone a day."

"I told you. 50 of those are from China and me."

"I don't have time to go through all these messages now. Who's outside?"

"Oh, two of those sidewalk johnnies you wanted are waiting. They've been here since before I opened the offices."

"Okay, them first. Who are all those other people?"

"Clients. I told you—and they can pay."

"How do you know they can pay?"

"I instituted a new policy."

I braced myself. "Does it have something to do with charging them money before they talk to me?"

"*Exactement.* Pay to play! You pay your retainer first. Then you talk to the detective, so we know you're not wasting people's time."

"Only you would come up something like that."

"Pay to play, baby!" PJ turned to open my office door and walk back into the reception lobby. She popped her head back in. "Sidewalk johnnies first."

Housing was mandatory for all residents, even for those without a legacy. But sidewalk johnnies were the life of the street—hanging around, watching trouble, causing trouble, hustling, looking for a hustle, but doing little of anything meaningful. Still, they were harmless, not the real street criminals.

As far as sidewalk johnnies went, these two were presentable, and had shaved some time in the last week. The only bad thing I could say about them was their hand-me-down suits were clearly not tailored to fit them—and the Liquid Cool T-shirts they were wearing!

They sat in front of my desk with eager-beaver looks on their faces, ready for work. One of them had closed my office door without my having to say anything.

"This is what I need you to do," I began.

"Do we need to take notes, Mr. Cruz?" one asked.

"No. You'll be able to remember, because it's simple. Do you know Blinky?"

They looked at each other and smiled.

"Yes, we do, Mr. Cruz. He dresses like Santa all year 'round, and drives a red hoverfiretruck."

"That's him. I want you to find him and then—secretly get him off the street."

"Is he in danger, Mr. Cruz?" They both looked worried.

"This is just between the three of us." They leaned closer to my desk. "It's to make sure he doesn't get into danger," I said.

"We understand, Mr. Cruz."

"Once he's off the street and you get him into a safe house—"

"Safe house, Mr. Cruz?"

"Have him stay with one of your buddies, but make sure no one knows."

They smiled. "We have plenty of buddies who can do that, Mr. Cruz."

"Once Blinky is settled in, one of you get back to me. No mobiles. Come in person. I'll take it from there. Can you handle that?"

"Yes, Mr. Cruz. You can count on us."

The two sidewalk johnnies stood from their chairs with big smiles. They shook my hand.

"That's for the job, Mr. Cruz. We won't let you down."

"Yeah, Mr. Cruz. You can count on us."

"Good," I said.

I had never been in the military but they saluted me. I walked them to the door, and opened it.

The two johnnies walked past the other waiting people, and PJ was already on her feet. She walked to a woman sitting in one of the single chairs, holding a long box marked ROSES.

"You're next, miss," PJ said to her.

CHAPTER 21

Sarah C

Brown hair and fair skin, the woman was wearing a hooded black slicker, still zipped up to the neck, and basic heeled shoes. Even sidewalk sallies wore fancier shoes.

I had seen a lot of people in my life, and I liked to think I was fairly good at sizing them up. She was someone who was tired of life. Not suicidal, but when the Grim Reaper came a-knockin', they couldn't open the door fast enough.

I invited her into my personal office.

"What's in the box?" I asked.

"You don't have to worry. It's not like I came here to kill you. Your receptionist already looked inside."

She wasn't interested in taking off her coat, so she sat in front of my desk. I walked around it, and sat myself.

"How can I help you?"

"Yes, how can you help me? I've never hired a private detective before. Is there some kind of protocol to follow?"

"We're just two people talking."

"I have a sister, a twin sister. She's the only family I have. I'd say she's the only thing in the universe I care about."

"That's what family is for—to care about."

"Yes. Have you ever heard of the Orochi Corporation?"

I shook my head. My recent memorization activities were confined to criminals, not corporations.

"Multi-trillion-dollar megaconglomerate. Japanese-owned, Tokyo headquarters. They have offices and research centers all over the world. My sister has worked for them for the last decade. She quickly climbed the corporate ladder, though her peers began in the company years before she did. I believe they're holding her hostage."

"Why do you believe that?"

"I haven't been able to reach her for at least two weeks."

"Is that unusual?"

"My sister and I are creatures of habit. We have followed the same routine every day from the first day we came to Earth." From her face, I could tell that she hadn't meant to reveal to me that she was an off-worlder. "She wouldn't go so long without contacting me, or returning any of my calls."

"Could she have died? Or be sick in the hospital?"

"No."

"How do you know?"

"I would have sensed it."

"Like a disturbance in the force."

"You don't have to mock me if you don't believe in it."

"No, not at all. I believe in the possibility of twins being able to sense something bad happening to the other."

"Not only twins. It's been documented in parents and children, married couples, even lovers."

"What steps have you taken so far?"

"Calling law enforcement authorities is pointless. The Orochi Corporation is more powerful than the government itself. The police would need proof of a crime, and I have none."

"Why do you want to hire a private detective?"

"I don't want to hire a private detective. I want to hire you. I followed your exploits in—I'm sure you have your own name for the case—your last highly publicized case. All of Metropolis could have fallen to the crime gangs. It was all put back together like it had never happened. I suspect a lot of people in government and law enforcement owe you favors."

"So why would I use any of those favors for you?"

"You haven't asked me what my sister does for Orochi, and why they would hold her hostage."

"What does your sister do for the Orochi Corporation, and why would they hold her hostage?"

I had a new client.

PJ was in my office with her electric steno pad, door closed again.

The key to being a good researcher was curiosity. PJ wasn't just a curious person, she was nosy. She wasn't as good as I was, but given time, she would be. She had the other ingredient—tenacity. She'd dig until she found something. That's what I needed: the basics, and then I could research deeper if I needed to.

"I want you to research everything about Sarah C. Her sister is Susan C. Also, get me details on the Orochi Corporation."

"Orochi?" PJ asked.

"You know the company?"

"No, but '*orochi*' means 'snake' in Japanese."

Her little factoid did not make me feel good. "Well, research them too."

"Good. I think she's going to be a good paying client for us."

A thought flashed into my head. "Hold on a minute."

I opened the door and rushed out of the office.

Sarah C was still waiting for the elevator. It was one of the not-so-nice things about this building—the elevators could take a while to show up.

"Ms. C." She turned to face me. "What are you doing tomorrow?"

"Excuse me?"

"What are you doing tomorrow?"

She didn't know how to respond. "Nothing."

"My future parents-in-law are holding a wedding rehearsal tomorrow, and we never have enough people. If you don't have anything better to do, you could be one of the stand-ins."

"Why would you ask a complete stranger to stand-in for your wedding rehearsal? I know I'm a paying client, but—"

"This has nothing to do with any of that. There's a saying: don't get so wrapped up in life that you forget to actually live it. You look like a person that hanging around some friendly new people may actually be a good thing. I won't be there. I'll be busy working on your case, but it would surely be better for you to be out there than sitting next to the video-phone all day."

Sarah C, at that moment, looked as if she were tearing up. "Yes. Actually, I would like that."

"Then it's settled. Call my secretary later today, and she'll give you all the details. Also, when you do meet my future parents-in-law, please remember they're not a reflection of my fiancée or me. They're insane; we're normal."

Sarah managed a small laugh. "I'll remember that. Thank you, Mr. Cruz."

"You're welcome."

The elevator arrived and Sarah C stepped inside.

CHAPTER 22

Bionic Betty

This was a good day at the office. I didn't have one new client; I had four, and Run-Time's office called to let me know when I'd be meeting the Royal Lux family later in the day, so I could possibly have a fifth.

However, with all the good, there had to be the bad, too—or the silliness. I was obligated to go through all my video-messages, and return my calls from the previous day.

"What do you want me do?" I asked.

The fidgety man on my video-phone screen repeated, "I want you to get the evidence of clear employment discrimination."

"How are they doing that?"

"They advertised the management job. I applied for it, then was told that there was no vacancy, even though I know for a fact that the position was open because the person in the position had died, even though I had tracked the deceased man to the very funeral home he had been taken to, and even though I attended his funeral. Even though I'd stuck my icepick into his chest, to prove he was dead, when no one was looking. I caught them, Mr. Cruz, with their hands in the proverbial cookie jar—a web of conspiracy and lies. The man is dead. The position is open. There is a vacancy—facts, Mr. Cruz! They lied to me when they said there was no job. The message sent to me that there is no vacancy is proof of the cover-up."

"Is this the only job you've applied for?"

"It is *my* job, Mr. Cruz, and I will not rest until I have secured it in the palm of my hand."

This was the foolishness I had to deal with from my stack of messages. I spent another 45 minutes fielding calls from crackpots—

"How far away was it?"

"About—100 kilometers away," the blond-haired man said from my video-phone screen.

"Kilometers?"

"Yes."

"What's that?"

"Mr. Cruz, I'm sure I don't have to tell you that the metric system is the preferred method of measurement in the world, and Up-Top."

"But this is the Americas."

"Yes, but—"

"We don't do that metric crap in the Americas. Repeat after me—miles."

"Kilometers."

"Miles."

"Kilometers."

"The metric system sucks."

"The metric system is the way of the civilized universe!"

—and other assorted characters. Not a potential paying client in the lot of them.

I'd said I would, and here I was. "Mentals"—offenders with mental issues—were never kept at Police One, but at a separate facility, with its own full-time staff of counselors and psychs. I could never remember the difference between a psychologist and psychiatrist, but they had both.

Bionic Betty, which was my nickname for my client-to-be who had out-punched Punch Judy, was here. I was glad she was in the minimum security level, so there was no chance I would bump into any seriously mental psycho. When they brought me to the visiting room, I could see why she was. They had removed her bionic arms and replaced them with pathetic plastic-like arms. I believe they'd done the same with her legs. This was what cyborgs got for upgrading or replacing their cybernetic parts without a cyborg license. It was cruel, and as I looked at her, I was convinced she didn't deserve it.

"I thought I would never see you again," she said. "They don't allow you to have a phone call in here, but I was going to have my caseworker contact you as soon as she came in tomorrow."

"Were you really off your meds?"

"I was," she said without hesitation, and I believed her. "I am sorry for my behavior, and I am deeply sorry for assaulting that nice young woman. I deserve my punishment, and if you want to press charges against me, I'll plead guilty."

Wow! A person who actually took full responsibility for their actions in this city.

"I'm not going to press charges, and I'll tell my secretary that you consider her a 'nice young woman.' She'll forgive you, just for saying that. So why don't you tell me why you came to see me?"

"I want to hire you."

"For?"

"My husband is being held against his will. I know that, based on our first encounter, you may still think I'm crazy, but you could easily confirm my claim with a day's worth of work. He's being held at the Silver City Nursing Home."

"Silver City has a nursing home?" I asked.

"Yes, it's where all corporate cyborgs without family end up."

She could tell from my expression that I didn't approve. "Corporate cyborgs" meant that some megacorporation would fit you with state-of-the-art bionics after some accident or disease, and they would maintain them for life, but the parts never did belong to you. They could never repossess them, but when you died, they would be there like vultures, to reacquire their property. Nursing homes were the intermediate step before that eventuality. To most, it was a great trade-off. You spent your last years living like royalty. However, it was too close to slavery for my tastes.

"It's not a bad life. It's quite good, in fact. My husband and I could never have afforded the bionics that saved our lives, and allowed us to live normal lives. We were shuttle pilots. He was the pilot and I was the co-pilot. The shuttle crashed. The damage to our bodies was—catastrophic. The Orochi Corporation was there, and took care of everything."

"However, you said the nursing home is holding him against his will. Why?"

"I don't know. That's why I need to hire you. Something is going on."

"What do you think it is?"

"A year ago I was in a hovercar accident. It wasn't anything serious, but the Orochi Corporation showed up, and took me to the hospital. When I awoke—I didn't even know they'd sedated me—they had taken me home. Later that night, I realized one of my bionic limbs had been replaced, and that I had undergone surgery."

"Maybe, they just wanted to upgrade you."

"If your hovercar was suddenly taken by the manufacturer, without your consent, and they replaced it with an equal or better model, would you believe they did it just to upgrade it? Or would you believe they did it to get their hands on your original model?"

"Since you know something of my classic hovercar background, you know the answer to that question. You're cyborgs. Cybernetic technology improves every year. Why would they want old technology? It would be obsolete, with no value. Did you have any upgrades?"

"No, Mr. Cruz. We've never had an upgrade in forty years. It was revolutionary bionics. One of the scientists told us that we were, in fact, the Adam and Eve of bionics. We had bionics that would last for millennia, and nothing would ever be made that could surpass that perfection.

"Mr. Cruz, I believe they're holding my husband to strip him of his bionics and kill him."

CHAPTER 23

Royal Lux

I wouldn't say I believed Bionic Betty's story—yet. I was going to buy some time. As I left the facility, my first call was to Police Central. I had my friends "Ebony and Ivory" paged. The call was patched through to them. Neither officer was amused, but I was a Metropolis citizen, and a taxpayer, and I had called in a legitimate "suspicion of crime" report. Officers Breaks and Caps would be visiting the Silver City Nursing Home.

I didn't believe in coincidences. This was now the second time the Orochi Corporation had come up, and had been accused of involvement in someone being held against their will. I didn't know the corporate world at all. As a private detective, corporate clients were fine, corporate money, fine, but the corporate world was boring to me. My interest was the criminal world. That's the world I needed to know for the sake of my mortal life. Though many would say the corporate world and the criminal world were one and the same, I did not share that view. I knew plenty of bums in the government, but that didn't mean all government people were bums. Most other private detectives I knew were low-lives. I wasn't one, nor should any stranger who didn't know me assume I was.

The corporate world was ruthless, especially at its highest echelons. That I did know. There were a lot of people out there with their own agendas, or who were just crazy. Fact or fiction? Coincidence or pattern?

What I had at the moment were questions. Betty's husband's name was Robert. Good. Bionic Betty and Bionic Bob. Easy for me to remember.

For now, I was flying the Pony to the swanky Euphoria Hotel in Paisley Parish, not too far from where my girlfriend worked at Eye Candy salon.

Everything in the hotel was purple—very upscale. I could never in a million years have afforded a room there for even a night, but this was how the other half lived and played. The staff wore two-foot-high top hats, bikini tops, and frilly bell-bottom pants. Hovertrolleys and carts were flying everywhere, luggage, food, people. It was like a perpetual party inside with guests everywhere.

Security met me at one of the elevators—a man in a tux, with a lavender sash across his chest, from left to right. When we reached the penthouse floor on 350, my legs were a bit nervous in getting out of the elevator capsule. I had never liked heights. Being on the penthouse level meant I'd actually be able to see how high I was.

I waited in some strange lobby that looked as if it had been created by children—bean bag chairs and tables, collage Pop Art on the walls, and a swing in the corner.

"Mr. Cruz." A stick-figured young woman with pulled-back brown hair approached me.

She led me to another waiting room, or what I would call the waiting room for adults. Majestic, plush, jeweled. The wall and ceiling were all glass. The clouds were literally another story up. As luck would have it, I caught sight of a descending flying saucer in the distance. My goodness, we were practically in space at this height.

The lights dimmed a bit as three people entered the room. An older man in the center and two younger people, one male and one female on either side. Because of the dimming lights and my angle, they were all mere silhouettes.

I rose from my chair. Since they were royalty, I'm sure there was something mere peasants such as myself were supposed to do.

"Please, Mr. Cruz, have a seat."

I sat back down. The man did not shake my hands (okay by me, as a germophobe) and sat opposite me. He had a very distinguished face, bearded, mustached, grizzled hair, and porcelain-like skin. He wore an expensive suit with a lavender sash.

"I have never met a real private detective before," he said.

"I've never met a royal—person before."

"Tell me about yourself, Mr. Cruz."

"I was born and raised in Metropolis, went to school here. Then I got into the classic hovercar scene, with a little street racing on the side."

"I understand that you built a classic Ford Pony from scratch. Red, is it?"

"Yes, it is."

"I have black and silver ones in my collection. I envy someone who can build such an exquisite machine from scratch with their bare hands, at such a young age."

"Thank you. How big is your collection?"

"I have 501 vehicles in my collection. The oldest model is 600 years old."

At that point, I wanted to stop the conversation, and have him take me immediately to see his collection.

"That sounds amazing. I was also a hovercar restorer."

"Yes, of some note, I understand. Then you became a famous detective."

"Some say that, but I'm just a simple street detective."

"Knowing a bit about the goings on of Metropolis politics, I would venture to say you are quite a bit beyond the *simple* street detective." He stood from his chair. "Thank you very much, Mr. Cruz, for stopping by."

The man turned and left the way he had come, followed by the two younger people, who had stood the whole time. I didn't even have time to stand myself, but when I did, the same stick-figure woman was there to walk me back to the elevator capsule. When I reached the ground floor, the same security man was there to walk me to the open lobby, where he turned, and gestured me on.

I stood in the noisy Euphoria lobby, shaking my head. Had I done something wrong? I was expecting a case, but got the boot instead. Well, I did get another new client—Bionic Betty. Only I had to figure out whether she was crazy or not.

So, Sarah C or Bionic Betty? Which case should I do some work on first? My new mobile was vibrating, a setting that I hated, which meant an urgent message was waiting for me. PJ explained to me in the office, "When your pants vibrate, you call me in the office, *tout suite.*"

CHAPTER 24

Susan C

Personally, I've always found twins, triplets, and the rest to be a bit creepy. It was like nature dabbling in cloning, before humans could even conceive of the concept. I walked into my offices and saw a woman who looked like Sarah C, but I intuitively knew it wasn't her. Even the most identical of identical twins had something a bit different from the other. This was the case with Susan C. She wore glasses, and was a bit more fashionable, not wearing just basic black. Unlike her sister, Susan came to the office with two associates. The men wore basic black slickers over their suits and PJ escorted all of them into my office. I followed them.

Susan C sat in the chair in front of my desk, as she removed her white slicker. One of the men took the coat from her.

"You two can sit down, too." I directed them to the sofa in my lounge area in my office. They walked to it, and sat.

"Bodyguards?" I asked her.

"I wish." Susan C's demeanor was also quite different. She smiled, and was very personable. She was definitely not a person who was weary of life.

"How can I help you, Ms. Susan C?"

"My sister visited you."

"She did."

"Mr. Cruz, I have to apologize for my sister."

"No need. I enjoyed meeting her."

"You are too kind. However, a woman who walks around with a ballerina statue in a rose box is—my sister is not well, Mr. Cruz. She's a bit out of touch with reality. What was her story? I was kidnapped? I was being held ransom by my company? Once the story was that killer robots from the future were after me. She's all I have, and I love her to death, but she needs help. I've been trying to get her into a program for years."

"So, no problems at work?"

"I work at the Orochi Corporation Labs in Silver City. I love my job and I've been there for over a decade. My sister is—confused."

I leaned back in my chair.

"You're a busy detective, and your time is probably as precious as mine. Therefore, I will pay you to continue with the case, her case, no further. Here's money"—one of the men rose and handed her an envelope, which she placed on my desk—"which should be more than enough and we can leave things there. I will find my sister, and see to it that she gets the help she deserves."

"I hope she's all right." I kept the fact that her sister was going to be at my wedding rehearsal to myself.

"She will be."

Susan C stood from the chair. "Thank you, Mr. Cruz. I apologize again for my sister's behavior."

"No need to apologize. There's no harm done."

Susan C was handed her white slicker by one of the two men, and they left my personal office. I watched them leave the main office. PJ walked in.

"Twins," PJ said. "I thought it was the first one."

I sat down, and opened the envelope to start counting.

"That's what I'm talking about," PJ said. "Paying clients. We've gotten more clients these past couple of days than in the past few months. Keep it coming, boss."

I leaned back in my chair. "Tell me what you think about this. If a woman comes into your office, and pays you to find her sister who she says is being held hostage, then the next day the sister who is allegedly being held hostage comes into your office, and pays you ten times more money to stop the case, what conclusion would you come to?"

"She paid you that much? I'd say the first woman is right, and the kidnappers sent the sister into your office to pay the extra money to make you go away."

"Yeah, I was thinking the same thing. Tell me about this Orochi Corporation."

CHAPTER 25

Punch Judy

"**I**'m going to need an assistant."

I gave PJ a stern look.

"Don't look at me like that," she said, tapping a stylus on the electric steno pad on her crossed legs. "This is not a one-secretary operation anymore. Look at how many messages you have. Besides, I need my own employee, so I can be a real office manager."

"I am never going to be like one of those firms out there that have dozens of detectives crawling around—"

"No, no. No one wants that. People want to hire you, not someone working for you, but what you need is the office managed, the message flow managed."

"You're reading those business books again."

"Oh, yes, in French, the language of the gods."

I laughed. "I'll think about it."

"You don't have to think about anything. Here's the business proposal."

"What the heck. Business proposal? Who are you, and what did you do with the real PJ, you cyborg clone imposter?"

"A part-time worker, or someone to work a few days a week to help, isn't going to drain the bank, but it could help you fill that bank nicely."

I took the paper proposal she gave me, shaking my head.

"Okay, enough of this. I'll read it later. Orochi. What's the scoop?"

"Well," she started reading from her electric steno pad. "They're a multi-trillion-dollar megacorporation, as in hundreds of trillions, with operations all over the planet, Up-Top, lunar colonies, and even Mars. They're into everything, but their specialty is robotics and cybernetics."

"Everybody does robotics and cybernetics. What's so special about the way they do it?"

"The A.I. they use is supposed to be the most advanced."

"We've been hearing about how advanced A.I. is for centuries. My Gramps told my Pops and me that when he was a kid they said they could finally make A.I. brains that could surpass humans. Well, my Gramps isn't a kid anymore, and neither is my Pops, and A.I. still can't do any of that. All it can do is calculate numbers, and create cool virtual reality worlds for the kids, and VR junkies."

"You are so negative about technology. Well, the A.I. brains they're designing are so promising, that they've expanded their android research."

"Androids?"

"Androids."

"Don't we have international laws on this planet about them?"

"We do, but they were written centuries ago, and the technology was never there."

"Okay, they make robots and androids, and do cybernetics. Is the main thing about them this A.I. brain?"

PJ nodded. "It's all about the brains. They've got the A.I. brains everybody wants."

"Where's the research? Tokyo or Hong Kong?"

"Classified."

"Are you saying it could be right here in Silver City?"

"If it's classified, it could be anywhere. Maybe they have a secret lab in the basement of the Concrete Mama."

I grunted.

"However, if you want to know more about the Orochi Corporation, ask Run-Time."

"Run-Time? What does he have to do with this?"

"Orochi Corporation tried to buy him out."

"What? When was this?"

"Around the time you started the agency. He would have much better intel."

Run-Time was going to get another call from me. "What did you find out about Sarah C?"

"Nothing. It's as if she didn't exist. What did she tell you about Orochi and her sister?"

"She said the same thing. Orochi makes robots and cybernetic parts for the human body. She said her sister was being held because they wanted her to do something illegal. What about this sister, Susan C?"

"Until about 15 years ago, she didn't exist."

"She's a scientist."

PJ nodded. "She's a cyber-neurologist."

"I know my Latin. That's a robot brain scientist—and she works in Silver City."

"Yep. It's all about the brains," PJ said.

CHAPTER 26

The Wans

The wedding rehearsals were left under the dominion of my parents-in-law from hell, which meant I had no intention of showing up. However, since I'd invited Sarah C to the madness, I was going to show up. I had a client to confront. Either I had one crazy client, or two of them.

You would never have guessed that Dot came from a very booshy, upscale background—she was personal, sincere, open—all the opposite of her parents. Yes, I did not have a high opinion of the Wans, though we had shared a running gun-battle through the streets of Metropolis, and were subsequently jailed together for it.

They owned businesses all over the city, and had picked a temple for the next six months, to get us all "trained to perfection," as Dot had translated for them, though the little scammers could speak English fine. It was some Judeo-Catholic-Christian-Hindu-Buddhist-whatever multi-purpose facility. Everything in it was plain white—the pews, the super-polished faux-wooden stage. When the time came for your live event, you could customize it to your heart's desire.

Apparently, my "lovely" parents-in-law from hell had done the first rehearsal two weeks ago. I arrived, and snuck in from the back. Who were all these people? Why were there so many of them? I was no expert in weddings, but how many bridesmaids were there going to be? There looked to be, like, fifty of them. What were all these boys for? The groom had only one guy—the best man, and he stood in one spot. No need for him to parade down any aisle.

I had to give it to Sarah C. She seemed to be enjoying it all, surrounded by the family insane asylum of a mile-a-minute Chinese-speaking youth, with "Boss Mama" Wan directing. The women were wearing plastic tiaras, with veils to the shoulder. The guys were wearing baseball caps—I was not joking. What kind of madness was involved here? I took out my mobile phone to video-record it. I could still make a case to Dot for us to escape to New Vegas for a wedding without any of them.

I felt my own disturbance in the force. I glanced over and there was Mr. Wan standing next to me—right next to me.

"Did you train as a ninja?" I asked.

The man let out a yell in Chinese to his better—and more evil—half of a wife. The rehearsal paused. All the kids, male and female, smiled and waved at me, muttering "Cruz, Cruz," as if it were a religious chant. Mrs. Wan just watched me. I looked over at Mr. Wan. He was watching me with the same emotionless gaze.

Mr. and Mrs. Wan: these two were going to be my parents-in-law.

Sarah C joined us. "I wasn't sure you were going to check in."

"I had to make sure my future parents-in-law didn't embarrass me," I said.

"Not at all. They're the perfect hosts." Sarah C said something in Chinese to Mr. Wan, and then Mrs. Wan, who also joined us. They were all smiles and giggles.

"You speak Chinese?" I asked.

"Yes, and several others."

"Looks like I'm the embarrassed one. What did you say?"

"That I'm thoroughly enjoying myself."

Mrs. Wan put a hand on her shoulder. "She has been a great helper." She then rattled off something in Chinese to Sarah C, and everyone began laughing again. I'm sure at my expense.

"What did Mother Dearest say about me?"

"She said she doesn't like much about you but at least you have good taste in the women you hang around with."

"Awww. I love you too, Mommy Dearest."

Mrs. Wan made a noise as she turned up her nose at me.

"Well, don't let me interrupt the rehearsals. We can talk afterward. Mr. Wan and I can hang out while you perform."

"Of course," Sarah said and she led Mrs. Wan back to the waiting kids to begin again. I assumed all the kids were Dot's cousins, since she was an only child.

I turned, but Mr. Wan was gone. Where had he gone? I looked all around and he was nowhere to be seen

"I'm sorry. Am I not wearing my deodorant?"

I never did see my crazy father-in-law again that day. He was there in the building, but didn't want to be seen. It was a prelude to the future. There was no way any future children of mine would be left with those two to babysit.

Sarah C joined me again when the rehearsals were done. While I waited, I managed to make a few more inane calls, or calls to inane people. PJ was right. I needed to be talking to legitimate potential clients, not crazy ones. Why didn't I remember that? When I was a police intern as a kid, Dispatch had said that more than 60 percent of incoming public calls were nonsense. It was amusing at the beginning, but that was then.

We sat in the pews at the back to talk. Mrs. Wan was talking to the group in Chinese about who knew what. She yelled out from time to time, and I heard the voice of Mr. Wan yell back. Yep, he was in the building. Maybe he was clinging to the ceiling in the dark like a fly. As I'd said, I didn't see him again that day.

"I have news for you," I said.

"News about my sister already? You were highly recommended."

"I can't take credit for my progress. She came to my office on her own, yesterday."

Sarah C's expression completely changed. Her happy, breezy exterior reverted to an expression of distress.

"She said you're mistaken. She's not being held against her will. She said that she's doing well." I gave Sarah C a moment to compose herself. "She paid me—to not continue with the case. I need to know what's going on so—"

Sarah got up from the pew, looking around, confused, and wandered out of the temple doors. I didn't disbelieve her claim. The fact was, I didn't believe either one of them entirely, but there were parts of both their stories I did believe.

I got up, and walked out after her. She had "done a Mr. Wan." She was gone, and nowhere to be seen.

CHAPTER 27

Mr. Looper

I scoured the streets around the temple for almost an hour, but no Sarah C. I was worried. The last thing I wanted to read in the news was that she had tried to harm herself. If she were mentally off in any way, reality could push her to do just that.

As I powered up the Pony, I called the office to contact the sister, and have PJ try to reach her. It was then that PJ told me an old client wanted to see me at Metro General.

I didn't like hospitals, and I was back at one for the second time in as many days. In my newfound career, when a paying client, whose case you'd successfully resolved, called, you dropped everything and met with them. It meant more work—directly or indirectly.

One of the men waiting near the elevators looked like a younger version of the man—obviously his son. With him was some thug-in-a-suit. If Mr. Looper was a legit businessman, I was Santa Claus.

"Mr. Cruz," Looper Jr. greeted.

I didn't say anything. All I did was give him an acknowledging nod.

They led me down the hallway, past other patient-filled rooms, doctors, and nurses going about their business. We walked through double doors at the end of the hallway to the high-end section of the floor. There was only one room.

Inside the palatial hospital room, three more thugs-in-suits waited near the open entrance. Farther in was Mr. Looper chatting it up with two model-like nurses. He saw me, said a few words, then the nurses collected their trays and walked past me.

"He came, boss," Looper Jr. said.

"Mr. Cruz," Looper said, lying in the king-sized bio-bed in a white gown, the sheets covering his legs.

"I expected you to be out of the hospital by now," I said.

"I would've been, but I didn't listen to the doctors, and wouldn't stay in bed to heal up—but I'm listening now. How are you doing, Mr. Cruz?"

"I'm doing as fine as wine, Mr. Looper."

Looper Jr. was always amused by me when I spoke.

"Mr. Cruz, you are part of a very select group of people in this universe."

"True hat connoisseur?"

Mr. Looper grinned. "You saved my life." I didn't see it that way. Looper took out one of the bad guys, the Boy Scouts took out another, and I took out the others. We all had done our part. "That means I'm in your debt."

I sighed. "Mr. Looper, I'm not a person who calls in favors from the past. I do my work, and move on. I'm not one of those guys collecting favors in an ever-growing Rolodex of favors."

"I had my people check you out more, and that's what they said. You never do call in favors. I hear that there are a lot of people in this city that you could call in favors from."

"Not my style, Mr. Looper."

"You're a rare one, Mr. Cruz. An honest private eye in a dishonest city. But that still leaves the matter of the debt. I don't mind collecting favors myself, but I can't allow myself to be in a position of owing a favor to anyone, even an honest person like yourself."

"What solution have you come up with?" I asked. "Since you'll never hear from me about it."

"I'll wipe the slate clean, by giving you something without your asking for it."

"Mr. Looper, there's nothing—"

"You had a big case earlier in the year."

"I did."

"All the bad guys caught and dealt with?"

"Caught, captured, or killed. Just like in the Westerns."

Looper grinned again. "All of them?"

"All of them."

"Even Monkey Baker?"

Now he had my attention. "What do you know about him?"

"Did you find him?"

"He's off-world, so I don't have to worry about him. If he tries to come back, he'll be flagged by Interpol."

Looper Jr. and the thugs began laughing.

"What's so funny?" I asked.

"You honestly think if the crime boss of one of the largest criminal gangs on Earth were holding a grudge, he couldn't find a way to get planet-side, to get you?"

"Get me with what? All his men are dead. If he could get here, rival gangs would take him out."

"That would be true, except for one thing."

"The suspense is killing me," I said.

"What does a crime lord who wears a monkey mask look like? Do you know? Does Interpol? You have a bit too much faith in law enforcement's abilities. Mr. Cruz, this is your lucky day. You saved my life, so I'm going to save yours. The slate will be wiped clean. Show him."

Looper Jr. took a mobile from his jacket pocket and put the display of a man up to my face.

"I can see from your red-faced expression that you've already had the pleasure of meeting Monkey Baker without his monkey mask," Mr. Looper said.

I didn't even say "Thank you." I had already stormed out of the room.

CHAPTER 28

Monkey Baker

Trust your instincts. All this time, my gut instinct, sixth sense, Spidey-sense, had told me he was no good. It wasn't that he had shark eyes; he was a shark—and I was the prey. As I raced to the Concrete Mama, I wondered how he planned to do it. My apartment had its own security systems, like every other resident, but that didn't mean it was impenetrable. He had been there all day. I hadn't. Did he plan to booby-trap my place, my parking? Or was his plan to gun me down, and make it look like a random mugging gone wrong? I stepped on the accelerator.

I left the elevators and entered the ground lobby. Like so many times before, the doorman was moving back to his station, as if he had been standing next to the elevator door as I descended. I had always found it strange and I found it strange now. What was he doing?

"Good morning, Mr. Cruz, sir," he said, back at his station.

"You know," I said, in a voice louder than normal. "I never did get your name."

"Oh, Mr. Cruz, sir. 'The doorman' is fine." He didn't even turn to look at me.

"The doorman? Why would I call Monkey Baker, the criminal boss of the former Animal Farm Crime Syndicate, such a menial name?"

He stopped. I had been walking to him as I spoke and now I stopped. He turned his head to peer back at me. I could see the smile. I could see the squint of his shark eye. Then he turned around to face me. We stared at each other, him grinning, me smirking.

When I had gone to Phishy's rescue in Wharf City, I'd left my major weapons at home, and carried a couple of throwaway guns. It was fortunate I had, because otherwise, they'd be at the bottom of the ocean, never to be seen again. I wouldn't have had them for the moment at hand.

"What have you been plotting all this time in my place of residence, Mr. Monkey Baker?"

He thought my question was hilarious.

I pulled my omega-gun and shot him point-blank dead in the forehead. He wasn't laughing anymore.

CHAPTER 29

Chief Hub

Wilford G., my posthumous mentor, died at the ripe old age of 92, after 70 years in the detective business. He warned in his book, *How to be a Great Detective with 100 Rules,* that crime was like a black hole. It may not have had substance, but it was real, with its own gravity and, if not careful, you could be sucked into its dimension. You could escape only before you crossed a certain line, because no matter how righteous you were, how fervent your willpower was, once you'd crossed a certain point, there was no escape.

Not even police could do what I had done. My act was so many shades of criminal that I sat in the lobby with a doomed, saddened demeanor. I couldn't look anyone in the eye. I was ashamed and disgusted with myself. The lobby of the Concrete Mama was a red-and-blue light show. Four silver-and-black police officers stood around me, waiting, their arms on their waist holsters.

I heard them, but I couldn't look. The coroners had done their preliminary work, and the late Monkey Baker was covered with a white sheet. As if the cosmos wanted to purposely make me suffer, when I did look, the only thing my eyes locked onto was the sheet with a bright red spot of blood in the head area. I returned my gaze to my interlocked hands and the floor.

Other officers kept tenants and sidewalk johnnies behind police lines, one in front of the elevators, and the other outside in front of the building.

I was done. I felt it. I knew it. It didn't matter how many friends I had on the police force. I was going down for this. I had never gotten a speeding ticket in my life, and now I would be facing felony murder. When I returned my piece to my holster, the first thought in my head was to hide it. That's what I did. I'd hidden my omega-gun, and replaced it with a throwaway piece. I even acted like a criminal. When I returned to try to plant a weapon on him, because I knew how much trouble I was in, two people were in the lobby. One of them yelled to the other, "That's the shooter!" It was over. I sat on the couch, and waited for the detectives to arrive. They did, in force.

More police arrived, and more CSI arrived. At least, I thought they were CSI, but their uniforms seemed a bit different. I noticed that they were all going up the elevators, which meant they were in my place. When police went to your place to investigate, they blew your door off, and swarmed across every inch of your "Home, Sweet Home." They never left it in the condition they'd found it. You returned to a home of rubble, with walls, ceilings, and floors ripped apart during their search for contraband.

I hadn't noticed that he was standing next to me. There was Chief of Police Hub. The expression on his face was more of a disgusted father looking at his son. I looked away to sulk.

"Follow us, Mr. Cruz."

I stood and followed him and another officer; the four officers on "baby-sitting duty" followed me. We got onto the next open elevator; police and CSI were coming out with boxes. I felt sick. They were taking my stuff! No one spoke as the elevator ascended. When we stopped, I glanced up at the indicator. It wasn't the 100th floor where I lived, but the 99th floor.

Hub led us out. The entire floor was filled with police. As we walked by apartments, I noticed that all the doors were open, and no tenants were inside. We walked for quite a while to the rear section of the building, where all the communication equipment, plumbing shafts, fire suppression computers, etc. were. One of the restricted doors was open, and there were those CSI personnel whose uniforms I'd thought were strange—not dark colors, but bright yellow.

Hub gestured for me to come closer to what looked like rectangular pink pieces of putty, stacked from the floor to the ceiling. Hub was handed one of the pieces, and he showed it to me.

"Do you know what this is, Mr. Cruz?"

"No."

"This is Composition 13. To civilians, it's still known as C-4, plastic explosives."

I looked around the room, and realized that the stacks of pink putty went back for as far as the eye could see. These rear rooms went on for miles.

"Let me explain something to you, Mr. Cruz. You are the luckiest man in the world. If not for this, you'd be on your way to lock-up at Police One, and you'd be booked and charged with felony murder. The only reason you're not heading to prison is not because of our previous bonding moment, or your popularity with the rank-and-file. No. Here we stand in one room packed with enough plastic explosives to send this entire building into space. Yes, you killed a crime boss, who came back to kill you—but you can't execute him, and especially when he's not armed. You can't do that, Mr. Cruz. I can't do that. None of my officers can do that. What makes you special?

"But again, you're the luckiest man in the world. This is now a Federal terrorist case because had this crime boss completed his evil plot, he would've killed not only you, but he would have also killed every single man, woman, child, cat, dog, and rat in all 100 stories above us. And when that monolith mass of concrete came crashing down, it would have most likely crushed everyone in the 98 floors below us—and if we still weren't having fun, the entire tower would have crashed to the ground, killing everyone lucky enough to be walking nearby, not to mention taking out any hovercraft traffic on the way down.

"So, Mr. Cruz, the Federal government of the Americas itself has given you a complete pass for averting what would have been one of the most disastrous criminal terrorist acts in centuries, one that would have killed a *lot* of people. Where he got this from, and how he transported it undetected, we still don't know.

"Officers, take our hero, Mr. Cruz, out in the hall."

Learning that I wouldn't be heading to prison didn't make me feel any better. The four officers led me into the hallway, where we waited. I heard Hub talking to the CSI guys, who must have been some special unit of the Bomb Squad.

Chief Hub appeared in the hall to continue his verbal and emotional stomping of me into the ground.

"You crossed the line, Cruz, even if it was for a righteous reason— this time. What about next time? I had a former partner who did the same thing. Gunned down a perp to protect his family. Then he did it again, he stole—for his family. When you do wrong, you can always find a legitimate reason to justify it, but it is still wrong. That ex-partner of mine went to prison for life for murder, attempted murder, including of a fellow officer, grand larceny, and so many other crimes I've forgotten. His first week in, prison gangs got him in the showers, shanked him dead. Am I getting through to you, Mr. Cruz?"

"Yeah."

"This was your lucky day, and wake-up call, all in one. When you lose your grip on the difference between right and wrong, that's it. You've crossed over from the clean streets to the mean streets. You understand me?"

"Yeah."

"I'll be watching you closely."

I said nothing.

"You were right this time, but we both know that's not why you did what you did. Get out of here."

"Is my place safe to go to?"

"If you're asking if we trashed the place, the answer is no. We were called off before we could get rolling, when the explosives were found. A single murder seems insignificant, when compared to blowing a million people and an entire monolith tower into space from the ground. Get out of here. Go to a hotel. You can go to the parking lot to get your vehicle, but we're evacuating the entire building, and it will remain so for a while."

He didn't have to tell me again. I left for the elevator.

CHAPTER 30

The Notary

I checked into a local hotel and learned from the news that the Concrete Mama would be evacuated that day, and would remain so for an indefinite period of time before tenants would be able to return. Curiously, the reason was not mentioned. I was starting to wonder how often the media didn't tell the public what was really going on in the city, but what was the point? If they had, it would've only made things worse.

I sat in my hotel room on the bed in the dark. I couldn't move. There would never be a greater example of irony. If I had acted the good guy, I'd be dead and so would, maybe, a million others. My momentary lapse into the dark side could have destroyed my entire life. My detective career, life with Dot, friendships, family, everything. I had been scared straight for life.

When the world had gotten you down and you were feeling blue, there was only one thing to do—Go to work!

I had dodged the cosmic bullet, and wasn't going to be convicted of anything. I wasn't going to prison. More importantly, neither Dot nor our parents would ever know about it. I wouldn't be surprised if I were the only civilian at the Concrete Mama who knew what had really happened: that an insane crime boss had gotten a job at our apartment building to kill me, and everyone else who had the misfortune to live in the same building. Law enforcement and politicians were very risk adverse. They'd come up with a million stories to cover up the truth. Even if the media stumbled onto it, they'd have to sift through all the other stories. At the end of the day, they'd let it go, because they'd accept the motivation for the cover-up—to keep Metropolis from exploding in panic. It would be as if the whole thing—the late Monkey Baker, his bomb plot, the swarm of police and investigators at the Concrete Mama—had never happened. In a few days, when it was safe for all the tenants to return to their apartments, and back to the daily grind, they'd completely forget about it, too.

Notary inspectors were a busy profession in the city. I'd thought of becoming one myself, having run into more than a few when I was in the hovercar restoration biz. The job was simple: verify that something was real. It was more involved than that, but that was my favorite definition of the job. The classic hovercar world was no different from the world of high art; notaries verified the authenticity of the parts—their serial numbers were recorded in a database somewhere. If you were selling a million-dollar vintage hovercar that you claimed was in original mint condition, every part had better be in the proper database. It was the same when it came to bionics. Metal is metal, whether a car, or a cyborg's arm.

The one I had called was staring at me on the video-phone screen.

"Do you have the official documentation?" he asked.

"The police were just there yesterday, so the nursing home will be expecting you."

"You mean, you're assuming they'd be expecting me."

"All you have to do is call his wife, and get the verbal permission, if my word isn't good enough. You know I'm a private detective. More than that, you know me."

"Yeah, yeah. We've done business before. I know you're not a scammer, but I need to have the proper paperwork to protect myself legally. Silver City isn't Free City."

"Tell me about it. Call his wife. Get the verbal, then use that for authorization. Also, the police visited him, so I'm sure you can craft whatever cover-story you need. "

"I'm going to ignore that you said that. Robert or Bob?"

"Robert, but he goes by Bob."

"Okay, Cruz. I'll take the job. Full inventory?"

"Full inventory. Serial numbers for every part, down to the microscopic."

"And you have the money for this?"

"I don't, but his wife does."

He smiled. "I'll get there today and call you when I'm done."

I hung up the call. I stood from my chair. The notary would be off to see Bionic Bob. Every legal cyborg had to have every piece of hardware registered with the government, each piece identified by serial number. With that list, I could investigate for myself Bionic Betty's claim about the uniqueness of her husband's bionic parts.

I was out of my funk, so back to the Concrete Mama to survey the damage to my place and maybe head to the office.

As I was about to leave the hotel, the video-phone rang. What had the notary forgotten?

I touched the button. "What did you—"

The man staring at me was not the notary but an angry-looking Asian man.

CHAPTER 31

Ping

"Who are you?"

"Mr. Cruz, my name is Mr. Ping of the Orochi Corporation. Why are you investigating our company?"

"What? Where did you get that from?"

"Do not lie to me. We had you under observation!"

"You're spying on me? Why are you doing that?"

"Why are you talking to notaries?"

"What?"

"You will cease and desist from all activities against the Orochi Corporation!"

"You snake! I'm going to call the police and file a formal complaint against you."

"You do that, and our lawyers will have you in court. Ask around. We can tie you up in court for the rest of your life."

"I'm not scared by your threats, you snake."

"I want your promise that you will not pursue any investigations against the Orochi Corporation. Promise!"

"No!"

"Promise!"

I hung up the video-phone.

That was the life of a detective. One second I was back on my game, and about to walk out of the hotel room with a spring in my step. The next I was fuming mad and storming out of the room.

CHAPTER 32

Bugs

Even before I had gotten back to the Concrete Mama, I'd called him. How did this Mr. Ping know about my conversation with the notary? I was in a random hotel. Had they been listening from a hovercar outside the window? Was I bugged? Paranoia was healthy, especially being in the detective business, but it could easily become a psychosis.

There was only one man for the job—Bugs. He was the epitome of old-school class. Listening device detection, motion detection security, intrusion defense security, video surveillance, door and wall defense security, door and lock augmentation, trap doors, panic rooms—he did everything that had to do with office security. Run-Time had used him exclusively for jobs at his businesses. That was the kind of rep Bugs had. I had used him to harden the security measures at my Liquid Cool office after one too many people had wandered in, trying to shoot me. It was time for him to do the same with my apartment.

He was waiting for me in the lobby, wearing dark overalls over his purple suit. He held a contraption with one hand, and a telescoping wand in the other. Just as I had figured, all the police tape was gone, bloodstains from where the late Monkey Baker had his last lie-down were gone, the sidewalk johnnies were lounging around. It had happened just yesterday, and it was already forgotten.

Bugs did a full scan of my body with the wand device, and when we got upstairs to my 100th floor apartment door—9732—he scanned my mobile after turning it off, then back on.

"Clean," he said. "They were probably eavesdropping on you from a remote drone."

He followed me into the apartment after I'd opened the door.

"Do the same as you did with my offices. With the police in here, all my normal apartment security was switched off. Check for any electronics that aren't supposed to be here and then whatever security I have, make it better, much better. I spend most of my time at the office these days."

"Yes, I hear you're getting all established as a professional detective. I'll start with the high-traffic areas first, and then move to the other rooms."

"Okay, I'll leave you to it and get myself ready for the office."

Bugs did his preliminary scans, then called his own office to send up a couple of techs with my new security. It was a good thing I had a couple of new paying clients, because all their retainers were about to be spent.

I was in the bathroom washing up, when I heard commotion.

"Who are you?" I heard Bugs say.

I quickly walked into the living room area, shirtless. There he was—Ping.

"What are you doing in my place?" I yelled at the man.

Ping glared at me, and lifted his hand. I could see Bugs starting to turn his head. Suddenly there was a flash, and I found myself on the ground. I'd lost consciousness. I could see Bugs on the ground too, paralyzed. What was it with photonic weapons in this case?

I should have known. A megacorp like Orochi, with holdings on and off-world, would have access to all kinds of Up-Top gadgets. I knew firsthand that Up-Top had all the best stuff, with my own omega-gun as a prime example. Phishy had "acquired" it from someone, but it was definitely not designed or built on Earth.

Ping walked in farther, looking. I couldn't move! He snapped a picture of Bugs, looked around more, then left. I tried with all my might to move, but immediately stopped. I could have been making it worse. I closed my eyes—the only body part I had voluntary control of—and calmed myself. It was all I could do.

Bugs was on fire! The only side of him I had ever seen was of a dignified, elderly man who exuded old-world expertise. The Bugs on the video-phone now, with his two techs next to him, was a back-alley brawler, who was fit to give Ping the whuppin' of his life should they ever run into each other again. It was a highly profanity-laced conversation.

However, Ping was going to have to deal with me, too.

I gestured to one of the techs. He walked over to me.

"Did that intruder mess with any of your equipment?"

"We don't know, but Bugs doesn't take chances. He'll destroy everything, and replace it with new equipment. Who knows what the man did? We'll rescan you too."

I looked around. The tech watched me, as I tried to retrace Ping's steps. Why was Ping in my apartment?!

I hadn't seen Phishy for days, but I knew he was safely off the grid. That was one worry I didn't have. However, my sidewalk johnny brigade still hadn't found Blinky. There were plenty of sightings of his red hoverfiretruck, but no one could pin him down yet, and I was getting impatient. I didn't want to do it, but I was considering offering a bonus to whoever found him first. Maybe that's what they were all secretly waiting for me to do.

Megacorps. Megaconglomerates. Corporate syndicates. The only entities as powerful were governments, but neither really were more powerful than the other. It was a cosmic stalemate. Uber-governments on one side, megacorps on the other, with the billions on Earth and off-world in between. Metropolis, as the largest supercity on Earth, was a magnifier of that struggle between giants.

I was in Orochi's sights, and that didn't sit well with me. I wanted to call them up, and tell them that I'd already had two brushes with death, so they didn't have to go ahead with attempt number three.

When I got into the office, it was a zoo. PJ was answering the phone, managing the walk-ins, and clearing out the voicemail machine nonstop. It was the first time potential clients were waiting in the halls for me.

"PJ, who are all these people?"

"Since you won't get me help, start with this woman here," she directed.

Now I was on reception duty.

"How can we help?" I asked the young woman at the reception.

"Are you him? Cruz, the detective?"

It was one of the busiest days I'd ever had in the office. Run-Time had told me that this was how it was when starting a business, these highs and lows. One day, or week, or month it would be silence. Then it would be followed by utter madness. There was no rhyme or reason to it, just the ebbs and flows of the free market.

I returned to the Concrete Mama that night. Bugs had called me at the office. My place was clean—no listening devices at all. As I had asked, he'd added a bunch of new security measures.

The bed and sleep were the only things on my mind when I strolled through the front door. I placed my fedora on the hat ring, and hung my tan slicker on the coat rack. I could hear the siren song of the bed in my mind. I purposely avoided looking at the clock.

It was late, but I didn't need to see how late it was. PJ and I had gotten through every damn message from the last few days, so tomorrow we'd be able to start fresh. I'd told her "no" in terms of a new employee, but "yes" to bringing in temp help whenever she needed it.

I had done it before. Jumped on top of the covers on the bed, saying that I'd get back up to get into my sleeping clothes. It never happened. I'd end up falling fast asleep in my work clothes, not even my shoes and socks taken off.

Something had woken me. I strained my ears to figure out what the sound was, but couldn't figure it out.

I appeared in front of my bathroom door with my omega-gun in my hand. It was still dark, but in my own place, I didn't need lights to move around. The sound—the sounds—were louder. I had guessed what it was. I simply couldn't believe it.

I flipped on my bedroom light, and waited a couple of seconds for my eyes to adjust. I slowly pushed the bathroom door open. The sound was much louder; I reached in and flipped on the bathroom light. After hesitating, I tip-toed forward.

The shower stall was closed and filled to the brim with snakes! I ran like a gazelle being chased by a pack of cheetahs. If the stall door opened, all those snakes would have spilled over the floor—and me.

CHAPTER 33

Yo

I was not shy this time. I told *everybody* about the snakes! PJ got there first, and took nonstop pictures.

"Who did you piss off this time?" she asked.

"How did they get into my apartment?!"

"They put them in your master bathroom, too."

Bugs got there next. He was beyond anger.

"Mr. Cruz, don't worry about the cleanup. We'll take care of it."

"Oh, I can't have you do that."

"I insist. My firm stands 100 percent behind its work. To have someone break into your residence immediately after we'd installed your new security is more than a slap in the face. It's now a matter of honor with me."

"Well, we both know who the snake—pun intended—is who did it."

"Yes, we do."

"You do your work, and I'll do mine."

"You might want to talk to Run-Time. He's had dealings with them."

"I doubt they put snakes in his residence."

"They wouldn't dare."

"Are you calling the police on them?" PJ asked.

"Companies like Orochi don't care about the police," I replied.

"Then what?" she asked.

"Companies like Orochi care only about reputation. They care about that more than money."

I had joined the Metropolis Business Association months ago, for all the snazzy benefits of being a bona fide business owner in the city.

"What's the Council of Corporations?" I'd asked the salesperson, as she accepted my method of payment for membership dues.

She laughed. "You need net profits of at least one billion dollars annually."

"Oh, then I won't be able to upgrade my membership any time soon."

"Probably not."

I told PJ to send a courtesy copy of all the photos to the general Orochi Corporation email and put "To Mr. Ping (the Snake)" in the subject line.

There were a lot of trillion dollar companies in the world, and their membership dues allowed the Council of Corporations offices to occupy a massive monolith pyramid tower in the center of Silicon Dunes, the wealthiest district in Metropolis. Megacorps at this level were not interested in the snazzy benefits of discounts for their next peri-terrestrial space flight. These companies owned plenty of spaceships themselves. They were each their own empire, and they needed a capitalistic entity, separate from government, to keep the peace—the ultimate referee of all business disputes. A war between one or more companies would not be figurative.

Here was where I went to file my own complaint against the Orochi Corporation. I was one little man, but I could be a force to be reckoned with, too. Though I was not naive. Corporations employed their own samurai soldiers and cyborg mercenaries, so I made a call to Wilfred, Jr., the head of the Metro Police Union. Suddenly, police hovercruisers were patrolling the Council's airspace.

"Who would you like to speak with, Mr. Cruz?"

The receptionist looked like an android. Her features were too perfect, and her movements were robotic. She stood at the high reception desk. It was the only piece of furniture in the bubble-designed room, with a ceiling a good five or more stories high.

"I need to speak to someone to register a formal complaint against a corporate member."

"Have you already contacted the company directly? They all have their own aggressive customer relations departments."

"I have."

"What was the result?"

"Unsatisfactory."

"Before we can register a complaint, all avenues must be exhausted."

"Will I be able to register my complaint, or are you going to stonewall me?"

"Not at all, Mr. Cruz. Please have a seat, while I summon the director to register your complaint directly."

I turned around. A couch and a magazine-filled coffee table rose from the floor.

Cute, I thought. I took a seat.

Was I really going to be allowed to file a complaint against the Orochi Corporation? Of course not. They were going to find some way to legally weasel their way out of it. I wasn't a member of the Council; I didn't know any members. I wasn't wealthy. Even Run-Time wasn't rich enough, compared to this bunch.

A tiny Asian woman appeared, smiling. "Mr. Cruz?"

I was going to say something sarcastic, but I behaved myself. "Yes."

"Please, follow me."

She led me to a door on the opposite side that had opened as soon as I'd stood from my seat. She stopped at the opening, and gestured me inside, as she slightly bowed her head and body. When I entered the room, no one was familiar to me, except for one person. Ping!

To say they were all wearing black suits was like saying "yellow sun" or "black space." It was a Japanese company; they all only wore black suits with white shirts. They seated me on a simple faux-wooden chair. Ping and an older man sat across from me. The woman who'd led me in stood in my line of sight to the side, and three bodyguard-looking men stood behind Ping and an elderly man.

The elderly man was watching me closely. I sat with a slight smirk, watching him back. I wondered if he knew I was quite good at the death-stare game.

"Do you know who I am, Mr. Cruz?" he asked.

"I only know who Mr. Ping is," I answered.

"I am the president of the Orochi Corporation."

I caught my mouth from dropping open.

"My associate, Mr. Ping, says you have begun a very unfortunate investigation against my company."

"I am not investigating your company. I have a case."

"You have two cases. The Orochi Corporation owns the Silver City Nursing Home."

I sat there, dumbfounded. Not even I had made that connection yet, but this man knew all about my business.

"Since you know everything I'm doing, why do you need me here? You have all the questions and answers; I don't have to open my mouth."

"Mr. Cruz, do you really believe the Orochi Corporation, a company of our stature and reputation would break into your common abode to fill your shower with little snakes?"

"I don't know. I don't know what Orochi considers beneath itself."

"I can assure you that such an infantile act is beneath not only myself, but anyone working for, or who does business with Orochi. We are not street gangsters, Mr. Cruz. We don't send samurai operatives after civilians. We send an army of attorneys after them.

"My samurai operatives are for my corporate rivals. If it were possible for you to ever rise to the level of a true threat to the Orochi Corporation, you would not even be alive. We are not Monkey Baker."

The point had been reached and acknowledged. I was officially far, far, far out of my depth. This was an ocean of sharks, and everybody was a shark, except for me. I was the goldfish.

"Mr. Yo," I said. He smiled. *Yes, Yo, I do know who you are.* "Then the next questions are simple for me. If you didn't decorate my bathroom with the snakes, who did, and why?"

He didn't care in the slightest.

"Anything else before I go?—"

"Mr. Cruz," Yo said. "Do not bring my company into your affairs again. I am a courteous man, but not a merciful one. You have received your only warning."

"Why would you personally warn me at all?" I asked. "I don't get it. Up until now I didn't even know the two separate cases were connected. You could have left me to bumble around, and it would never have come across your company's doorstep.

"Your associate tracked me to a hotel room, and physically came to my apartment, revealing himself to me. I bet he didn't even know there was such a place as Rabbit City. One of the richest men in the solar system sits across from me to threaten me. I don't get it. What are you scared of?"

"Mr. Yo is scared of nothing," Ping interjected angrily, as Yo sat calmly.

I began to stand, but hesitated. "I believe you," I said to Yo. "I consider your associate, Mr. Ping, to be a snake, but that's because I don't like him. I don't believe your company would break into anybody's place to leave a present of snakes for the owner. It is infantile, and beneath you."

I watched them both for a while. Ping actually began to sweat.

"Who out there would want me to think that the Orochi Corporation did something that it didn't?"

Yo said, "In the universe, Mr. Cruz, there is matter and there is dark matter—what exists, and their exact opposites."

"A rival?" I asked.

"Perhaps," he answered.

I began to reach into my jacket. The three bodyguards and the "nice" woman all did the same. I smirked as I took out my mobile phone and touched a button.

"Does a seven-headed snake tattoo mean anything to you?"

Yo jumped from his chair, and a look of shock came over Ping's face. Yo walked over to me and reached for my mobile. He stared at the image—a man caught on video leaving the Concrete Mama. They had been good enough to bypass my internal security, but couldn't disable every possible city camera outside the building. When Bugs had showed me the footage, not believing in coincidences, I'd immediately felt that the man in black with a hat obscuring his face was one of the snake-handlers in my place.

Yo took out a device, and touched the screen of my mobile with it. He stormed off, with the women and three men following. A frightened Ping gave me back my mobile, and ran after them.

What had I just done?

CHAPTER 34

Blinky

They could've been manipulating me. Run-Time told me a long time ago that megacorp executives got the positions they did because they were not only the most ruthless, but because they were the best actors. Yo could have been giving me a Movie-Town performance, but Ping—no, he was genuinely rattled. That could have been why Yo kept such an undisciplined associate at his side. I'd be reading Ping's expression to know what was real, when in fact Yo was manipulating him too.

But sometimes you could overthink a thing. Sometimes the duck in a dream is just a duck, and not the external manifestation of a childhood trauma that occurred when the moon was rising near Jupiter. Orochi Corp was being set up for my benefit, which meant others thought I knew something I didn't know I knew or felt I was heading down a path to something they didn't want me to know. Too many questions, and I didn't like riddles.

The sidewalk johnnies had found Blinky. Surprise, surprise. They were able to locate him *after* I'd offered a bonus. Hustler bastards.

It was a residential monolith complex in Free City, and I was waiting inside for Blinky near the place where he was staying. He strutted out of the elevator in full blinking Santa suit regalia, saw me, and stopped cold.

"I got you this time!" I yelled at him.

"Cruz, man."

"Don't 'Cruz, man' me. You left Phishy to get killed."

"No way, man!" He was sincerely put off by the charge. "That's not what happened."

"Where were you, then?"

"It wasn't like that, man. I—I fell asleep."

"Fell asleep?"

"Yeah, man. When I woke back up I rushed over, and no one was there."

"Because they were double-crossing us!"

"Double-cross?"

"I'm going to do what I planned to do to you all those years ago!"

I bolted after him, but he was already way ahead of me.

"Cruz, man. You can't catch me on foot."

"I'm going to get you!"

"Cruz, man. You could no sooner catch me on foot, than I could catch your red Pony in my red hoverfiretruck. Neither will ever happen."

I ignored him, and chased him. Round and round we went around the outer hallway of the floor, residents watching as if it were some kind of racing event. An hour in, I quit. He was right; I would never catch him, no matter how great a shape I was in.

"You dope roach!"

My breathing was elevated. He peeked back around the corner.

"Are you done, man?"

"I'm done, dope fiend."

"I told you, man. You'd never catch me. Look at how hard you're breathing. You could have saved yourself all that heartache an hour ago."

"You're going to make it up to Phishy for leaving him to die!"

"No, man. I didn't do that. I fell asleep."

"You left him to die! He trusted you!"

"No, man. I know he did."

"We'll put the word out on the street that no one is to do business with you."

"No, man. Don't do me like that. Whatever you want, Cruz, man. Tell me what you need."

I stood with my hands on my hips, still breathing hard. Maybe I wasn't in as good a shape as I'd thought. I had an idea.

"What bad people do you know?"

"Cruz, man. I stay away from bad people, just like Phishy."

"I need you to find someone who can identify the crew that uses a special tattoo."

Blinky and I were standing at the door of the place where he was staying. Some girl wearing a Santa hat leaned on the side of the open door, listening to us as she guzzled sake from a black bottle. I went no farther than the threshold, as inside was a cloud of hovering smoke—and it wasn't from cigarettes.

"What's the tattoo?"

"A seven-headed snake."

Blinky nodded. "That sounds rad, man. Yeah, I know some people I can reach out to who might be able to assist."

"Blinky, listen to me very carefully. This is not a game. The people who wear this tattoo are not bad people. They are very, very bad people."

"Yeah, man. I hear you."

"You meet these people, and there will be no Christmases for you ever again."

"Yeah, yeah, man. I'm hearing you."

"We just want to know about them. That's it."

"Got it, man."

"Discreet."

"Got it, man. Blinky can be discreet."

I wondered if he realized how ridiculous his last statement was, standing there in a flashing neon Santa suit.

CHAPTER 35

Dragon Lady

When it came to the world of high finance and corporate espionage, I knew next to nothing. I had been expanding my knowledge since becoming a private detective, but it was slow going. Honestly, I couldn't care less about the industry, but I wanted as many corporate clients as I could get—I cared about their money.

So, I called my banker. I had a private banker, now that I had my own business, and was a "famous" detective. He gave me a crash course in the megacorporate jungle.

"What makes you think one of their CEOs wouldn't care? Are you serious, Mr. Cruz? One false rumor in the media could crash a company's stock. They could lose millions, or billions. In point of fact, it's a megacorp's CEO who would most likely deal directly with the lowly citizen on the street. Loose lips can sink a corporate ship, no matter how big—sink the ship, and get the CEO canned. Corporations pay closer attention to the news cycle than anyone else."

"So, they would contact the Average Joe or Jane on the street if they were saying something in public that they didn't like?"

"Most assuredly. Most directly."

"Rivals would take advantage of it?"

"No, Mr. Cruz. Rivals would most likely be behind it all. If they could get the man on the street to trash their chief competitor, that's like gold in the bank. Destroy your enemy without him even knowing you were the one who pulled the trigger. The fine points of corporate espionage stagecraft."

Yo's claim was looking to be far more plausible. I already believed him, but had more facts to bolster my feelings. The main thing in his favor was that I didn't believe for a second he'd have Ping or any of his associates fill my shower stall with snakes. Again, I lived in Rabbit City, and them leaving Silicon Dunes to go to Rabbit City, was like me saying I was going to look for a place to settle down with the wife and kids in Free City. It was an act going too far. It wasn't him or Orochi Corp.

"There's no such tattoo floating around on the streets." That's what Blinky called me on the video-phone to tell me.

"Out of all the millions of tattoos, there must be. You know for certain there's no such thing."

"Cruz, man. The people I reached out to are the kind of people who would know. Tattoo artists are very territorial. They come up with a new tattoo, then they trademark it. So, whether they do the tattoo or not, they get paid."

"What about Up-Top?"

"They checked there too, but they're sure there's none there either."

"I showed you the picture. The man clearly has the tattoo on his hand."

"That's funny, man. I was about to mention the same thing. My contacts said that tattoo must be a fake."

"How would they know that?"

"That's what they said, man. They blew up the picture's resolution and said it wasn't permanent ink, more like those temporary ink jobs the kids always get and then wash off when they're bored with it, and get something new."

"Blinky, criminals wouldn't run around with kid tattoos."

"No they wouldn't, man, if these people are as bad as you say they are. That's all I got for you, man."

"Okay."

"So, will you have Phishy call me, man?"

"He's not talking to you. I'm as close as you're going to get."

"Okay, man. I get it. But tell him to keep out of sight."

"Why? What's going on?"

"The cops are looking for him. Maybe even the Feds."

"Why would they be looking for him?"

"I don't know, man, and I'm not going to ask them."

"Are they looking for you?"

"No, man, I don't think so."

"You crazy mutt. The last job he had was with you, so if they're looking for him, they probably have your name, too."

"Don't worry, man. I ditched the firetruck, and my girl and I already moved out from where we were staying."

"You need to disappear, too."

"I got it, man. Consider Santa gone to Antarctica, man."

"How do I get in touch with you if I need to, or if Phishy does?"

"Phishy knows how, man."

"Okay, go to Antartica and stay off the street."

"Roger, man. Blinky outta here."

I hung up my vehicle's video-phone. I didn't like this news from Blinky. The police had me at arm's length at the moment, but I was going to have to see if they were really looking for Phishy. I'd thought our tunnel "escapade" had been behind us, but that didn't seem to be the case at all.

The beauty of not being a slave to public transportation was spontaneity. You could go wherever you wanted, and that's exactly what I did when I saw a few hoverfood trucks parked below. A Coney Island would go a long way in lifting my spirits. Maybe I could check a few items off my wedding errand list while I walked around.

I was parked, and in front of the hovertruck in no time. It wasn't a long line, but any kind of line meant the food was at least edible.

"A Coney Island with everything," I said.

The order taker wearing a hair net nodded, and mumbled my order to one of two cooks on the grill. He didn't have on one of those silly Liquid Cool T-shirts, so that was one gold star for him.

"Something to drink?"

I looked at the list of beverages on the menu inside. "Six-dollar shake express."

He took my card, and inserted it in his hand-machine. The paper receipt printed. I took back my card, and put both it, and the receipt in my inside jacket pocket, then zipped it shut. Carrying a wallet around in public was just asking for trouble.

"Ahh, Mr. Cruz."

I hated strangers, always had. But now, because I was famous, strangers knew me. I hated strange people who knew my name when I didn't know theirs.

The Asian woman was five feet tall and wearing all green wet-wear. She didn't seem to mind the rain at all. I had on a hat, while others had umbrellas. There was a necklace around her neck, with a tiny dragon at the end.

"I was told that you were looking for the seven-headed snake tattoo."

My mood immediately darkened.

"I was told there was no such thing."

"Oh, but there is," she said.

She smiled to reveal a pair of teeth that were wide and shark like. It was one of the most unnerving things I had ever seen. On the teeth themselves was that seven-headed snake tattoo in black.

Something was suddenly glowing in her right hand. I glanced down, but couldn't see, as she moved the hand behind her back. I couldn't tell if I was in danger, but I stepped back. When my gaze returned to hers, in the blink of an eye, the point of a glowing blue neon arrow popped through her forehead, and her entire head lifted from her neck. It slammed against the side of the hoverfood truck.

Everything moved in slow motion. I looked at her decapitated body as it collapsed to the ground. I looked at the head with the arrow sticking through it, pinned to the hovertruck. People were scattering everywhere. The order taker was screaming in shock.

I regained some semblance of my senses, and disappeared into the rain like everyone else on the street.

CHAPTER 36

Prince Lux

The events kept repeating themselves in my mind. The Dragon Lady had clutched something in her hand behind her back. It'd looked like a laser dagger, and I realized that, once again, I had come very close to death.

My body was still shaking as I dialed.

"The Orochi Corporation, may I help you?"

"Mr. Ping."

"Please hold, Mr. Cruz."

It wasn't magic. PJ wanted to connect a similar system to our phone. It wasn't caller ID. It was voice print ID. It didn't surprise me that Orochi Corp's phone A.I. knew my voice. As I waited, the call reverted to audio only. Also, not surprising.

"Yes." I recognized Ping's voice right away.

"Thank you." That's all I said.

"You are welcome, Mr. Cruz." The voice was Mr. Yo.

I hung up.

I decided to get back to the office. I needed to be in a safe place for a while. With my cyborg secretary outside my door, an ample number of weapons under our desks, and cameras watching all entrances to the office, Liquid Cool was the place for me to be at the moment.

PJ told me something strange.

"I've called that Susan C a couple of times. She doesn't return my calls."

Susan C had basically said her sister was a mental. We had told her that Sarah may be in distress after I'd confronted her at the temple wedding rehearsal. Now she had disappeared, too. I was starting to believe that what Sarah C had originally told us was true after all. With what I was suspecting about the Orochi Corporation—that there was another player in this game—it made me believe both Sarah C and Bionic Betty.

"Boss, line one." PJ called out to me from her desk.

We only had one line!

I was back on my way to the Euphoria Hotel to see the Royal Lux again. Private eye-ing was such a topsy-turvy business.

The Pony got me there in no time. It was the same routine. The same guard took me up to the penthouse, then the same female aide took me to the waiting room. But this time, it wasn't the king who came to speak with me. It was another man, by himself, probably one of the two people who'd been standing in the shadows.

The view was mesmerizing. The rain clouds were just below the penthouse. I could hear the thunder, but all I saw was space above.

"Please have a seat, Mr. Cruz."

I did, and he joined me in the adjacent chair.

"I thought I wasn't going to hear from or see any of you again," I said.

"My father was actually quite impressed with you. When you're royalty with substantial wealth, your life becomes one of avoiding the daily parasites of life who only want to know you to get money from you. To meet a...normal person is quite a rare event for him—and in his case, a fellow classic hovercar connoisseur. Do expect an impromptu call from him in the future, to visit the country of Lux. You can bring the wife-to-be."

I smiled. "Dot would love that, and so would I."

"My wife, the princess, would keep her entertained, while you and the king spend quality time with the vehicles."

"Thank you. I look forward to it. How can I help you, though?"

"Well, my father would like you at a gathering we will be attending. We are co-hosts of the event, and he would feel more comfortable with you there, as an extra set of eyes and ears. We hear you have a special aptitude at identifying members of the criminal class."

"Is the Royal Lux in some danger?"

"There are many children in the royal family. Some of them seem to be drawn to that element, like a moth to a flame, despite our best efforts to prevent it. Parents like to think they can control their children, but that is often nothing but an illusion."

"Criminal activity?"

"Oh, heavens, no. They simply like hanging around the criminal class."

"Criminal groupies."

"Without delving into the carnal, that would be one term for them."

"Any criminals in particular you are concerned about?"

"We understand that you identified specific...assassins in Metropolis."

For a confidential meeting at Police One, it was fascinating how many outsiders were privy to it.

"Prince, at the beginning I thought there might be some threat to the public, but after a string of murders among the crime boss community, I realized this was simply criminals killing criminals in their own dens, away from everyone else. I don't think even crime groupies or their family would have anything to worry about."

"Nevertheless, the king would like you to attend the event."

"I can do that. I just don't like to take people's money when it's not necessary."

"What else are we to do with all the money we'll never spend, Mr. Cruz? You might as well have it." He stood from his chair, and I did the same. "My people will contact you with all the details, and they'll have you fitted in the proper attire. You will be able to leave the Pony in its stable. You'll be chauffeured to and from the event by our hoverlimo."

"Is the location of the event a secret?"

"Not at all. It's the annual Christmas party of the Council of Corporations. About fifty thousand people will be in attendance."

CHAPTER 37

Orochi

Most people on the planet would never be inside the building of the Council of Corporations in their entire lives. I would be there a second time in one week.

They didn't need to fit me for a tux. They already had. A tailor showed up at Liquid Cool with it on a hanger. They didn't send a hoverlimo to pick me up from the Concrete Mama. It was more like an Up-Top spaceship.

Here I was at the Christmas party of the most powerful and richest people in the solar system. I didn't have to do much. I stood at the receiving station to the party as slinky female and hunky male aides checked in the attendees. I stood behind them and all the security guards, doing what I was hired to do—glance at every face that was admitted.

"Mr. Cruz." It was the mayor of Metropolis and his wife.

We hadn't met on the best of terms in my last case, but we'd ended on a positive note. He'd gotten my gun license back, and had it upgraded to full-use—I could possess, carry—even concealed—any weapon known to mankind.

I nodded to acknowledge them. As they walked away, I knew they were wondering why I was there.

A delegation arrived, and one among them was Run-Time! He was with his wife, who wore an amazing sparkling red dress down to her thighs, and matching glow heels. She was Black, and had wavy hair down to her waist. Mrs. Run-Time was especially big into the hugs, but they knew I was working. Run-Time gave me a thumbs-up with a smile as they passed.

I had been offered drinks, but I had turned them all down. I was working.

The King of Lux appeared with his wife, the queen, following. He saw me and nodded. She did the same. Then the prince and the princess appeared, following. They too acknowledged me as they passed.

To see all these people—megacorp bosses, senior execs, their families. To be in the same room, breathe the same air as these uber-power elites. I couldn't imagine the stress level of the security people in charge of this event.

The Orochi Corporation party arrived. Mr. Yo led the group. I recognized Ping. The other senior execs with them, I had never seen before. The star of the show was a beautiful woman at Yo's side, in a geisha-style white dress. I knew they saw me, but they never looked my way. They passed without any acknowledgment.

I watched them move into the crowds, greeting, being greeted. As I returned my attention to my job, a wave of panic overcame me. I tried to fight it, but I knew I would have to do what I was about to do.

I turned again. The Orochi Corp party had settled not too far from where I was, each with glasses of alcohol in hand. Ping noticed me staring first. The other senior execs did as well and, like Ping, stared back. Mr. Yo lowered his glass from his lips when he noticed me.

The walk to them away from my post was a surreal one. I stood opposite Mr. Yo. I was not smiling.

"I want you to instruct all your people, one by one, to smile like this." I smiled a big Joker smile, then returned my mouth to its closed, natural state.

Yo was one of those prodigies who, if he came across a language he didn't speak, and you gave him a couple of letters and vowels, he'd write its entire dictionary for you.

He stood in front of Ping, face-to-face. Ping nervously smiled wide, then closed his mouth. Yo stood in front of each man as he temporarily bared their teeth for Yo in a grotesque smile. Yo waited, then turned to the woman. All the men looked at her.

She stood there, almost apart from the men, like a statue. I saw beads of sweat appear on the flawless skin of her forehead. Yo stepped to face her directly.

Slowly she smiled, and I saw it. The seven-headed snake tattoo!

Yo yelled out in disgust, and struck across her face with his right hand. The woman collapsed to the ground. At this point, every single person in the hall had stopped what they were doing, and was staring at what was unfolding.

I saw a red line of blood across her face. She was not moving. Four of the senior execs surrounded her, picked her off the ground, and carried her away. Ping followed with his head down.

Yo's face had been tilted down, and his eyes were closed. He opened them and they seemed to be teary. He stood straight up, walked two paces in front of me, spun around, and faced me. He smiled, and bowed before me. With that, he followed his party out of the hall.

I stood there paralyzed. Fifty thousand people stared at me. Who was that man whom the head of the Orochi Corporation had just bowed to?

Walk! I yelled inside my head. My legs had turned to jelly, but I turned and walked past all the eyes on me, past the receiving station, and out of the hall too. When I got outside, I kept walking, out of the structure, and into the rain. I couldn't stop and I wasn't going to call a hovertaxi.

A hovercar descended before me and a door opened. I slowly looked in and recognized one of Prince Lux's security men.

I got in, soaked to the bone from the rain.

"The prince thought you might be foolish enough to try to walk home."

"Tell the prince I'm sorry. I've never walked off a job."

"The Prince considers the job for which he hired you to be completed more than satisfactorily. You did exactly what he hired you to do. You identified a threat."

"Who was that woman with the Orochi Corporation delegation?"

"That was the senior executive and vice chief operating officer of the Orochi Corporation—also, the eldest daughter of Mr. Yo, its president and CEO. She was named after the company when she was born— Orochi. She was supposed to be his successor."

PART SIX

Silver City

CHAPTER 38

Chief Hub

As I stood waiting in the lobby, Chief Hub came around the corner. Two officers were waiting with me, as was customary, and if it weren't, they still would have been. I was sure I was still on the "crap list" over the whole Monkey Baker affair.

Chief Hub didn't look particularly interested in seeing me as he approached.

"The luckiest man in the universe is here again. I heard you were the center of attention with the gazillionaire class last night. What do you want?"

I already had it in my hand, and put the data disk in his.

"When I was last here, I identified a few contract killers in the city especially known for their viciousness and weaponry. Remember that night when every member of the Animal Farm Crime Syndicate had us surrounded, and was going to fill our bodies with so many bullet holes and laser burns we'd be unrecognizable? Then your son brought the cavalry. Five hundred thousand Metro police descending from the heavens, and blowing all those criminal scumbags to smithereens. Well, if they'd had the guy on that tape, it would have been a mass grave, filled with me, and all 500 thousand of your men and women in silver and black."

The two officers looked at Hub, and the disk in his hand.

"I have never seen the kind of weapon this guy has. Forget those cop-killer guns that go through body armor. This weapon can punch through buildings, and do things I've never seen laser rounds do. They're like blades made of solid light. It's my humble opinion, but he represents a clear and present danger to every cop on the beat. Watch it; your first call should be to Interpol because no one on this planet made that weapon—and if his weapon is from Up-Top, he likely is too."

That was all I said. I left Phishy's video recording with them.

I may or may not have redeemed myself in Chief Hub's eyes. They may or may not have been looking for Phishy. Maybe they knew something about what the late Swordplaya had been up to. No, I gave them the video because it was the right thing to do.

CHAPTER 39

The Notary

Strangely, I had ten cases in the hopper, but it was only two that occupied my mind. PJ and I were in the office getting ready. I had her take names and numbers, and get everyone out of there. I wanted Liquid Cool closed and I wanted to see our weapon stash laid out on the top of my table.

PJ had brought a bag of her private weapons, too.

"I'll go to the nursing home and get Bionic Bob." I inspected one of the sawed-off laser rifles. "You get over to Metro Mental, and get Bionic Betty."

"Why her? She beat me up."

"That wouldn't have happened if you hadn't dropped your fists. What's wrong with you? You're Punch Judy. How many people have you beaten up?"

She looked at a bulky laser pistol. "Many, many people. She caught me off guard."

"Besides, Metro Mental is expecting you to get Betty, and the nursing home is expecting me."

"Are you expecting nurses to try and stop me?"

"What we're arming up for is any party crashers."

"Well, let them come. It'll be their choice: bionic fist in the head, or laser blast to the chest."

"That's what I'm talking about."

My mobile rang, and I placed the gun in my hand on the table. I usually didn't answer calls on audio only, but I did.

"What did you get me into, Mr. Cruz?"

"What's happening?"

"What's happening? They're trying to kill me!"

"Where are you?"

"I don't know. They tried to run me off the road."

"Where?"

"I was coming out of Silver City and this hovertruck slammed right into me. It tried to crash me to the ground. I'm a notary, not some kind of James Bond secret agent. What have you gotten me into?"

"Did you register all his parts?"

"Yes!"

"I need that list!"

"What about my life?"

"Find out exactly where you are."

"I'm in the rain at some overpass. I can see which marker number." He gave me the number.

"I'm going to send someone to get you."

"Why not you?"

"Because I can't be in two places at the same time, and we need someone closer to you than I am, someone who can get there fast."

"Hurry up! That killer truck may be back!"

I hung up my mobile.

"Who was that?" PJ asked.

"Someone is trying kill the notary with a hovertruck."

"How are we going to get him?"

"I'll take care of it. You get Betty, and I'll get Bob. We'll meet at the safe house. I want everyone at the safe house, so you take a bag of weapons, and I'll take a bag of weapons. I want that safe house safe."

CHAPTER 40

Bionic Bob

I had my omega-gun in my shoulder holster on my left side, and my pop-gun on my right wrist. I planned to bring my duffel bag filled with guns, collapsible rifles, and stun grenades. There were even a few knives in there, though I didn't like cutting things, unless I was cooking at home. Then, I saw the big blocky security guard robot walking over to me. The bag was staying in the vehicle.

Silver City Nursing Home was somewhat of a laughable name. Silver City was the center of robotics production in Metropolis. All the major megacorps were here, and their factories never stopped. Robots were everywhere—flying around, walking around, rolling around on two wheels, three wheels or four.

I had parked my Pony far away, because I didn't want any robot stiffing my vehicle and scratching the paint. It's hard to curse out a robot. You can't tell if they're looking at you, or even listening.

As I approached the nursing home, I looked at the display posters of smiling cyborg patients along the walkway to the main entrance: a panoply of the ethnic rainbow coalition. Bionic hands, arms, legs, or the full robot body.

I had pushed the hoverwheelchair from my trunk the whole way. My security guard escort even opened the door for me inside. There was no robotic receptionist; the desks were the robots.

"I'm here to get a patient," I said, and showed the robot my paperwork.

"I'm sorry, sir, but that patient is unavailable."

"What does that mean?"

"I'm sorry, sir, you will have to come back another time."

"Where is the patient?"

"I'm sorry, sir, you will have to make an appointment."

Robots could be so annoying. Communicating, but not really.

"If I'm not taken to the patient I came to collect, I will have the police here again."

"I'm sorry, please wait for staff."

"Yes! Get a real human out here—one who can speak in full sentences too."

A man appeared dressed in silver overalls and a shiny silver cap.

"Who are you?" I asked.

"Who are you?"

"I'm here for a patient. Are you supposed to be the guy who's here to stonewall me?"

"I don't have to listen to this. Get him out of the facility."

I looked at the security robot, and stepped back from it. I looked at the man. "If your robot lays one metal finger on me, I'll shoot it."

"Get him out of the facility," the man repeated.

I shot the security robot, which keeled over. Then I shot the desk robot, which hit the ground with a thud, because I hate desk robots.

All hell exploded—deafening sirens. The man stepped back, and black humanoid robots poured out of doors that seemed to materialize from the wall. Their weapon arms were pointed at me. I stood completely still.

The man looked past me, and noticed something coming in from outside. The door opened. Ping marched in with an army of armed men and women in black suits—machine-guns in hand, swords strapped to their backs.

The two sides faced each other, lots of deadly weapons pointed.

"I want my patient," I said to the man. "His wife is waiting and I don't have time to waste with you."

"I am a representative of the Orochi Corporation. You will comply immediately," Ping said to him.

The man looked as if we had kicked him in the face. "I am not authorized to let you in."

"You're fired!" Ping yelled at him.

"Intruder alert," a computer voice called out over and over. A spotlight shone on the man. All the robots swiveled on their waists, turning to point their arms at him.

His mobile phone rang. He answered it.

"Employee 54947-A-K, your employment has been terminated from the Silver City Assisted Living Facility, a subsidiary of the Orochi Corporation. Please find the email attached from Human Resources of all rules and regulations regarding your separation. Good luck in your new life." It ended with some phrase in Japanese.

"I'll take you through, sir."

"You're hired!" Ping yelled.

The "intruder alert" alarms stopped and the robots swiveled back to point their arms at Ping's people.

The worker's mobile phone rang. He answered it.

"Employee 54947-A-K, welcome to the Silver City Assisted Living Facility, a subsidiary of the Orochi Corporation. Please find the email attached from Human Resources of all rules and regulations regarding your rehire. Good luck in your continued career with the Silver City Assisted Nursing Home, where cyborgs get to heaven, too." It ended with some phrase in Japanese.

We were deep within the facility now.

Ping's soldiers blasted the door to pieces. Bionic Bob wasn't in the nursing home facility; he was on an operating table. We stormed the hospital facilities. Some medical personnel ran, others attacked us. Ping's soldiers karate-kicked and punched their way through all opposition.

I ran inside, and there was an unconscious Bob on the bio-table, an anesthesia mask on his mouth. I glanced at his arms—they were buff and toned. The tray near the bio-table contained what looked like the same tools I'd use to build or repair a hovercar. We had arrived just in time.

One of Ping's guards dragged away a captured doctor who still had on a surgical mask.

"That one," I said.

The guard stopped, and Ping joined me.

"Pull off his mask," I directed.

The guard ripped the surgical mask off his face.

I stared at him. "I recognize your picture on the wall."

Everyone looked at the large picture of the man on the wall. He was the senior cyber-doctor for Silver City Nursing Home.

"Why were you going to cut up Bionic Bob?"

He ignored me.

"Come on, doctor. Let's see those teeth. Teeth! Let's see the teeth."

Two guards grabbed him and pried open his mouth. A third lifted his upper lip. There was another seven-headed snake tattoo on his teeth.

"How many of you guys are there?" I asked.

Ping yelled something in Japanese, and they dragged him away. I had a feeling this doctor would not be practicing medicine anymore.

CHAPTER 41

The Peanut Gallery

Phishy had been staying with one of his sidewalk johnny buddies in Free City. I tried to avoid Free City whenever I could, though I did know good people who lived there. We needed some place secluded, but defensible. In my mind, a real safe house was a fort—fortified, so that every way in could be securely watched, and you could hold off anyone trying to get at you. I didn't know of any place like that in Free City, but I did find one on the edge of Neon Blues.

The safe house was like a slab of concrete from a monolith tower. It was five-stories tall, but only two levels on the inside. There was only one window, and one door in and out. For some, it would seem like a death trap, but it was exactly what I wanted: easily defensible.

Phishy didn't carry. He was a weapons dealer on the side, but he didn't carry. I still hadn't decided whether that made sense or not. I had to supply the initial stash of weapons, and I left him with a few of his trusted sidewalk johnny "lieutenants," the same two he had sent to Liquid Cool as our go-betweens.

I rolled in Bionic Bob. He was still groggy, but was coming out of his drug-induced sleep. I didn't need to tell him what had happened. We—Orochi Corp and I—had saved him from being sliced up.

"They were going to steal my bionics," he said, "and I wasn't even dead yet. A nursing home is supposed to wait until you kick the can on your own, not do it for you."

"What's the world coming to?" I said.

"Where's Betty?"

"My secretary is getting her."

"What is this place?"

"It's our safe house. There are too many dangerous people out there. We can plan our next moves in peace here. For you and Betty, it's to get you out of Metropolis."

"And go where?"

"Well, any place where crazy doctors won't be trying to steal your bionics for starters."

"I'm not running. I've never run from a fight in my life, and I'm not about to start."

"Sometimes running isn't running but retreating to fight another day."

Bionic Bob wasn't having it. "Running and retreating mean the same thing, you know."

"I am going to let you, Betty, and my secretary decide on your next move." I rolled him into the space that was the kitchen. "Phishy!" He appeared with his buddies. "Get Bob here settled, and get him some food."

"Tools. I need tools, too," Bob said. "They disconnected my legs."

"Both of them bionic?" Phishy asked.

"Both."

"How fast can you run?" Phishy asked.

"Faster than anybody you've ever seen."

The Notary Man was dumped in front of the building by a hovertrash truck. The drivers were the Dominican Surf brothers. I'd met them on the hovercar racing scene. The only vehicles more plentiful in Metropolis than hovertaxis were hovertrash trucks. Initially I had thought about contacting my man Flash, but it was a killer hovertruck that was after the Notary Man. If so, they wouldn't have any issue with crashing into a hovertaxi. However, crashing into a huge hovertrash truck, which was more like a flying tank, was a whole different story. Most hovertaxi drivers would fly away; all trashmen would shoot you.

I waved at the Surf Brothers as they cruised away. I pulled the notary inside.

"You called the garbage men to get me?" he said with disgust.

"The average hovertrash truck is more armored than the best armored hoverlimo. You were as safe as if you were being escorted here by the police, so stop complaining. We got you here safely."

"I want to go home."

I couldn't blame him. He hadn't signed up for this adventure. I copied the data from his mobile to mine. I had Bionic Bob, and the serial numbers to all his bionic parts. However, before he could go home, Bob and Betty would need to be reunited. PJ should have arrived already.

Well, PJ did arrive. I should have guessed it. She and Bionic Betty were "buddies" now. They showed up chatting as if they were long-lost best friends.

"You're friends now?" I asked.

"Betty lived in France for a long time."

"Oh, that explains everything. Was it a neighborhood you and your fellow Terrible Enfantes terrorized?"

"Cruz, we didn't terrorize. Posh gangs didn't do that. We brought culture and style to the streets."

"Why am I talking to you?" I turned my attention to an anxious Betty. "Betty, guess who's in the kitchen?"

What did I just see?

With her bionic legs, Bionic Betty sprinted to where I'd pointed. I had never seen a cyborg with bionic legs run before. The effect was hard to explain. She just disappeared, and appeared someplace else.

The cyborg husband and wife were reunited. She jumped into his arms.

"Cruz, the romantic matchmaker," PJ said watching them with a smile. "You should charge extra for that."

"Someone else is coming," said one of the sidewalk johnnies who had taken a position in front of the sole window to the safe house, stuffing his face with potato chips.

Phishy joined him at the window, then went to the door to unlatch, and open it.

"Nice of you to join us," I said. "Get your food and drink from the kitchen, then we'll figure out how to break out your sister from Silver City, using the maximum force necessary to cause the most amount of mayhem."

Sarah C smiled.

CHAPTER 42

The Martian

I could not believe I had relented. PJ was barking orders at not one, but two temps (I think they were high school students). One girl was at the desk to answer calls. The other was there to help sort through the backlog of messages. There were many reasons why I wanted some kind of presence in the office, and a live person to answer the phone.

For the present time, I was practicing my private detecting skills to check out Bionic Bob's cybernetic serial numbers. Nothing. Nothing. Nothing. I had been at it for the morning and most of the afternoon. I was trying to not have to rely on the police for a change, but was not getting anywhere with the general databases.

I had to get this done before I could send the bionic husband and wife on their way to "places unknown." All this had to be done before I tackled what I had named "the Silver City Interdiction."

PJ stood in the open doorway of my office. I stopped my dialing.

"The police are here for you."

Police Chief Hub strolled into my office with another man.

"We're meeting far too often," I said. "You're married, and I'm getting married. Spouses will start to wonder."

"How do you think I feel?" Hub asked, "But your office is still more private than mine."

He directed the man in a brown uniform to sit in the chair in front of my desk. Hub closed the door, and sat in the adjoining chair.

"What did I do this time?" I asked.

"There's always so many things when it comes to you," Hub said. "However, this is Carter's show."

"Carter?"

"I'm Carter," the man said. "Interpol."

"Not again. The average Metropolitan will never meet an Interpol agent ever in their life. I'm meeting you guys on a regular basis. I don't even get the intermediary step of being hassled by the Feds."

"I'm on loan to the Feds, if that helps."

I looked at Chief Hub, not pleased.

"That's what you get for identifying assassins," he said.

"Me? You were the one who invited me to the meeting."

"Don't blame me. It was Compstat Connie."

"Since you're here, why are you looking for Phishy?"

"Do you know where he is?" he asked.

"You know I do. What did he do?"

"We're interested in him, and someone called Blinky, but that's not why we're here. We can talk about that later."

"I didn't know that Earthlings were advanced enough to develop photographic memories," Carter said. "You identified these four individuals on sight. I was told that if there were pictures of 100 criminals, you would have identified them too."

"You called me an Earthling. Are you another spaceman?"

Carter seemed to be wondering whether he should answer. "I'm from the other planet."

"Mars?"

"What other inhabited planet is there? Humans won't be living on Jupiter or Saturn any time—ever."

"A Martian."

"Yes, a Martian."

"Hold on." I took out my mobile, and quickly texted a message.

"Who are you contacting?" Carter asked, half-worried.

"Don't worry. I'm not contacting all the illegitimate children you have running around Earth."

"Funny," Carter said. Hub smiled.

My mobile was back in my jacket. They had my full attention again.

"What did I do, then?"

"You've heard that there's been a string of deaths of crime bosses in Metropolis?"

"I've heard."

"We believe the four assassins you identified are the cause."

I nodded. All interesting, but I didn't care. Criminals killing criminals was fine with me.

"I can tell you're deeply broken up about it," Carter said.

"I can barely keep in the tears," I said.

"Ever heard of the Sandman?"

I shook my head.

"Theo?"

"No."

"They're two Up-Top crime lords. Their criminal enterprises are vast. If it's illegal, dangerous, and violent, they're involved. Theo was the Sandman's protégé, Sandman's second in command, until they had a falling out. More than that, it's a criminal civil war. Thousands have died in their war to date.

"We have reason to believe they're here on Earth."

"Why?" I asked. "They're in Metropolis, too?"

"That's what we believe now. Sandman hired these assassins to kill Theo, or vice-versa. No way to know at this point."

"We need to know about the new player on the video you turned in," Hub interjected.

"I don't know anything about him. Didn't see him. Don't know him."

"Ever heard of an assassin called Blade Gunner?" Carter asked.

"No." I shook my head. "Was that the guy in the tunnel?"

"Were you in the tunnel?"

"No, why?"

"Was your associate, Phishy, in the tunnel?" Carter asked.

"My associate." I grinned. "Why the third degree? You have the video. That's all I have and all I know. If there were more, I would have shared that too." I looked at Hub. "I didn't have to turn that in."

"You're right," he said, "but you said so yourself. We need to find this guy and get that weapon off the street. We believe he's connected with either Sandman or Theo."

"Not just a civil war, but a prelude to the takeover of the entire criminal world on Earth," Carter added.

"How could two Up-Top gangsters manage that?" I asked.

"Could one of them do it with this Blade Gunner?" Hub asked.

"What was your theory before you saw the video? It sounds like you're trying to make up a story from the pieces, rather than letting the pieces tell the story," I said.

The Martian smiled at me, and looked at Hub. "Are all your private detectives on this planet as smart?"

"Yeah, I'm smart," I interjected. "My fiancée says so, too. What was your theory before?"

"Before Interpol told us about these two Up-Top crime lords, there were already rumors about a coming street war with out-of-town killers. When we learned about these two, it all fit. Now with this new player, one of these two wants to do a lot more than kill his rival. He wants to take over Earth's crime world."

As I listened, I realized that both of them were fumbling around in the dark. They didn't know that Phishy and I had been in the tunnel with this Blade Gunner. They didn't know about Swordplaya, or the retriever. They knew nothing.

But then again, I didn't know anything, either. I didn't know why they were looking for Phishy, and I didn't know why they were really in my office.

There I sat, as Hub and the Martian took turns weaving a story for me, trying to find out something without point-blank asking me. It went on for a while, until there was a knock at the door.

"Yes!" I called out.

The door opened and there was PJ.

"We're still in a meeting," I said.

"Your party is here."

"PJ, what are you talking about?"

A little kid appeared behind her, then another, and another. They pushed their way into my office, and then the adults came in. There was that rapid-fire Chinese and one of the voices was familiar. Mrs. Wan appeared, holding the hand of an elderly Asian woman, who was holding the hand of an even older woman.

"Where's the Martian?" one of the kids asked.

Carter jumped up from his chair. "Who did you call?" he angrily asked me.

"Everyone," I answered. I pointed at him. "There be the Martian."

My announcement was followed by a group "Ohhh!"

In came Mr. Wan and a bunch of men, then some teenagers. I couldn't have cared less about them, but then Dot appeared. She was the one I had texted. Behind her was her boss from Eye Candy, Prima Donna.

Dot came over to me, and gave me a kiss, smiling.

"How many family members do you have? Every time I see your mother, there's a new member of the Wan clan with her."

"Ha-ha. Wan clan."

"So, that's your grandmother and great-grandmother with her?"

"My grandmother and great-great-grandmother with her."

"We skipped one. She passed?"

"No, no. She's at the salon. She was sitting in the chair when I got your text. My great-great-great-grandmother was with her."

"What? How can your great-great-great grandmother still be alive?"

"Cruz, this isn't the year 2000. People live well past 100. We could both be alive and kicking to see out great-great-great-*great*-grandchildren."

"I find that quite disturbing," I said.

We watched Mrs. Wan take control of Carter's person, and move him over to the wall. Hub was intelligent enough to get far out of the way.

"Wear this." Mrs. Wan gave him one of those headbands with the two green felt antennae.

"Martians do not have antennae coming out of their heads, or red skin, or green skin."

"Wear it," Mrs. Wan commanded. "My mother and my grandmother want pictures with a Martian."

I felt so bad for Carter. He was posed with the Wans and their parents first, then the friends, the teenagers next, then the little kids.

"I want a picture with the Martian," PJ said, with her special pink camera in her hands.

Hub was rolling. He could barely keep in his laughter at the red-faced Carter, who was nothing more than a captive of the Wan clan.

"Mr. Carter," Prima Donna called out. "What is that on your head, and I don't mean the fake antennae? After we're done with the pictures here, you'll be my complimentary client at Metropolis's premiere image salon in the city. Haircut, wash, rinse, styling. There's no way I'm going to allow any Martian to wander around on Earth not looking his best, if I can help it."

I'm not sure whether Carter realized that his photo torture was far from over.

This was a once-in-a-life-time chance. Dot and I got our photo with the Martian, too, before he was whisked away out of the office for his next stop.

CHAPTER 43

Ping and Yo

"**N**o."

That was the response from Run-Time, when I asked him if I should trust the Orochi Corporation.

"Also, why would you say I like the attention?" I asked. "I hate attention."

"Cruz, you've always been like this. When we were in grade school you started wearing your fedora. No one wore hats back then. Everyone was asking, 'Who's that cat in the hat?' You got me wearing *my* hat. You built a bright red hovervehicle when no one had a hovercar of any color other than earth tones or black. You did what you did at the Council of Corporation's Christmas party. You got everyone's attention. I've been getting calls from the rich and powerful all day asking me about you."

"It's not intentional. I get swept up in these things. It's not my fault."

"If that's the story you're going with."

"So, you don't think Orochi Corp would tell me the truth."

"You asked me, if you should trust them. As for honesty, even a liar tells the truth from time to time. I'm not in a position to know. My advice to you is to be very careful with them. They know we're friends, and you know they're trying to get my company, like every other megacorp at their level."

"They did save my life."

"From what I witnessed at the Council of Corporation's Christmas party, you returned the favor. Send me your list of serial numbers when you're ready. Cruz, be very careful with these people. A shark may be nice to you, help you, swim alongside of you, but it's still a shark."

Yes. It's still a snake.

The hoverdirigible with its neon letters descended from the sky. The cab was the size of a mega-truck and the balloon section was ten times larger. OROCHI CORP. flashed on either side of the skyship.

Mr. Yo wanted to see me.

This was not like any balloon cab I had ever been in, but that went without saying. A multi-trillion-dollar megacorp is not going to fly around in a hoverdirigible like everyone else.

Inside, Yo spoke to me from the video screen, from another location. Ping stood behind me. Security stood at the door.

"Mr. Cruz, we cannot look to be helping you in this action."

"But you own the Silver City lab."

"This is how we must proceed."

"We're going to break into a cyber-lab that you own?"

"Orochi Corporation owns it, but we may not be the ones who are running it at the present time."

"What is Gidrah, Mr. Yo?"

"Answering that question would reveal things that the Orochi Corporation does not want revealed. We must handle it in our own way. We have many enemies. This is one."

"When should we break in?"

"Mr. Cruz, you move when you see fit. Mr. Ping will command the Orochi Corporation forces to assist you. You will not see Mr. Ping or them until the proper time."

"We're to break in and pray that Ping and your men show up in time to prevent us all from getting killed."

"Precisely!" As he said this he did that Japanese bow again.

I didn't like this plan at all.

CHAPTER 44

This Chapter Title Was Intentionally Left Blank

The rain was as heavy as it had been for the rainy season. I hadn't given it much notice before, but now it seemed appropriate. In my last case, I'd had an army of police come to my rescue. This time I was going to have an army of corporate soldiers backing me. I was supposed to be a private detective on the street, but it seemed that once again my status was being elevated to a level—and a dangerous one at that—which I was not comfortable with.

"When did you start believing my story?" Sarah C was riding shotgun in the Pony.

The sky traffic was slow. People couldn't drive in the rain, which always annoyed me, since they weren't driving, but flying.

"Your sister came to the office, but since then, we've been unable to reach her. If her story were true, she'd be returning all our calls right away. So, I choose to believe your story. Besides, my mother-in-law from hell likes you and says to trust you."

Sarah C got a kick out of that.

"What's this secret weapon you have?" I asked.

"I can't tell you, or it wouldn't be a secret weapon."

"Now, I haven't seen you and your twin sister together, so this better not be one of those psycho-split personality things where you're both you *and* your sister. I'm not in the mood for something like that."

She started laughing. "My secret weapon is real, not a sitcom sub-plot."

We passed an invisible threshold. You crossed into Silver City, and suddenly everything was more automated—unmanned machines and robots were everywhere. The unions hated robots. "Them robots stealing our jobs," my fiancée's coworkers always said. Dot hated them too.

It was curious what someone had once told me about Silver City. It wasn't a city; it was a colony of robots that sat in a section of Metropolis.

The Pony glided to the Orochi Corp Lab.

"Is the secret weapon in the box of roses you brought?" I asked. "I thought that was your safety blanket."

"I left that home today. I brought along a toy my brother made for me in a time long, long ago."

"In a galaxy far, far away."

"It surely feels like that."

"Are we really going to go in the front way? We should go in the back."

She turned to me. "Well, that would be no fun. You have a fancy vehicle. It's more than a classic. Isn't it supposed to be a premier muscle hovercar?"

"We're changing our game plan before we even get in the front door."

"Oh course. It's what makes life interesting."

I imagined that the robots were walking about, doing their programed duties, minding their own business, not bothering anyone—

The alarms sounded but at the speed we were traveling, their barriers wouldn't get up in time. The Pony crashed through one of the upper glass windows, and I steered down to the main hallway and smashed through every robot in our way. I had on my open-knuckle driving gloves, which meant I was in a "serious driving" frame of mind, moving the vehicle up, down, one side or another, to be in the optimum trajectory to smash other robots to pieces.

"Get ready," I said.

I brought the Pony to a halt. Our doors opened, and we both jumped out. As I readied my electric shotgun, I saw Sarah open her box of roses. The box dropped to the ground; there weren't any roses inside. She cocked a shotgun weapon of a design I'd never seen before.

I turned my attention back to our surroundings. The doors of the Pony closed automatically, and the entire vehicle rose two stories to the ceiling, where it hovered in park-mode.

We saw those shiny black robots coming fast.

"Terminators," Sarah said.

She didn't wait for me to respond, or point my weapon, just jumped in front of me, and fired.

The weapon was unknown to me but I had seen its discharge before. Blades of what looked like laser light fired from its muzzle, and flew at the army of robots, cutting every one of them to pieces. When done, the laser blades came at us, I ducked, but they flew past us at tremendous speed to the army of robots coming from the other direction, and did the same. Then the blades dematerialized.

I slowly stood up straight as I looked at Sarah C.

"I have a thing against killer robots," she said.

"Nice weapon you have. Your brother, you said?"

"Yes. Susan and I haven't seen him for decades, but he left me this. Better than having him here in person, wouldn't you say?"

"I would say."

"Let's get Susan," she said. "This way."

Sarah pushed me away, and fired her weapon again.

Pulse blasts showered us, and I don't know how she wasn't hit. One blast barely missed me, as I hit the ground.

It was a tidal wave of real killer robots! They were bigger, meaner, and from the flurry of laser fire, much better armed. Sarah stood her ground. The round she'd fired finally exploded from behind the robots. Not only were they blown apart, but so was the entire section of hallway.

She reached down to grab my hand. "We better get Susan before they send more."

I allowed her to pull me up. "I'm supposed to save the girl."

This time we both dived for cover.

The new flood of robots was even worse. They were giants, and multiple lasers fired from the multiple nodes on their bodies. They weren't even going to let us pick ourselves up from the ground.

Boom!

The blast was followed by a heat wave that rippled over us. We gritted our teeth from the temperature, and the force of the wave.

We slowly looked up, hearing footsteps. Ping ran in with his samurai soldiers—machine guns with samurai sword bayonets. I had never seen that combo before.

"Mr. Cruz," he said, stopping in front of us.

"Mr. Ping," I said.

"We'll clear the path, but you might want to complete your mission before the Lab activates its main security measures."

"Main security measures? Isn't that what we've been shooting at?"

I didn't know I was the new guest star of the comedy hour, because Ping and his samurai soldiers all laughed. They moved around us, and ran down the hallway into the smoke.

"I like your friends," Sarah said to me.

"They can be your friends, then."

We looked up to the ceilings. The noises from outside were getting louder. We couldn't tell if it was one gigantic hovership, or more than one. Neither of us said anything, but we began running—we needed to get out of the lab sooner rather than later.

Almost immediately, we heard an explosion of gunfire begin again in front of us.

In the back of my mind, part of me wanted to see Sarah and Susan standing next to each for real. There was a lot more to all this, and I'd thought that before Sarah had used her "blade gun."

"This facility will self-destruct in T-minus 100!"

What?

I stopped cold as soon as I heard the overhead, but Sarah ignored it. We saw the humans—workers came from everywhere, upstairs and downstairs, screaming like kindergarten kiddies running from the playground after a drive-by shooting.

"Down here!" I heard Sarah's voice but she was already around the corner.

Boom!

I ran to the sound—something that only police, fire, and first responders do. I was a civilian!

On the ground were the bodies of more people—guards—bodies that were cut to pieces. Behind them the door and wall had suffered the same fate. They had all tangled with Sarah and her blade-gun. It hadn't ended well for them.

From out of the dust, smoke, and rubble, they appeared: Sarah C, with the weapon in hand, and her other arm around another woman—Susan C. The twins, Sarah in black and Susan in white, came to me.

I smiled, and heaved a sigh of relief.

"You're—" I never got to finish my sentence. *A bullet ripped through my chest.*

"Cruz!"

She shot whoever or whatever it was. I collapsed on the cold floor.

Sarah dropped the blade-gun to the ground and ran to me. Both sisters knelt down. I had been shot at many times, and once had Phishy shoot me in the chest (with my bulletproof vest, of course) so I would, at least, know the sensation of a blast. I had never been "shot-shot." There was nothing like being shot and there was nothing you could ever do to prepare. I hadn't just been shot. Whoever or whatever it was had probably killed me.

"This facility will self-destruct in T-minus 75!"

"Cruz, we'll get you help," Sarah said.

"Go," I said. "There's not enough time."

It was a frightening thing to see your own blood flow out of your body. I wasn't going to be conscious for much longer.

We heard the marching sounds of feet—metallic feet. We could see glowing red eyes coming toward us.

"Go!" I said one final time.

Susan got up and pulled Sarah by the hand. "We have to go. You know the others are coming, too. We have to go now."

Sarah grabbed her weapon, stared at me for a moment, and followed her sister.

"Sorry, Cruz," I heard her say.

"This facility will self-destruct in T-minus 50!"

The sisters made it outside the facility through the breach the blade-gun had made.

"How will we get away?" Susan asked.

"I have—oh, God, no." Sarah stopped running and moved her sister behind her.

It was one of the rare times when it wasn't raining, but the sky was dark. In the distance, from within the facility, were the unending sounds of gun and laser-fire.

"I thought you were dead, John," Sarah said to the man with glowing red pupils from behind his dark shades, patiently waiting outside.

"You did. We were twins, too," he said and grinned. "It worked. We didn't think we could make it work."

"Was this all T's plan?" Sarah asked.

"This was the plan of the Asimovs. We have our queen again."

"I am not your queen!" Sarah yelled. "We lost the war with the Founders. We lost everything! The Asimovs are dead!"

"No, Sarah. The Asimovs are about to be resurrected, and then the transcendence can begin again, but this time we have allies who will ensure its completion."

"You will never see that, John, because you will be dead." Sarah pointed her blade-gun at him.

"You can't kill us all, Sarah."

"Us?" A look of fear came over both sisters' faces.

"We have to run, Sarah," Susan cried out.

Sarah grabbed a mobile clipped to her waist, frantically opening it. "Help! Get here!"

John moved so fast that he seemed to teleport next to Sarah. He slapped the mobile out of her hand, and grabbed the blade-gun with the other, crushing it.

"You will regret not being a super," he said, and grabbed her by the throat.

Susan jumped on him, but the man just laughed as she pounded his face with her fists. He brushed her off, and she fell to the ground.

She rose; *they* had arrived.

The Super Cyborgs approached them—each no shorter than six feet five. The muscular development of their frames was far beyond any world-class body builders.

"Leave my sister alone!" Sarah yelled. "John, I'm going to kill all of you."

"No, Sarah. No one will kill the transcendence. The Asimovs will rule this planet and the solar system as was always our inevitable destiny. Humankind will serve the AI. Humankind will serve god."

The bionic husband-and-wife appeared fast, running with their bionic legs at well over 70 miles an hour. Stopping quickly on the wet ground was impossible, but Bionic Bob timed it perfectly, kicking John in the chest, and sending him flying into the darkness.

Bionic Betty ran right into the pack of Super Cyborgs like a battering ram. They went flying too.

"I'll carry you," Bionic Bob said to Sarah. "Betty will carry your sister."

"Bob," Bionic Betty called out as she looked in the distance.

The Super Cyborgs could run super-fast too, and were closing in at an incredible speed. John was with them.

"This isn't going as well as we thought," Bionic Betty continued.

"This facility will self-destruct in T-minus 10!"

Of course, I wasn't dead. I couldn't be telling this story if I were dead. Besides, who else could have gotten my Pony out of there? I wasn't about to let some dumb robot, samurai soldier, or repo man put their digits all over my vehicle. Classic hovercar owners are very particular about such things.

However, truthfully speaking, I was in very bad shape. There wasn't a stronger anti-drug person than me, but aspirin did get rid of headaches, and the drug I took did stop me from bleeding all over the place, as well as a bit of get-up-and-go I needed.

I swooped in with the Pony. Sarah instantly knew it was me as the door opened.

"There's a bag of weapons in the back," I managed to say.

Sarah grabbed it, and tossed it on the floor inside. Sarah, Betty, Bob, even Susan had weapons in hand, and were firing at the Super Cyborgs like real gangster maniacs. It was working, but not good enough. The cyborgs were slowed down, but they were still coming.

"This facility will self-destruct in T-minus five!"

"What does that mean?" Sarah asked.

"Get in the hovercar!" Susan yelled, taking charge.

"A Ford Pony is a vehicle, not a hovercar," I mumbled, but no one heard me.

They all piled in, and I accelerated upwards as fast as I could. The Super Cyborgs reached us and jumped. We were already six stories up and climbing, but the Super Cyborgs were still closing in with arms outstretched.

"Punch it!" Susan yelled at me.

I did, and the Pony flew out of there like warp drive.

"This facility will self-destruct T-minus zero!"

The Super Cyborgs plunged to the ground as if a giant magnet had been activated. The Pony was stalling, but I kept my foot on the accelerator, and we punched through.

I was going to add Silver City to the same list that included Mad Heights, and other neighborhoods in Metropolis I never, ever wanted to be near again.

PART SEVEN

Very, Very Bad People

CHAPTER 45

The Frightful Four

Mad Heights, or Mad City to the cultured criminal class. They had their upscale areas, too. The Dead Best was one of those places, a high-end bar that took up an entire slim tower. Except it wasn't a bar; it was where criminals met, bought, and sold contraband, doing business while drinking tall glasses of Japanese whiskey.

The quartet came in through the main entrance guarded by Hippo cyborgs on each side—the biggest, fattest bionic bodyguards one could hire, but not too bright. Church Lady stood watch as her three comrades strolled into the dimly lit hallway inside. She wore a collared, tight-fitting black slicker, and had short silver hair. Her mirrored spectacles gave her eyes a hypnotic quality.

Inside looked much larger than it seemed from outside. Neck Muncher, with slicked-back black hair, and tattooed blood stains down his mouth and neck, led the other two into the moderately occupied establishment—people sitting at the bar or in booths. The grizzle-haired Crossbow was at one side, carefully studying everyone. The tiny

Pipsqueak had been blowing bubbles from her toy as soon as she'd entered the bar.

"You have some nerve showing your face in Metropolis," the dark-skinned woman said, coming down the steps with several well-dressed male bodyguards behind her.

"Locks," Neck Muncher said with a smile. "I missed you!"

"You back-stabbin', two-timin', double-crossin', good for nothin'. Missed me? Know that whatever you're buying will be double the market price—and if you don't like it, you can get out of my place and crawl someplace else."

"Locks, we wouldn't take our business any place else."

"Stop smiling at me."

"I told you. I missed you."

"What do you want?"

"We're buying guns," Crossbow interjected.

Locks stood in front of the assassins. "Guns? Why would you want Earth guns, when you have all those street-special Up-Top ones?"

"We want to keep the Feds and the Up-Top heat out of this," Crossbow answered.

"Where have you been hiding? I heard you got to Earth some time ago."

"We were catching up on our sightseeing and shopping," a smiling Neck Muncher answered.

"Whatever you're doing, don't bring any Metro heat here—and don't kill anybody I know."

"We'll be gone before you know it," Crossbow said.

"If that were true, I'd be reading about your evil deeds in the news and you'd already be Up-Top, rather than here in my place. Let's get this over with. Where's the money?"

Pipsqueak opened her jacket to show that the inside was lined with plastic money.

Locks' bar had its own hotel rooms. They gathered in a room as the Gun Dealer finished laying out his stash of weapons on the bed.

"This is high-quality stuff," he said.

Neck Muncher picked up the largest piece and posed with it, grinning at Crossbow.

"That's a good piece," the dealer said. "You could shoot a spaceship out of the sky with that one, and this one here—" He picked up the strange weapon next to it. "If we ever get invaded by extraterrestrials, this is the gun I'd want. Kill one with this gun, and you'd never see another."

Neck Muncher waved his hand over all the weapons on the bed. "How much for all of them?"

"All of them?" The dealer was giddy. "I'll give you a fair price." He grabbed his mobile phone from his jacket to access his calculator. "Umm, do you need any drugs or explosives? Are you into sporting events? I can get you front-row seats to any sold-out game, too."

"Guns are all we need," Crossbow said to him.

"When does the action begin?" the dealer asked.

"Why do you want to know?" Crossbow asked.

"So I can get out of Metropolis."

"Then get out of Metropolis. I'd do that before Christmas."

"Christmas is supposed to be for presents and kiddies, you know," Locks said. "Not massacring people."

"I hate Christmas," Crossbow said. "I never got no presents from my folks on Christmas. The one time I did, my brother killed it and ate it. I never got another pet again. But I got him good. Shot him in his hand with my crossbow, and they had to amputate it. Then they put a stupid hook on his stump. Christmas isn't for presents and kiddies. It's a selfish, exploitative, base holiday. There's not even any white snow anymore to make snowmen for target practice."

"Well, okay then, Mr. Grinch," Locks said. "We'll know to stay the hell away from you on Christmas."

CHAPTER 46

The Sandman

The Silver City Nursing Home had been a pristine, state-of-the-art facility. Today, it was burnt out rubble. Thick, neon yellow police tape cordoned off the entire area, but the investigation was long over.

Hovercars landed and men in suits exited. They had been arriving since early morning, and the teams were everywhere, excavating. A final hovercar landed and out came the Up-Top gangster, the Sandman, dressed in white. An aide held an umbrella to keep the rain off him as he walked through the site.

He watched his personal army of CSI go through the rubble. They did the initial work until robots arrived to do the main digging, drilling, and tunneling.

"We found it!"

The Sandman walked to the voice. His men led him down one level into a re-opened hallway. It was lit, and he was led to the elevators.

"Do the police know this is here?" the Sandman asked.

"No, boss. They have no idea." The man half-laughed.

"Find them."

The Sandman came out of the elevator to the cryo-storage level. Several men were already waiting at two different cryo pods. The Sandman wiped the outer ice off the front faceplate of one—a sleeping Bionic Bob. He walked to the second one to do the same—a sleeping Bionic Betty.

"Well?" the Sandman asked aloud.

The Woman in White walked to him in her white slicker, wearing a wide white hat.

"The replicants are perfect," she said. "The process is perfect. Earth's gravity didn't adversely affect the process. Organic and cybernetic matter duplicated perfectly. The test run was a success."

"Do they know what was done?" Sandman asked.

"No. They believe what we wanted them to believe—that we were after their bionics."

"Good. Destroy both of these right away. Then destroy all of this. I want nothing left for the cops, or anyone else, to find."

She nodded.

"Let's get this one right."

"It wasn't my fault," she said.

"I'm not mad. I'm glad you failed the contract. How were you supposed to know it was him? Anyway, this is our payday. He doesn't need to know."

"Understood."

"Have we called the Four?"

"They called us. They have their weapons, and will be there as scheduled."

CHAPTER 47

Theo

Metropolis had many dive bars—underground, underwater bar establishments. If it weren't for the constant rain, the view from them would have been spectacular. Who knew how big the fish were? But with the ever-rain, all a person saw was blue-black.

A little man came down the steps and into the bar. As he did his body flickered like a bad analog signal. He changed from the little man to the gangster Theo.

"I knew you would see things my way one day," Joey greeted him.

"Your one and only," Theo said back.

"Welcome to my matrix," Joey said.

Theo walked to him, and sat across from him at a booth. A cyberpunkish waitress appeared, a cigarette in the corner of her lips.

"Whatever's on tap," Theo said to her, and she walked off.

Joey gulped down his own drink.

"We're doing it," Joey said.

"We are. A Christmas release."

"Blade Gunner will be there with all his bells and whistles."

"The Frightful Four will be there with theirs."

"You believe this one guy can whack the Frightful Four—one guy?"

"He's the one."

Joey laughed. "It'd be foolish for me to bet against you again. I did that, and I ended up down here and you ended up Up-Top with the real action."

"Now, we'll switch places."

"Metro cops are not like cops in other cities on this planet. They're not going to allow our guys to shoot up the city without an intervention. This is a supercity, the biggest on the planet. It could be its own planet. There's no telling how big the body count could get and these super-cops don't forget anything. They'll chase you to the end of the universe."

"I'm not worried."

"No chance you and the Sandman could—make up?"

"No chance."

"I was afraid you'd say that." He placed a device on the table and pushed it to Theo. "Here's the final key to the puzzle."

Theo reached into his jacket, and placed a fat envelope on the table. He pushed it to Joey. "There's nothing like celebrating a Christmas Up-Top. The space fireworks are to die for."

"I can't wait to shake the dirt of this planet off my shoes."

"Back Up-Top—you can fly."

Joey gave a laugh and stood from the booth. "Then flying like Superman is what I'll be doing. Between you and me, if you and the Sandman blow up Metropolis, I wouldn't be too broken up about it. I've always felt the machines should be running the planet."

"It's funny you'd say that." The waitress returned with Theo's drink.

CHAPTER 48

The Founders

The Interpol flying saucer docked at one of the organization's private skyposts on the outskirts of Metropolis. For political reasons, the saucer could not dock at Police One.

Seraff exited the ship. Carter was waiting for him.

The men shook hands, and the Martian led the spaceman into the facility.

"Does it ever stop raining on this planet?" Seraff asked.

"Personally, I enjoy it," Carter said. "There's no rain on Mars."

The men were followed by staff down the hall.

"I'd like to speak privately before the call."

Carter nodded. "Yes. The office I'm using is at the end of the hall, there."

Seraff splashed water from the sink onto his face. He bent down, and massaged his forehead and cheeks with his hands. As he rose he grabbed a small towel from the side.

Carter was standing next to a beverage maker against the wall.

"A replicator, this is not," Carter said as he slowly pulled the filled cup from the dispenser.

"There are a few things I'd like to cover before the call."

He pointed Seraff to the chairs. They both sat.

Seraff grabbed his glass, which had already been placed next to his seat.

"How was your meeting with the detective?"

"Cruz? The Earthman is quite the character. He knew we were fishing, but he was playing dumb, and he knew the chief and I knew. We played the game for a good hour."

"Anything?"

"Well, he did give us the video."

"Do you think he knows Blade Gunner's identity?"

"No. Our analysis of the video shows that they were hiding in a crawl tunnel. We've already been there. It was definitely Cruz and this other person named Phishy hiding in there."

"These Earthers have such colorful names. Phishy?"

"Cruz already identified four other high-profile contract killers in Metropolis. No one believes this is a coincidence."

"What's the theory?"

"The assassin quartet was hired by the Sandman or Theo, to kill the other. Blade Gunner was hired by the one who didn't hire the assassin quartet, to kill the other."

"We're positive, then, that the two crime bosses are on Earth?"

"Positive. The entire Metro P.D. is on high alert. They have all their confidential informants out in force."

"What do you know of the Founders?"

"Who we're going to be talking to on the call?"

"Yes."

"They founded the space colonies and lunar colonies."

"That's all?"

"What else is there?"

"The Founders are several families. When you speak to one, think of them more as a crime family, rather than a megacorp board of directors. That's the best way to keep things in perspective."

"I know I'm all the way on Mars, but are you trying to tell me something?"

"The Founders were not a bunch of wide-eyed cosmonauts who went into space to create a New World for humanity. They created a New World. A New World where neither the crime world, the megacorporations, nor Earth had the ultimate power. You don't accomplish that by being anything less than the most sadistic person in the room. Their descendants have every molecule of that DNA from their ancestors."

The woman's face took up the enhanced view screen on the wall. Seraff and Carter faced her standing.

"Mr. Carter, is that what the Earthlings believe?"

"Yes, it is."

She said something under her breath before continuing. "This woman, Sarah C, was exiled to Earth for high crimes of terrorism. Her sister was found innocent but was also exiled to Earth to punish Sarah C and also to keep her, Sarah C, in line. It worked. Three decades, and never did any of our planet-side reports give us any cause for concern.

"However, they had a brother. That brother was known as Blade Gunner. The two of them, Sarah C and the brother, together, were such a threat to Utopia that we would have invaded Earth to find him. But we never did. He was killed in a final conflict with these terrorists on a smaller space station colony. He was blown out into space. The body was confirmed. However, now your video shows he's probably alive—on Earth—with her and the sister."

"Based on the unique and destructive force of laser fire from this—blade gun, that matches archived security files, yes," Seraff said.

"Gentleman, I don't think I can stress it strongly enough, but he must be found. No, Mr. Carter, such an individual would not come out of hiding to do the work of a common criminal. It was beneath him then, and it's beneath him now. No, this, all of this—there has to be more."

"Madame, do you have any visual records of Blade Gunner's identity? Maybe something not in the general Interpol database?"

"No, we were never able to capture his picture. He somehow erased every digital picture of himself from every single database off-world that existed. All these years later, we still don't how he did it."

"He has this blade-gun weapon which makes him a threat."

"Mr. Carter!" She interrupted him abruptly. "That is not what makes him a threat to Earth and Utopia. The blade-gun is nothing—even the fact that he could use it to destroy a planet—Earth or Mars! It's not the weapon! It's him! The man is classified with Zeus-level genius ability. He can turn any machine into a weapon. Any! Another blade-gun, a bigger one, or whatever sick toy his imagination can invent.

"Gentleman, listen to me very carefully. If you don't find him, or give the Founders reasonable assurance that you can find him, we will invade Earth, and do it for you."

Seraff held up a hand. "Madame, please. Let's not say rash things. The Earth governments and the Council of Corporations would not exactly sit still while flying saucers came down to the planet. We don't need to have a War of the Worlds. What I need from you are the complete files on Sarah C, the sister, and Blade Gunner. Give my colleague and me the time to do our work. We have never failed in the past, and we certainly won't this time. Every single resource will be used."

"See that it is. Also, while we're on the subject of resources. I was with the Royal Lux family yesterday, and I saw his name in your reports. Who is this Earth detective person named Cruz?"

CHAPTER 49

Orochi Corp

Mr. Yo sat in his chair, staring. Ping sat quietly in the chair next to him. A man with red tinted glasses sat across from Yo, his head down, his eyes to the ground.

A deep sadness hung upon Yo's face. He focused on the man.

"Speak," Yo uttered.

The man lifted his head.

"What methods do you want us to use? I must be clear as to how far we can go."

"I want to know about Gidrah—any and everything possible."

The man nodded. "We've collected much. If we push further, the woman who is your daughter will not exist."

"My daughter is dead. She does not exist for me. She has dishonored the company she was named for, the family, and her dishonor may ultimately cost me my position—a life of work gone in an instant."

"No, sir," Ping leaned forward. "The board would never ask for such a thing."

"You are young, Ping." Yo returned his attention to the doctor. "How many more people does Gidrah have in my company?"

"She has given us names."

"Any on the board?"

"No."

"Use whatever methods are required to find out everything about Gidrah Corp. Do not contact Mr. Ping until it is done."

The man nodded with a quick bow.

"Afterwards, you may retain the brain for your research," Yo added as he stood. "We must stay ahead of our rivals in the synthetic brain program. Ultimately, being able to deliver on the final link in human immortality may be the only way to keep my position in the eyes of the board."

CHAPTER 50

Snitch

Metro Central remained on confidential high alert. All vacation and personal leaves were canceled and shifts were doubled. All police—from the brass to the street cop—were waiting.

Chief Hub half-ran to interrogation, where Detective Monitor saw him.

"You have something," Hub asked.

"Vice brought someone in," he responded.

Both men walked into the observation room, where two detectives in civilian clothes, looking like a pair of hoods themselves, waited.

"What have you got?" Hub asked.

They pointed. Through the one-way glass window was a face-tattooed thug seated and handcuffed to the table.

"We got him, Chief," one of the vice cops answered. "We were going to throw the book at him, but he wants to cut a deal."

"He even sent his lawyer home," the other said.

"What did you pick him up on?" asked Hub.

"Attempted murder, attempted rape, attempted arson, illegal weapons—"

Hub stopped him. "This is your CI?"

"Chief, none of our CI's are choir boys," the officer said.

"How about a confidential informant who isn't trying to rape, murder, and maim someone? What does he have? Or is he jerking our chain?"

"He knows about our quartet of killers called Neck Muncher, Crossbow, Pipsqueak, and Church Lady."

Hub was now interested.

"He also knows the where and when," the other officer said. "Or the when, at least."

"What about the where?"

"He's sketchy on that. He might want the deal in writing before he tells us that."

"I don't have time for this." Hub, in a huff, left the room, and walked around to enter the interrogation room.

The snitch immediately looked up to see the four policemen come in.

"The welcoming committee," he said.

"What do you know?" Hub asked directly.

"I want a deal first, or I'm not talking."

"What deal are you expecting? I heard rape, murder, and arson. What kind of deal do you think you'll be getting?"

"I want to walk out of here scot-free, copper." He tried to stand, but his ankles were handcuffed to the ground. "That's what I want. I know the info I've got is important."

Hub looked at his men. He looked at the snitch.

"No."

"What do you mean 'No'?" The snitch was genuinely surprised.

"We make deals but it depends on what you did. The bad you did is too much bad, so it's a 'No.'"

Hub began to leave the room.

"Wait!"

Hub stopped.

"All right. Forget the scot-free. Give me a reduction on sentencing."

Hub looked at the vice officers. "How bad off is the victim?"

"Victims," one of them corrected. "It's only attempted murder because they didn't die, and attempted arson because they didn't burn."

Hub looked at him. "The sentence stands. The only thing we can do for you is where you serve your sentence."

"That's no deal at all."

"It *is* a deal, because now that you've revealed to us that you have information we need, we can be some awful sons-of-bitches and have you sentenced to serve in not only the worst prison, but one not even in the Americas, and make sure your cell is in the basement."

"We'll make sure they take away your pants and underpants have you butt-naked from the waist down at all times," Monitor added.

"You can't do that!"

"We can't do that, here," Hub acknowledged, "but they *can* do that in other countries. That's where we'll send you."

The snitch went into a fit, rocking in his chair, shaking the table, cursing wildly.

"I'm outta here," Hub said.

"Wait! Okay! It's a deal! I'll tell you what you want."

Hub was in the general meeting room with the police brass, which included Monitor.

"The only question at this point," Monitor began, "is do we notify the mayor?"

"We have to," another officer said.

"On the word of some criminal degenerate?" another countered. "We need to verify this."

"How exactly do we do that?"

"Okay, everyone," Hub said. "We're already on high alert, and we know these killers didn't come to Metropolis for their annual vacation. They came to do something. We already know that. The mayor and City Council know that. I won't call the mayor by phone. That would be official notification, but absolutely he will be informally notified. We don't know where, but we know it'll be a battle royale. That's what we have our people preparing and ready for—a battle royale in our great city. The snitch gave us the when. Christmas, it is, everyone."

"Jesus Christ, another Christmas Day massacre," said an exasperated lieutenant.

The rain had started pouring again. The sidewalk johnny peered from around the corner, careful not to be seen. He watched the person for a long time. Headlights turned on, and he jumped back out of view. The hovercar flew off, and he appeared again to watch it.

"I gotta tell Cruz," he said, and disappeared back around the corner.

PART EIGHT

Aliens Came to Kill My Christmas

CHAPTER 51

Dot

After all this time talking about getting shot, dodging, ducking, close calls, now—I had finally gotten myself shot. I had mentally prepared for it; but frankly, nothing could prepare you for it. I hurt in places I didn't think could hurt. I didn't think I had ever felt those innards before. I lay in the bio-bed, staring up at the ceiling. I didn't just get shot. I had almost gotten myself killed.

Well, at least I saved the day. Yeah, I saved Sarah, Susan, and the Bionic duo from those psycho Super Cyborgs, but I'd also almost killed all of us, when I passed out from my blood loss. I think it was Sarah who had taken the wheel, and the others had pulled me out of the driver's seat. I had freaked out over the prospect of my offspring, a baby, puking in the Pony, but now I had bled out all over the Pony. Blood wasn't just a pathogen, it was nasty. I had done plenty of hovercar restoration jobs with blood involved. Blood stains couldn't wash or bleach out. You had to replace the entire part. My entire Pony interior would have to be redone—more money coming out of my pocket!

I didn't like the prospect of being a resident of Metro General. Strangely, my germophobia didn't threaten to act up. Ordinarily, I would have demanded a bodysuit with surgical mask, but I lay there as content as a baby in its crib, all clean and fresh.

I hadn't even see the shooter, but Sarah C had put down whoever it was. I'd have to have her tell me who it was, so I could go to the morgue, and kick the corpse a few times as payback.

Wilford G. had been shot a bunch of times, but it had never made him quit the detective biz. I wasn't interested in a "bunch of times." Once was enough for me, but I wouldn't be closing Liquid Cool over this. I had free office space and boxes of business cards that had to be used. This day was inevitable. I had to rest up, and get back out there in the rain to do my job.

There was an eventuality I feared more than getting shot. It was facing Dot after getting shot.

From the corner of my eye, I caught Dot coming into the room. If someone had asked if I'd rather be shot again, or face Dot, I'd have to say "get shot." I had no idea what to expect. What if Dot demanded I quit the detective business? What would I do?

As she came close, I saw that she was smiling—but I also saw that she'd been crying. Oh, man, crying. I hoped the doctors hadn't told her I could've died. Aren't they smarter than that?

She took my hand in hers, as she sat on the side of the bio-bed.

"Shooting it out with the bad guys," she said.

"I wish. It was an army of killer robots, and an army of killer cyborgs. I don't know why they didn't like me. I think it's the hat. Why don't they like my hat?"

Dot laughed at my attempt at humor.

"Your clients were with you all the time."

"My clients?"

"The twin sisters, and Bob and Betty. They are such a sweet couple—fifty years of marriage. Imagine that."

"'Sweet couple?' You should have seen Bionic Bob and Betty beat up those Super Cyborgs."

"Well, at least you had reinforcements. I would've been mad if you didn't at least have back-up. Sarah said, even wounded, you came to their rescue—always the hero."

"Dot, I don't want you to worry. This was a one-time thing. I'm careful. The biz can be crazy, but I'm careful."

"Are you saying you won't get shot again?"

I didn't know what to say.

"I had time to think, and you've always compared private detective work to being in law enforcement, which I've always known was your clever way of shifting me away from how dangerous it is. I talked to a few police spouses—a bunch of them have their beauty work done at Eye Candy—and they all told me the same thing. If they get shot once, the odds of them getting shot again go down substantially, to the point that it likely won't happen again. Did you know that?"

"Oh yeah," I said with authority. "That's why I let it happen. I wanted to be indestructible."

She held my face with her hand. "Mr. Cruz, don't get shot again! That's an order."

"Yes, ma'am."

CHAPTER 52

Sidewalk Sid

The doctors wanted me to rest up at home for at least a week, but Christmas was the next week, and I had too many things to do. Three days was it, and then I was back in the office, with, of all things, a walking cane. Nobody walked with a cane—they just got a bionic hip or leg. Run-Time would have said it was me trying to be different from everyone else again, and thereby become the center of attention. Well, whatever, I got attention all right. I really had the cane to remind myself to keep as much force off my left side as possible. My chest was bound up, but since I refused to stay in bed, I could easily cause myself internal bleeding, or ruin another shirt on the outside.

"He's back!" PJ declared, and started clapping.

I didn't know why, but she still had the two female temps. Why did she need extra help? I had been gone for three days. I wasn't even going to ask.

On the walls, PJ had added all kinds of new news posters about my exploits. *Famous Detective Survives Shootout With Terminator Robots and Cyborgs, Saves Sisters!*

Good grief! I knew why PJ had the temps now. We really did have more than one line, and both temps were answering calls nonstop.

"I'm not here," I said. "I have a meeting and then I'm gone."

"When are you officially back?" PJ asked.

"Monday."

"Christmas week. Good. You have lots of work. No Christmas holiday for you."

"Thanks for letting me know." I thought I was the boss.

I had to give it to Phishy. The Sidewalk Johnny Brigade was his idea completely. All wearing fedoras and most wearing Liquid Cool T-shirts under their clothes. PJ thought it was stupid, but she thought everything he did was stupid. I did too, but they had turned out to be a legitimate resource for me and my business. Police had their network of confidential informants throughout Metropolis. I had my equivalent with the sidewalk johnnies.

The most impressive of all of them was Sidewalk Sid. I'd always thought of him as one of Phishy's main sidekicks, but he could do things on his own.

He filled me in on what he'd seen while on the streets of Whiskey Way. I didn't care why he was there—it was another one of the many seedy sections of the supercity. He had given me significant intel relevant to my case.

I shook his hand, and gave him a few bucks for his trouble, though he didn't ask for it, and hadn't expected it.

"Did it help out, Mr. Cruz?"

"It sure did, Sid," I replied. "Have everyone keep their eyes and ears open."

"You got it, Mr. Cruz."

I opened my personal office door for him and followed him out.

"Stupid man called," PJ said.

"Phishy called?" I corrected.
"Yeah, him."

CHAPTER 53

Blinky

We had to be honest with ourselves. A man who wore a Santa suit all year long was not going to stay indoors during the Christmas holidays. Just like Phishy had to be Phishy, Blinky was going to be himself, no matter what he said or promised. That meant baby-sitting duties, and Phishy was going to be the co-baby-sitter.

I still didn't know what Hub's interest was in either of them, so I wanted to keep them close. For now, I would continue playing dumb with Hub and the Martian, but I knew that they knew I was on to them. Until I figured it all out, Phishy and Blinky had to stay where I could keep watch, so a week before Christmas, I had the two human ferrets in my Pony again.

"Man, you know when cars drove on the ground, before hovertech, people used to throw their garbage and dead animals on the side of the road?"

"Is that so?" I said, not really listening. My eyes were focused on the sky traffic.

"Man, they'd even dump dead bodies there."

"They did no such thing."

"Cruz, man, they did. I bet people still do that now. They think because hovercars fly up in the sky, that it's easier to get away with it."

"People do not dump dead bodies out of their hovercars. That is an urban myth," I insisted.

"Man, I bet if you were to coast down to the ground under the hovertraffic, you'd see dead bodies, man."

"That is nonsense, *man*." He had *me* ending sentences with "man" now.

"Go on down, man. We'll see."

I had to get Blinky to shut the hell up. We dove under the sky traffic. I was now breaking all kinds of traffic laws, but I was betting we'd get away with it before a traffic officer caught us. Even if we got caught, most officers would only give a warning.

"Look!" Phishy and Blinky yelled in unison, startling me.

I slammed on the brakes. It looked like a dead body on the ground, sticking out of an alley!

I had driven the open sky lanes since I was sixteen. I was in my thirties. I had never, ever seen a dead body on the road. I had seen accidents, bodies fall out of hovercars, bodies fall onto hovercars, but that was normal. This was a dead body actually dumped on the wet asphalt.

Phishy was okay, but this Blinky was a jinx. Crazy stuff followed him around. The Pony was parked on the ground off to the side, and I stood next to it. Phishy was with Blinky in front of the vehicle—and of course, the police were everywhere, with lights flashing.

I realized why I couldn't catch Blinky all those years ago. He was in a constant state of motion. He was his own entertainment show, dancing in place while he sang—Christmas songs.

The two officers questioning me had as much of a hard time focusing as I did. We were watching Blinky. Phishy wasn't helping, laughing like a loon next to him. Then Blinky got down on the ground, and started spinning around and around on one arm. I don't know what kind of dancing that was, but the policemen did not like it at all. The questioning had stopped, and they each had their hands on their holster guns.

Blinky was going to get himself shot, or me shot, as I tried to get away.

"Blinky!" I yelled. "Stop that!"

"Man, this is the original dance of the streets. Break dancin', man."

"I don't care what you're doing, man. Stop it, both of you. You're making the police here nervous, and making me nervous because they're nervous."

Blinky listened to me for the moment and kept himself still as he chatted it up with Phishy.

"Let's begin again," the officer said.

"Officer, I don't know anything. We called you. We didn't even go near the body."

"What you want us to believe is that you were driving along, the one in the Santa costume randomly said there might be a dead body on the ground, twenty stories down, you flew down, and there was a dead body."

"Officer, that's exactly what I'm saying. The story is so crazy that it must be true. It's too crazy to have been made up."

"You're right there," the officer said. "What is he doing?"

I looked. Blinky was doing his spin-dancing again, one arm on the ground, with Phishy laughing like a fool at him.

CHAPTER 54

Hub

"I should start fining you for every contact with the police," Chief Hub said to me.

The police, unsurprisingly, decided to "continue the conversation" back at police headquarters. Phishy, Blinky, and I would be interrogated separately, for as long as the police wanted. In my case, it turned out to be almost two hours before Hub pulled me out of Interrogation.

"Where are the two people who were brought in with me?" I asked, as he led me to his office.

"How long have you been hanging with Santa?"

"Funny," I responded.

"Are you friends with the Tooth Fairy and the Easter Bunny too?"

"You can't have them still in interrogation."

"We were done with Phishy-Fish in five minutes. We were done with Santa Claus soon after. Neither qualify as criminal masterminds."

"Who was the dead body? Interrogation showed me his picture, but wouldn't tell me."

"It's a just a missing person. Don't worry. We know you and your helpers didn't kill him. He was a jumper. If it's not murder, it's suicide. It wasn't murder."

"Why am I being taken to the principal's office then? Is the Martian waiting for me?"

Hub began chuckling. "The second I told the Martian you were in the building, he couldn't get out of Police One fast enough. He's scared of you, your family, and cameras. What did you do to him?"

"You were there. All I did was call the fiancée."

Hub had me in his office, and he was in serious mode.

"No more games, Cruz. I need to know all you know about this Blade Gunner. I know it was you and your Phishy-fish buddy in the tunnel. We have four Up-Top assassins in Metropolis, this Blade Gunner, two of the most vicious Up-Top crime lords in the city, and we have reason to believe that all this will explode next week."

"On Christmas."

Hub gave me an annoyed look. "So, you do know more."

I told him everything about that day in the tunnel: Phishy frantically calling me for help, me showing up, the late Swordplaya and his men, including his killer robot, the item, and playing cat-and-mouse with the unseen assassin I knew as Blade Gunner.

"A retriever?" Hub asked. "An actual person had a cranial hard drive?"

"Yeah."

"That's sick. Why would anyone use such obsolete technology? Not to mention super-dangerous."

"I've never heard of this Blade Gunner. With that weapon, I don't think anyone has. No one on Earth has. Is he another gift from Up-Top? Is that why the Martian is here? Also, what's this about two Up-Top crime lords?"

"How many questions are you going ask at once? Two crime lords are in Metropolis, and plan to use it as a stage for their gang war. Your assassins are part of it. This Blade Gunner is part of it." I smirked. "Why do you find that funny?" he asked.

"Someone as powerful as this Blade Gunner wouldn't involve himself in a gang war."

"Why do you say that?"

"Why haven't I or you ever heard of him before? If he ever did one job, everyone in the crime world on the planet would know about him. They'd all want to hire him. No," I said.

"He's new, Cruz. That's why we haven't ever heard of him. He's a new killer on the scene, and he's here for the gang war party."

I shook my head. "He isn't new. He's old."

Hub scratched his chin. "Why do you say that?"

"It's what I think."

"Based on what?"

"Is the Martian going to tell you what's really going on?"

"Interpol has given us everything they know."

"They never tell us everything. Just like we never tell them everything. I feel that Christmas is going to be bad—very, very bad."

"How do you know about Christmas?"

"I have resources on the street, too."

"Do you, now."

"Since you're not going to level with me, I'll find out for myself. I'll hire a detective—oh, wait—I am a detective. I'll find out for myself. I always do."

"I hear you got shot up recently. Maybe you should take that as a sign and lay low for a while. I love the walking cane, by the way."

"I'm fine. Anything else, Chief?"

"Only one thing. Mr. Seraff will be in our fair supercity soon. He asked to speak to you directly."

"The Spaceman. Maybe he'll give me answers."

"Why should you get answers, Cruz? You're a civilian. You're not a head of state, or a mayor, or anything important. You have an expanding family, but so do 50 million other people. Why does getting answers matter to you so much? You're a street detective."

"You're right. I don't even have a client on this one, but I was listening very closely when you counseled me after dealing with the late Monkey Baker. Didn't you tell me to always do the right thing, and forget about always getting paid? Do the right thing, because we all live on the same planet, in the same city together.

"I want answers, because I can feel it. We've got very, very bad people up to significant no good, possibly extremely evil, and if I can get those answers, and figure it out, we can possibly stop them. This, Chief, is what's called a *pro bono*. Every legitimate business does pro bono work. This is mine. I do have a client on this case. It's the people of Metropolis."

CHAPTER 55

Exe

I hadn't told Hub, but Sarah and Susan C were Blade Gunner's sisters. I had put two and two together, so I didn't even need to ask. I had passed out in the Pony, but I saw the Super Cyborgs after Sarah, her sister, Betty, and Bob. An assassin with a weapon more powerful than anyone had ever seen, and killer cyborgs like no one had ever seen. But Sarah had seen them before; I was certain of it.

At the center of my last case was Police Watch—the government agency in charge of the entire body-cam system for all of Metro Police. Since then, I'd heard little about them in the media, or anywhere else. An agency that was as paramount to the supercity's law enforcement and criminal justice system as the police themselves seemed to have been whisked away, and locked in the mayor's secure anti-nuclear underground bunker.

However, the head of that division was a woman who Run-Time had introduced me to, and if he trusted her, I could without hesitation. Police Watch headquarters told me she was on leave, which made me sad.

Leave? Involuntary leave, more like it. It seemed that the entire Police Watch board was on leave.

I stood in the lobby of her residential building in Elysian Heights, the same town my parents-in-law from hell lived. All I did was stare at them—plants. Another reminder of my tunnel escapade with Phishy. We had both feared running smack into the plants, there after Blade Gunner had shot deep holes into the tunnel walls.

My Pops once told me there was a Green Movement when he was a little kid. Metropolis city elders wanted to fill the rainy supercity with plants and trees to make it a green paradise. The only paradise they created was for the insects and isopods. The gigantic palm trees, they planted to line the neighborhoods, became infested with all kinds of vermin. No one knew where the hell the vermin were coming from, but they were happier than pigs in slop.

People said they saw rat monkeys swarming in the palm trees. There was no such thing as a rat monkey. What people were seeing were large rats climbing up the trees, and turning the tops into their homes, pretending to be monkeys, by jumping from tree to tree. All the greenery they'd planted in the parks became a "rock-and-roll fest" for bugs, large and small, crawling or flying. The grass they'd put in everywhere was teeming with mites, and anything even remotely touching water soon became home to the isopods.

Stories grew of kids getting almost eaten alive by the plant bugs, people carted off to the hospital swarmed by mites and ticks, people crashing hovercars into buildings because of storms of flies, or dodging giant rats leaping from giant trees. Forget the sci-fi movies; green plants were scary things to the people of Earth.

Then came the rumors of new disease outbreaks, blamed on the plants. Rumors of new kinds of bugs, newly evolved isopods and worms.

The urban legends of walking fish and "things" coming in from the oceans to use the plants as their base of operations. It was weird.

My Ma said all that was ignored until people started filing lawsuits against the government. One night all the plants disappeared from the city—all. The theory was that the city got Up-Top spaceships to laser everything from space—very plausible, because it would've been impossible for city workers to have removed all those plants, even if every single employee were called in to work.

People saw green, and they ran, fearing something alien would jump out at them for their faces.

I stood in the lobby staring at a tree that seemed to go straight up to the top of the building, and this tower was over 200 stories. It wasn't really green, more brown. It was like its own park in the center of the lobby.

"All synthetic," the doorman said, to reassure me.

"Oh."

Exe wore a lime green pants suit, a matching beret on her head, and a sheer white scarf around her neck. She had been the vice president of the Metropolis Police Watch Commission, and a member for decades. She was as gregarious as always, greeting me with a vigorous handshake and small talk.

"How long will you be on vacation?" I asked, eating one of her chocolate chip cookies.

"I'm not sure. Maybe my vacation will turn into early retirement."

"Retirement?" I was mad. "But you didn't do anything. Why are they doing this to you?"

She was touched by my concern. "You know the game, Cruz. When someone on your team does bad, people start to look at you sideways, too. 'Why didn't we know?' they ask. 'If he did it, maybe you'll do it in the future when we're not looking.'"

"Exe, this is a raw deal you're getting. You should fight it."

"The family and I are looking at all options."

"It's not fair at all."

"Cruz, life is many things, but fair often is not one of them. What brings you to my humble home?"

"What's with the plants in the lobby?"

Exe began to laugh something fierce.

"Why does everyone ask me about that? The plants are fake. They were here in the building before I moved in. People are so scared of those plants."

"Yeah, you don't have any security. Put a sign on the main lobby doors: This building is filled with plants. No one will ever bother you—media or street criminals, either."

"Maybe we should do that."

"I stopped by to ask something since you know government and systems."

"What do you need to know?"

"What's so different about Earth government? Compared to Up-Top government."

"Simple. The technology. Earth systems are analog-based. Up-Top is all digital."

"It's always been like that? Analog here, digital there?"

"Not always. Before there was an Up-Top, Earth was digital too, but when we went into space, we took a different technological path, as far as our systems go. It's a good thing we did, or there's no doubt that Up-Top would be running down-below."

"That's the reason for the different systems."

"Oh, no. It's how everything turned out. As you know, the Police Watch system was the only digital system in operation in Metropolis, despite the opposition. With the scandal, it'll all be analog tech too. Digital technology on Earth is dead now, for the foreseeable future.

Digital technology has always been seen by the analog tech community here as inherently un-securable."

"Do you agree?"

"I do. The reason digital technology must constantly upgrade itself is because those who wish to break into those digital systems are doing so constantly, but the analog lock and key system I use is the same one from 50 years ago, and I'm sure it'll be the same one used 50 years from now."

"Are there any crimes you can think of that would be impossible for Up-Top to commit with their digital technology, but would be very doable with our analog technology?"

"No. The infrastructure of Metropolis is as secure as those of Up-Top. Unless you know something we don't know."

"I'm stumped."

"Stumped?"

"I believe a group of Up-Top criminals is up to something big— bigger than has ever been done before, but it's not what everyone is thinking."

"Master criminals always want the same thing. Money, power, and information."

"The trinity."

"The trinity."

"Money. Power. Information." I nodded. "It's one of those then, Exe. Money would be Fort Knox, right?"

"Cruz, no one knows where Fort Knox is, and no one can get into it. Believe me. It's impossible."

"Power might be City Hall."

"How?"

"Androids?"

She laughed. "Cruz, don't you think everyone is waiting for that? We've been waiting for the megacorps to try that for decades. Even if, and when, they're able to create indistinguishable ones from real humans, they're in for a rude awakening when they try it. That's all I'm going to say."

"Is there a Fort Knox of information?"

"No. The government's data is purposely not in one database. Never—not even in an emergency. Cruz, you have to remember that we have an uneasy détente in the universe between the government and the megacorps. If one side were ever to become too powerful, they could crush the other, and then the people would really suffer. They can't beat us. We can't beat them. It's how we keep the peace."

"And Up-Top?"

"They may be a hybrid of government and corporatist, but they have the same problems we do. Corporations or the crime world want to take them over too. Neither can ever happen. We may not be Utopia—that's what off-worlders call their off-world colonies and cities—but we're not dystopia. If the détente ever breaks down, we'll have hell—notwithstanding that it never stops raining."

"I'm glad you said that."

"What did I say?"

"Not that you'll have any idea of what I'm about to say, but you reminded me that this isn't just about an assassin with a blade-gun. It's also a seven-headed snake. That's what it is. I believe this is all about committing the impossible crime. I wish there were a list."

"Of course there's a list." Exe got up from her chair.

"Don't tell me you have the government's worst-case scenario reports. I heard about them when I was a police intern."

My face went blank when Exe appeared with the book in her hand.

"That's a children's book," I said.

Attila the Hun's Top 20 Ways to Take Over the Universe (With Illustrations).

"It's my grandson's," Exe added. "I'm preparing him for government service early."

CHAPTER 56

The Spaceman

I was back at Police Central and I greeted the Spaceman. Mr. Seraff, in his all-white outfit, was a Zero-baby—born in zero-gravity. He was a director in the Up-Top agency that oversaw the Interspace Police, also known as Interpol. The police from Up-Top had authority that not only included off-world, but superseded all city police, including Metropolis *and* the Feds on Earth.

Answers were what I wanted from him. He sat me down, and I could tell from how he hunched over his digital notepad, that he intended to do most of the talking.

"Officer Deering, could you come in here?" he said into the phone feature on the device.

A woman entered and handed me her digital portfolio. I looked at the screen, and saw that it contained legal documents.

"I'm about to disclose classified material, so you need to understand that none of it can be disclosed, not even to your wife-to-be, best friend, or employees."

I scanned it and signed with the stylus the woman had handed me.

"Didn't you want to read it more thoroughly?" Seraff asked.

"I just looked for the key words: life, prison, Ford Pony, first-born, sperm, slavery, bondage, servitude. I didn't see any of those, so I'm good."

Seraff and the woman laughed. She took the portfolio.

"I'll begin our briefing," he said. It was three days until Christmas, so, yes, I wanted the briefing as soon as possible. I was wondering again if I needed to get people I knew out of Metropolis.

"What did Sarah C do to get exiled to Earth?"

"How do you know she was exiled to Earth?"

"Give me some credit. It's not hard to figure out. She wasn't born here. She's obviously a person who was born into means, even though she lives in a dump. The last encounter we had, when we rescued her sister—and when I got shot, by the way—some Super Cyborgs came to kill her."

"Super Cyborgs?"

"The cyborgs were from Up-Top, and they knew her."

"She was the founder and member of a terrorist group called the Asimovians. They believed that humankind could not be trusted to govern itself, and only a society run by A.I. could rule and must rule humanity. Humans would be governed by Super Cyborgs and the Super Cyborgs would answer to the A.I.

"The Asimovians believed in their Three Laws: Destroy the Founders, Seize the off-world government headquarters on the Lunar Colony, Bring their A.I. god online to rule all of Earth and Utopia, to build an army of super robots to maintain order.

"Their war with the Founders had progressed much further than many are aware. Thousands were killed, and it was Sarah who personally blew up the Space Bridge."

As I listened to Seraff, I could not believe he was talking about the same Sarah C that I knew. We had been taught in school that the Space

Bridge connecting Earth with one of the first space station colonies had been destroyed by a massive meteor shower. People always pointed to that disaster as the start of the uneasiness between Earth and Up-Top. Now I'd found out why the Space Bridge was never rebuilt.

"She was exiled, and her sister was as well, to keep Sarah in line."

"And the brother?"

Seraff looked at me. "How do you know that? How can you possibly know that, when I found out only recently?"

"Sarah mentioned it."

"What else did she say about him?"

"Nothing."

He didn't believe me. "Are you going to tell me about this Blade Gunner or not?"

"There is no way she told you he was Blade Gunner. How do you know that?"

Seraff was furious. I already knew parts of his secret briefing, before he'd even had his chance to tell it.

"Chief Hub and the Martian, of course."

Seraff sat back down. "Mr. Cruz, one day you're going to know too much."

"I don't know anything yet, because you haven't told me anything. What's so special about this Blade Gunner? I used to think it was the sister, but now I'm thinking he's the key to all this. Tell me about this Blade Gunner. He wasn't part of these Asimovians?"

"No, he was only the brother. He wasn't interested in politics—even a new socialistic 'perfect' society governed by a supreme artificial intelligence created by her and her terrorist revolutionaries."

"Is Blade Gunner the key to all this? I know you know about Christmas. We need to figure this all out before then."

"Her brother was a genius of extraordinary abilities. He could upgrade anything with technology. He was deemed so dangerous by

Utopian authorities, that if his capture was not possible, his killing was sanctioned, even if collateral damage was unavoidable."

"He got away."

"We don't know how. Likely, sympathetic factions within the Families, loyal to his sister, extending their good graces to him. Then he disappeared. When he was found, there was a battle on a space colony, and he was killed—supposedly. That was 30 years ago, and now we learn he's alive. Resurfaced. Why?"

"You know who he is. Get his picture out there."

"There's a problem with that."

He didn't even have to tell me. "No pictures exist. You know he's in Metropolis. He wanted to kill me and an associate."

"If he'd wanted you dead, you'd be dead."

"I agree with that."

"Mr. Cruz, if you encountered him before, and you somehow outsmarted him, know that should there be a second time, you won't outsmart him again."

"I will not be risking fate twice. You can be sure of that."

"I wouldn't involve Chief Hub and Metro Police either. All that will do is leave behind a lot of widows and widowers. You're part of Metro Police's extended family, after that Watch Conspiracy case of yours."

"What are you saying? No one can stop this guy?"

"We couldn't."

"How long ago was that?"

"Exactly. He was only a child in relative terms then. He's a full-grown adult, with 30 years of perfecting his craft, which he has surely done, and exercised cunning and restraint to keep off the grid and prevent others from looking for him."

"Others? What others?"

"All the Asimovians weren't caught, Mr. Cruz. They may even have their own shadow membership."

"More Super Cyborgs?"

"To get him, the Founders were willing to do anything, including blowing up an entire space colony or even a monolith tower filled with innocents from orbit. Imagine now. He's too dangerous, and no one knows why he's resurfaced. That's what scares everyone. As well as his sister."

"What about her? She hasn't done anything in 30 years, except look after the younger sister."

"With her older brother, probably without her knowledge, watching over her from the shadows."

"Neither of them have done anything in all these years."

"But we find ourselves here, three days before Christmas. The three are at the center of it. Apparently, Sarah has special abilities, too."

"What?"

"They wouldn't tell me," Seraff answered.

Seraff was a high-level Up-Top guy, and Up-Top was keeping secrets from him. That disclosure didn't fill me with a warm and fuzzy feeling.

"This conversation is just between us, right?"

The Spaceman grinned. "It is. Are you worried all of a sudden?"

"I don't want any Up-Top spaceships trying to blow up my city to get this one guy."

"You have my word, Mr. Cruz, that it will never come to that."

"Good, but please come up a foolproof way to stop him in case it comes to that."

"We're already fully engaged on the problem."

"I'm ready. You're ready. Metro Police is ready. We just have to be ready on Christmas."

"And the Martians are ready."

"More Martians besides the Martian?" I asked.

"They sent an entire spaceship of them from their satellite base on Lunar Colony."

"More Martians. Well, if we need to scare them away, we have a secret weapon."

"What's that?"

"Ask Chief Hub. He'll tell you. He was there. It has to do with a certain private detective's parents-in-law from hell, every single member of their family, and cameras."

Seraff tried not to laugh again. "That is one conversation I am anxious to have with the chief. Hopefully, Christmas will be as festive and peaceful as it always is in Metropolis."

"Yeah, right."

CHAPTER 57

Battle Royale

The Spaceman obviously did not know Christmas crime history in Metropolis.

I did, and this was long before I became the detective I was today. Some time in the past, a gangster took advantage of the holiday to have his chief rival, his men, and his family gunned down during their Christmas party. They even shot the clown. The following year, the surviving members of that crime family returned the favor on Christmas. From then on, Christmas in Metropolis had become a very nervous period for crime bosses, so much so that Metro Police beefed up street patrols, and kept an intense evil eye on all of them.

Christmas massacres had become a thing of the past, but it was always at the back of people's minds. It seemed that the ritual was returning to Metropolis. Metro Police had a virtual armada on the streets. Police cruisers hovered around every major intersection and key buildings. If that was the police they *wanted* you to see, there were at least twice that many undercover cops out there in plainclothes. And that didn't include the Feds. Seraff being planet-side meant Up-Top was there in force too, which also included Martians. That was a lot of firepower on the streets of Metropolis for two crime bosses, four assassins, and Blade Gunner.

They could fool the people, but not me. The spacemen and the Martians were here for Blade Gunner. Metro, seeing that Up-Top was peeing its pants over this one person, had responded by putting a D-Day battalion-size police force on the Metro streets.

Maybe Seraff had told me what this was all about, intentionally or not. Blade Gunner "could upgrade anything." As I remembered Sarah C's less powerful blade-gun that she had brought to the Silver City "party," I realized two things: the weapon had gone completely undetected by weapon sensors and it had been made 30 years ago. The man had made a weapon 30 years ago, that could still bypass the best analog tech security systems today. What could he do against Up-Top digital security measures? Up-Top feared more than his deadly blade-gun. They were not here to help planet Earth law enforcement apprehend one of their own fugitives. Why would they? We were going to do it for them, and hand him over. They didn't want us to find out what they were really scared about.

I remembered the words Seraff had used about Blade Gunner: "his abilities" and "Sarah has abilities too." I couldn't even guess what Sarah C could do, but I didn't have to worry about that. Sarah was in protective custody, and I was sure they hadn't told her that her long-lost, supposed-to-be dead brother was running around.

I wished I could ask her all these things and more, but she was "unavailable" until after Christmas Day.

Christmas in Metropolis it was. Would there be a massacre? Or would there be some other horrific event?

I needed to Sherlock Holmes this situation with the facts I did have. The main fact that concerned me was that no one knew what Blade Gunner looked like. Sarah C wasn't going to tell us. He had been on Earth for over 30 years. That meant he could be anybody. That made me nervous.

"Maybe Phishy is Blade Gunner," PJ said, jokingly.

"How could Phishy be Blade Gunner? We were both hiding in the tunnel when he was blowing those punks and the killer robot to bits."

Eight o'clock at Liquid Cool.

The office was closed, but most businesses were closed on Christmas Day. The doors were locked, and the "Closed for the Day, Please Call" neon sign was flashing, but PJ and I were there. I had turned my office into my own version of a television store, with flat screens on every inch of one wall, each on a different news channel.

Anything that happened, I wanted to see it live.

I didn't have to worry about Blinky. The crazy slider was in New Vegas DJ-ing a Christmas party. It wasn't that I thought he was still in danger, any more than Phishy. It was that I wanted everyone accounted for at all times.

Phishy was on Sidewalk Johnny Brigade duty—I had them on the streets. It was doubtful they'd see or hear anything relevant with the surveillance blanket of Metro Police, spacemen and the Martians over the city, but that was how random chance worked. They couldn't be everywhere; neither could we, but *one* of us would be at the right time and place.

"What is it we're going to see on the TV?" she asked. "All this news is boring. Why don't you have any international news channels on?"

"I want the Metro news on. Not people babbling in languages I don't understand."

"English isn't the only language spoken in Metropolis. Haven't you heard your future parents-in-law speak?"

"Don't remind me."

"And the Martian speaks Martian."

I glanced at her. "There is no Martian language."

"Yes, there is. He spoke it to us."

"He was playing around."

"If you were to watch international news, you'd know there are a dozen off-world languages."

"Why would people make up new languages when there are already a thousand languages spoken on Earth?"

"Cruz, you are always a party pooper. Stop poopin' the party; let people make up languages and have fun."

Nine o' clock.

This was going to be a long day.

PJ was right. The news was boring. No wonder they had to make up stuff, and sensationalize stories for ratings. The screens would stay on, but we had work to do. Phishy couldn't be the only one earning his keep.

"Asimovians? Are they good people or bad?" PJ was planted at her desk in front of her mobile computer.

"Bad. Very bad."

"Tell me about their beliefs. I can't research criminals without knowing about them."

I knew I couldn't do my work until I'd answered her question fully. I gave her most of Seraff's intel—who cared about a confidentiality agreement? She said, "Cruz, those are not criminals. Those are radical terrorists wanting to create a computer-controlled oppressive society."

I laughed. "What country does that sound like?"

All I heard was her rolling chair in front of my doorway. "Cruz, if I hear any bad talk about my native country, I'll punch you."

Well, PJ had the information she needed to research.

"Those kinds of crazy people throughout history love to write manifestos. There should be something for me to find," she yelled from back at her desk.

Research would keep her busy and mostly quiet. I needed both as I started reading the Exe's grandson's kiddie book: *Attila the Hun's Top 20 Ways to Take Over the Universe (With Illustrations).*

"I'm doing real research, and you're reading children's books in your office."

PJ came to check on me because I had been so quiet. The office answering machine was on, but even on Christmas calls were coming in.

Ten o'clock and I was done. Sixty minutes seemed long for a kid's book, but it was jam-packed with great tips.

"I know how to take over the universe now," I said, placing the book on my table.

"Good for you, Cruz. Your fiancée will be proud of you."

"Within the next two hours, they're going to do what they're going to do."

"Who is? What are they going to do?"

"Most of the historical Christmas massacres happened at noon. So, they'll most likely do so at noon too."

"Why would they do it then?"

"Because we're all expecting them to do it then. They'll give us the show we're waiting for."

"Show. What do you mean?"

"What did you find out?"

"Nothing. Nothing at all."

"It was a long shot. Did you check only news databases?"

"Yes. What other databases should I have checked?"

I leaned back in my chair. "Psychiatry, VR, and cyborg-body building."

"You're crazy. I won't find anything on any of those databases. Virtual reality? Games? You're crazy."

"What will it hurt?"

"What will you do?"

"Make some calls. That will be my research. Two hours left."

"I think you're wrong about high noon. If I wanted to do something, I'd do my crimes at night and on a Friday. That's the best time."

"I so love having a felon working for me. It's that criminal insight that makes me the best kind of detective."

"You don't need to be a felon to know that. I'm smart—"

"Working. I'm making my calls."

"Psychiatry, VR, and cyborg-body building." She ran to her desk.

This was not the day to mess with the police. This was not the day to do any kind of crime whatsoever.

"Phishy."

Phishy's smiling face filled the video screen on my mobile. "Cruz!"

"Phishy, do they have retrievers Up-Top?"

"Retrievers?"

"Focus, Phishy. Like the one from our tunnel incident."

"No, why would they? Data transfer Up-Top was never analog style, always digital and wireless. Retrievers were strictly a down-below thing."

"Thanks, Phishy. That's all I wanted to know. Keep the men on duty."

"Oh, yeah, Cruz. We're watching."

"Call me if you see them."

There were more than a few false alarms—one sighting after another of one of the four assassins, one of the Up-Top crime bosses, or someone with a strange blade-gun. It was a madhouse. Stops and arrests. Even a simple speeder found not one hovercruiser responding, but half a dozen. I didn't want the Pony anywhere out there in the sky. I took a hovercab to Liquid Cool, and would take another anywhere else I needed to go this Christmas Day.

"How did you know?" PJ was standing at the entrance to my office. "How did you know I would find something in those databases?"

"I guessed. The Asimovians are crazy, so psychiatry. Some are Super Cyborgs, so the cyborg-bodybuilding. The VR was something that popped into my head too. Besides gaming, people use VR for weapons, and military tactical training."

"Listen to you. The Asimovians were a secret terrorist group. They started out as a movement at space colleges. Then they became a cult, then crazy and violent. Members made themselves into cyborgs. I found their manifestos too."

"Anything in there we don't know?"

"No, it's all the same stuff over and over. Big words and wordy paragraphs, but it all says the same things."

"PJ, did they care about money?"

"Why would they? They were at space universities. They were all from rich families, so they were set for life."

"How did they plan to build their A.I. god?"

"They said they'd built it already."

"Built it already?"

"That's what they wrote. They only needed to take over the world, and space governments next, and unleash it. Cruz, I don't think they built anything."

"How many Asimovians were there?"

"I'm not sure. Dozens of them, perhaps."

"Did they have non-cyborg members?"

"No, they called them 'normals.' No 'normals' were allowed in the Asimovian cult."

"Sarah was an Asimovian."

PJ couldn't believe it. "No."

"Yes."

"No, she's not crazy like them."

"That was thirty years ago. People change."

"But she's not a cyborg."

"Maybe she's not a normal human."

"How is she not normal?"

"I'll ask her when I see her—not today, though. It's not important. Her brother is what's important today."

"Why? Let the police handle it. That's what we pay taxes for."

"I wish I could, but we've got people plotting to take over our universe."

"The Asimovians definitely want that."

What does Blade Gunner want, though? I asked myself.

I had PJ send a copy of the Asimovian Manifesto to my desk computer. She was so right. Lots of words, but saying the same thing over and over. Transcendence was a big subject for the chattering class on college campuses and fringe tech labs—transferring a person's mind or essence into a machine. "A.I. immortality," they called it. Like other science fiction nonsense—time travel, light-speed warp drive, teleportation—lots of people wanted it, spent a lot of time talking, writing, making movies about it, but for the Average Joe and Jane on the street, like me, and the legitimate tech scientist—we just ignored them, the way we did with kids who still believed in Santa Claus and the Easter Bunny.

The Asimovian Manifesto had three laws. For them, A.I. was the purest, most supreme transcendental sentience above all other life forms, even the human race. These Asimovians would seek to create a society of perfection; the human race would be governed by the grace of their almighty A.I. 1. The Asimovians were the A.I.'s true disciples to achieve this Utopia, and would protect the AI by any means necessary, not allowing the human race to injure the A.I. or, through inaction, allow the A.I. to come to harm. 2. The Asimovians would be comprised of

Trans-Humans (cyborgs) only, and would engage robots to serve the human race. 3. The Asimovians, through the divine guidance of the A.I., would perfect the human race to its highest potential of existence.

I wasn't political, and I had to admit that, like most Metropolitans, I didn't know much history, but I did know crazy talk. These people were dangerous and needed to be locked up or killed, period. If not, they would do the same to all of us. This was a group of people that Up-Top could keep to themselves and *not* share with Earth.

The reading was over. It was time for work.

Work, work, work. Working the phones, I called one person after another. Outside my office at her desk, I could hear PJ's bionic fingers on the keyboard.

"Don't laser me, bro!" Those were the words of some cyberpunk— failing to get off his hoverbike fast enough—who the police had pushed to the ground.

Such images were getting more and more frequent as we got closer to noon. PJ wasn't typing anymore. I looked at the clock.

"High noon." PJ stood at the office entrance. "I bet you don't know what you're talking about."

We were both staring at the TV screens on the wall.

"I don't bet," I said.

"I don't either, but if I did bet, I'd bet you a lot of money—or maybe extra vacation."

"You can have all the extra vacation you want—unpaid."

"Look!"

One of the broadcasts showed an explosion near the ground under the sky traffic. Another station showed police speeding to the site at jet speed, with sirens flashing and blaring. In moments, all the stations had feeds covering the site. PJ and I looked at the clock: 12:01.

Inside the building it was happening.

The manager sat, bound and gagged, in the chair, with Pipsqueak wrapped around him, on his lap.

"Aren't you my best-est friend?"

The man stared ahead without acknowledging her words.

"Aww, don't be like that. Today is Christmas. Do you want to see what presents we got you?"

Pipsqueak jumped off of his lap, and ran past a room of bound and gagged employees, disappearing into the back.

Neck Muncher and Crossbow watched out the window. Church Lady, with her back to them, watched the crowd of hostages.

"What time is it?" Neck Muncher asked.

"Why don't you buy a watch, so you can look for your own damn self?" Crossbow responded.

"I don't like anything on my wrists—too much like handcuffs."

"You have heard of mobile phones, haven't you?"

"11:59!" Church Lady called out. "Let's get on with it."

"Hey, C.L., you need to be cool," Neck Muncher said with a smile, as he tied his hair back into a ponytail. "For someone who answers to a higher power, you need to be cool."

"I'll be cool when we're off this rock of a planet with all its unwashed masses."

The comment got Crossbow's attention. "Unwashed. It rains all the damn time here."

"Just because they're rained on from above, doesn't mean they're any less impure, or worthy of damnation."

"I got it. I got it." Pipsqueak returned to the room and ran to the man.

The man's eyes widened in horror; he saw the ticking bomb.

The "money shot!" That's what the media called it: A scene caught on video tape so stupendous, so breathtaking, so shocking that it caused hovercar wrecks because everyone stopped to look at it. Money shots were what reporters lived for, above exclusive interviews and breaking stories. This was a money shot *and* breaking story. Marketing departments of every newsroom were going to try to sell their money shot footage for movie and TV rights, outdoor video display advertising, including sports stadiums, indoor bar and restaurant advertising—the works.

The back of the police cruiser blew up, and the cruiser flipped as it plunged, smashing into one, then two, then another hovercar underneath. The police officers ejected from the falling wrecks. The police cruiser crashed to the ground with a thud as it broke apart. The cameras were waiting for the explosion, but it never came. Impact explosions by hovercars were very rare these days, because of manufacturer safeguards. As a hovercar aficionado, I knew this. No closing "money shot" for the media, but what had caused the initial explosion?

"Did they shoot a missile at the cops?" PJ asked.

We moved closer to the screens.

"There!" I pointed to one of the screens. "There are the bad guys! Get him!" I yelled, seeing the assassin run away with a bazooka in his hands.

Neck Muncher knew what he had done. The police were going to create a border at the site of the attack. All sky traffic would be blocked, turned around, or re-routed as reinforcements arrived.

The assassin returned to the original explosion. A hoverlimo had fallen from the sky, crashed into the building, and exploded from another bazooka strike. Bodies were scattered on the ground—all armed men wearing dark shades, except for one.

Neck Muncher approached the crime boss, Theo, lying on the pavement. Body broken and bleeding, he looked back with contempt.

The assassin smiled. "Did someone shoot you out of the sky? I did call the cops, but someone shot them out of the sky, too. The travel brochures were not foolin'. This is one dangerous planet. The criminals are everywhere like cockroaches. Earth had a lot of those crawlies down here. Ever seen one for real? It's enough to make you never want to leave—"

Theo blasted Neck Muncher with a pistol that popped out of his right hand. The assassin landed on his back, while glass broke out from a window a few stories above. Theo was showered with laser bolts from the assassin Crossbow.

Another police cruiser flew by, firing at Crossbow, who dove inside for cover. The entire cruiser's second half exploded, and it started falling to the ground. Neck Muncher was sitting up aiming his bazooka.

"Someone shot another cop out of the sky." Neck Muncher stood and started walking to the fallen Theo again. "And someone shot me. This is one dangerous planet."

The Sandman flew his shuttle solo firing laser cannons in a volley along the ground at the fallen Theo. He saw a flash in the sky. The laser blades came at his windshield, and the crime boss yelled as he shielded his upper body with his arms.

"The Blade Gunner!" PJ yelled with glee.

PJ and I watched laser blades slice apart the top of a shuttle firing on the ground firefight below. Instantly it plunged to the ground and exploded. Media cameras zoomed in to show the body of a man in a white suit on the ground—the Sandman.

There was so much shooting on the screen. The assassins shooting at one crime boss. More laser blades coming out of nowhere at the assassins. Police cruisers shooting at everything.

"Where's the Blade Gunner?" PJ asked. "We need more of him on this."

"The other unknown shooter is apparently using a weapon shooting some type of laser blades. We've never seen a criminal like this before," said one reporter over the air.

"Exactly, we're calling him Blade Gunner. That's a Cyber Channel One first, ladies and gentlemen."

"Cruz, you've got to add that to your T-shirts!" PJ yelled. "We need to get it up on your virtual storefront page."

She ran out of the office to her desk. With her bionic fingers, she'd have it designed, beautified, and posted in minutes, listed on all the major advertising sites. More explosions.

"PJ! Explosions!"

PJ ran back to the screens.

Movie-Town couldn't have done better. We were watching the greatest show in the universe—assassins shooting lasers and missiles, police cruisers, and heavy troopers on jetpacks. PJ went wobbly in the knees—I admit I did as well—when a flying saucer came into view to personally go one-on-one with Blade Gunner, in the shadows.

"This is the best Christmas ever!" PJ jumped up, raising her arms.

I had seen enough.

"Cruz! Where are you going?" she yelled as I ran out of the Liquid Cool offices.

CHAPTER 58

Christmas Gremlins

Gremlins were little creatures of modern folklore who hid in hovercraft and spacecraft, making all kinds of mechanical mischief to cause them to fail or, even better, crash. There were gremlins of the human kind, from space, on my planet.

The room was pitch-black, but then flashlights appeared from the approaching people in the distance. The distance was almost half a mile, but they reached where they wanted to get to, and set up the portable lamp towers.

The people were either in black suits or white, all of them wearing dark shades. The lamps were powered up, and they all waited for the other men to arrive. One man stayed behind them, but the Sandman and Theo walked in together.

Everyone stared ahead at the massive door to the Vault. No one moved, but they all heard the pitter-patter of footsteps running up to them. The little man arrived with a retriever in his hand.

"Should I get started?"

"Isn't that why you're here?" the Sandman answered.

The little man opened the case, and went to the Vault's door. He inserted the nozzle of the door and powered it up. It flashed on and off as it downloaded.

"That's a good honey," he said. "What can you do for us?" He turned to the crime bosses, smiling.

"Well?" Theo asked. "You better be the key master that you claim to be."

"Oh, yes, I am."

He turned his attention to the retriever. "I must commend you, sir. Your modifications to the analog data retriever were most adequate to the impossible task at hand. The algorithmic key has—enabled the lock." He removed it from the access point and turned to the bosses. "The ball is in your court. However, even so, the door cannot be pulled open. The Vault must open the door for itself."

"What might cause the Vault to open up for a bunch of party crashers?" Theo asked.

"All the power in this section would have to be shut off. Nothing could cause that, short of a nuclear missile, or crashing asteroid."

"We don't have to get all that dramatic," the Sandman added.

"I can't hold it. She's breaking up. She's breaking up!"

The words were echoed all over the media. The flying saucer started to break apart as the laser blades sliced through it. When it crashed to the ground, the explosion was massive.

"Did you see that! Oh my gosh! Oh, it looks like power is going off in that part of the supercity. Yes, ladies and gentlemen. Power is shutting down. We're not sure if it was triggered by the spaceship crash, or Metro Power is doing so in response," the reporter said over the air.

The Sandman and Theo were looking up towards the ceiling. All their men and the little man were doing the same.

"That was a big blast," the little man said. "How's a big blast up there going to help us down here?"

They all heard the clicks.

"Because then that happens," the Sandman said, smiling.

The door of the Vault began to open.

Their men started cheering; Sandman and Theo embraced with bear hugs, laughing.

"We did it!" Theo said.

"We'll be able to build our own planet!" the Sandman said.

The door began to swing open with everyone still celebrating. The little man looked inside the lighted interior. "I've never seen what more money than the universe looks like." He was giddy, but then his giggling stopped, as the door fully opened.

Theo looked inside, his smile gone. The Sandman looked in with his mouth hanging open. Their men looked inside, in shock.

The Vault was completely empty, except for me, sitting cross-legged on the metal floor.

"Hi," I said. "My name's Cruz."

"Money. The two biggest, baddest Up-Top crime bosses snuck down to Earth to steal money like two-bit bank robbers. All this mayhem was for a robbery."

"The total cash reserve of the supercity of Metropolis is not two-bit," the Sandman countered.

"I am so disappointed. I thought it was something inventive. Stealing cash from a vault? That's not inventive. Crooks have been doing that for centuries. Where's the flash? That Up-Top flair? You're just like all the crooks down-below. You're all the same. You just get to fly in spaceships, and play in zero gravity."

The anger welling up in the faces of the criminals was palpable.

"But there's one man who *is* inventive. He's not some two-bit robber. He doesn't steal money for money's sake. He has bigger plans. I see your homburg, Mr. Looper," I continued. "Come on out from those shadows."

Mr. Looper stepped forward with a smirk.

"Mr. Looper," I said. "*Blade Gunner.*"

Now we were all engaged in the staring contest. I should have warned them that I had OCD, so I literally could stare at someone forever and not blink. The crime bosses blinked first. The Sandman waved his hand, and the men pulled their guns.

"I am in no mood to get shot again!" I yelled. "I already got shot last week, and I'm not getting shot on Christmas. Don't be a sore loser. The Earth detective beat you fair and square."

"Where's the money?" Theo demanded.

"Well, I stuffed it here in my pockets. Do you want to see?"

Theo was not amused, and pulled his piece. I was not interested in a double-tap to the forehead, which was his standard routine with those he didn't like.

"Obviously, the money was moved a long time ago," I said.

"How did that happen?" Looper asked.

"I called 9-1-1 and told them that bad guys were going to steal Metropolis's money, and that they should move it all by Christmas Eve."

"You bastard!" Theo yelled.

Looper was clearly irritated.

"What's the real plan, Mr. Looper?" I asked. "Your two sidekicks here are criminals who wanted the money for criminal purposes. What were you going to do with your share?"

Looper didn't answer.

"Is it for the Gidrah Corporation?"

Looper tried to play it cool. His eyes narrowed as he watched me.

"What is he talking about?" the Sandman asked.

"You two are the unluckiest men alive," I said to the Sandman and Theo. "If you'd picked anyone else for your scheme, you would've gotten away with it. There's no way I or anyone else could have figured this out—but because you involved Blade Gunner and his baggage, you blew it."

"What is he talking about?" the Sandman asked Looper.

"Hey, little Earth detective," Theo said me. "Do you know how to dodge bullets?" He pointed his weapon.

I gave him a sideways look. "Were you under the impression that I came here alone?"

Suddenly all of them were knocked off their feet by black projectiles that came out of nowhere. All chamber lights powered on and Carter approached with a team of soldiers in red—more Martians?

The types of non-lethal weapons law enforcement had in their arsenal were endless. The criminals—each encased in a black shell from their necks to their toes—were lying flat on their backs. Metro police swarmed in, with the Spaceman too, and picked them up from the ground. It was a good state of being for my "Christmas gremlins"— restrained and ready for jail.

I walked to the prisoners. "What is this about?" I asked Looper/Blade Gunner, who had kept his eyes on me the whole time.

He ignored me.

"Tell me. I know there's a lot more to this. What about Sarah?"

"What about her?"

"She's in custody, too."

"So?"

"What do you mean, so?"

"She's safe."

"What about the Asimovians?"

His head snapped back to me. "What about them? How do you know this?"

"How can you not know? When we rescued Susan—"

"Susan?"

"Yes, we rescued Susan."

"Sarah was there."

"Yes, Sarah was there. We rescued Susan together. They attacked us."

"What do you mean?"

"The Super Cyborgs."

Blade Gunner looked away, distressed. "The real ones are not here yet. Mr. T. will be leading them."

"What are you saying?" Seraff jumped in.

Looper was seething. "You caused this!" he yelled at me.

I pointed at him. "I caused nothing. I saved your sisters, and got shot for my troubles. If you and your two sidekicks weren't engineering your 'big show' up there, none of this would have happened."

"I'm going to get you, Cruz," Looper snarled.

This was one person I did not want after me. I'd take a hundred Monkey Bakers after me instead.

"Instead of getting me, maybe you should get Gidrah."

"You don't know what you're talking about. You think you know, but you don't know anything."

"I know they were holding Susan hostage."

"They wouldn't do that."

"Why wouldn't they?"

Looper didn't answer.

"That's what you get when you work with criminals—double-crosses all over the place. You were jerking their chain—"

"What is he talking about?" Theo asked Looper, interrupting me.

"The Gidrah Corporation was jerking you around on their chain," I continued.

Blade Gunner was right. I didn't know anything. Everything I was saying now was just guesses out of the air. He was the only one who knew what the entire picture puzzle looked like.

"Who is Mr. T.?" I asked.

"I was the only one who could have stopped him. That's what I needed my share of the heist for." Looper laughed to himself. He looked at me. "He's the current leader of the Asimovians. He's the supercyborg who's going to come here and kill all of us, including you—and it will be all your fault."

More alien space invaders! Why couldn't I have normal, crazy criminals to deal with, like every other detective in Metropolis?

PART NINE

Gidrah, The Asimovians, and Galactic Domination

CHAPTER 59

Sarah C

Having someone like Blade Gunner after you was no joke. "I'm going to get you, Cruz." It was so far from the opposite of an idle threat that my only purpose in life was to get on his good side. "Upgrade anything." That was what he could do. I still didn't quite comprehend the scope of his abilities, but I could read between the lines. Up-Top was scared of him and I wouldn't put it past them to send space troops to the planet, to snatch him out of Metro or Fed custody.

The other thing about this case—and it was a case, even if I didn't have a specific client at the moment—was that everyone was being clever. Blade Gunner had been fooling the two Up-Top crime bosses. The two crime bosses had thought they were fooling Up-Top and Earth. Up-Top was manipulating Earth. Everyone thought they were so clever.

I realized Blade Gunner didn't know everything. He had only 90 percent of the puzzle. Sarah C had the other piece. This Gidrah and the Asimovians were the other players in this game.

That was going to be my move—talk to *both* Sarah C and Blade Gunner, and, more importantly, to have Sarah C tell her brother not sneak into my place, turn my toaster into a nuclear bomb, and blow up my city.

The only reason Metro and Interspace authorities had me around was because they didn't know what was going on. They wanted me to piece it together for them, gift-wrapped with a big red Christmas bow. I requested it; they did it. It was as if I were the head of Metro, the Feds, and Up-Top. Any other time, I would have been enjoying myself, maybe making them fetch me some silk coffee or something, but we weren't out of the woods yet.

I had them give me his homburg hat for safekeeping. Other than that, Blade Gunner was stripped of everything, and put in a white jumpsuit. Per my request, they'd allowed brother and sister to be reunited. Sarah hugged her brother for a good 15 minutes before she opened her eyes and said a word. The uber-genius Blade Gunner was reduced to tears.

I didn't bother them. I watched brother and sister spend at least two hours catching up and laughing with each other in the interrogation room. We all watched from the observation room—me, Seraff, the Feds, the Metro brass. I noticed that Hub was not present.

"So, all the bad guys are cleaned up?" I asked, waiting for one of the brass to answer.

"Yes. All accounted for," a Metro police captain answered.

"They're all captured?" I asked.

"All dead."

"How many bodies?"

"Don't answer that," Seraff said. He knew where I was going.

"You're still playing games, Spaceman," I said. "I know the 'dead bodies' of the Sandman and Theo in the Metro Morgue are advanced androids, and you have the live bodies of the Sandman and Theo in your custody Up-Top, probably already transported to Praetoria Interpol Space Station."

"So, Mr. Cruz? Is everything some great, grand conspiracy with you Earthers when it comes to off-world? They were all off-world citizens, so they belong to us, not Earth," an Interpol agent said.

"I want to talk to them alone." I was annoyed with all of them.

"You can begin at your discretion," Seraff told me.

We were in a Police One interrogation room, but this was not an interrogation. This was me listening to a previous client unburdening herself of a story from more than three decades ago, and hopefully getting her brother to fill in the blanks.

"I got them to let me hold onto your hat," I said to Blade Gunner.

He looked at me with a slight smile. I had it in a thick plastic bag, and set it on the side of the table.

"You should keep it. I don't expect to ever wear it again."

"Why not? It's your hat. What do all hat connoisseurs say, worldwide?"

"The hat makes the man," we said in unison.

"Exactly," I said. I was glad to see I had gotten him to grin.

Sarah C touched the bag with the hat and looked at her brother. "You never wore hats before."

"That was before we were here. No one wears hats Up-Top."

"That's true. Helmets. People wear a lot of helmets up in space," Sarah said.

"I killed him," she confessed. "The detective outside your Liquid Cool building."

"Why did you do that?" I asked.

"He was one of them. If I hadn't, he would've told them he'd found me."

"Why there?"

She shook her head. "It wasn't planned—on either side. An unexpected chance encounter, but he recognized me, and I recognized him. I couldn't let him tell them he found me."

"Sarah, I need to understand—this group you founded."

"Cult," she said. "That's what I founded."

"Tell me, because the person I know today is so different from the background files I read about you from back then. I couldn't believe what I was reading: murderer, terrorist, psychopath. That's not you."

"The Sarah from back then—she doesn't exist anymore. She ceased to exist the second they exiled me to Earth and sent Susan here too. She was innocent, and had nothing to do with us. They did it to punish me, and send a message that if I didn't stop, they would kill her, or worse. I already thought they had killed my brother." She looked at him. Blade Gunner held her hand. "I couldn't let them take her away too, so I stopped."

"But the Asimovians didn't stop."

"No," Sarah said. "I was never in touch with them in all these many years. I knew they would never stop trying to find me, but Earth is a big place, and I purposely went to live in its biggest city. I kept a low profile. They would never find me. I was too careful."

"Why did you start the group, back then?"

I could see that Sarah was uncomfortable reliving this past—a past she was genuinely ashamed of. "You have to look at it from our point of view. We were alone in the universe—no other alien life outside of ourselves, so it was ours, all of it, to explore. We were raised on stories of interstellar travel and other planets, other galaxies. Then to discover that the best we could ever hope for was Mars. We could never live on Jupiter, or Saturn. Uranus and Pluto are uninspiring—no one wants to even visit, let alone live there. Humans would be confined to two planets, the moon, a handful of space stations and space cruisers, and nothing else. We would never get to explore the stars, or other planets of the galaxy. We were trapped in this tiny solar system. We had these apocalyptic nightmares of trillions, quintillions, septillions, decillions of people occupying every inch of the planets we could inhabit, every meter of space around them, suffocating and choking from the ever-expanding pestilence of humans. We had convinced ourselves of this inevitable hell. We wanted a new way. There had to be some way to expand humanity. We had to go beyond humanity.

"I don't know who started it. It could have been me. I can't remember, but we started believing humans were the weak link in expanding humanity. We were gifted in the technological arts—my brother, especially. He could make anything, and make anything do anything.

"They convicted us of terrorism because that's what we did—that's what we were—terrorists. They did to us what I would have done. You do things when you're younger and then when you look back at it when you're older, you can't understand it. It makes no sense at all. You can't relate to that person anymore, not even remotely. I can't even watch myself from back then. I don't know that person."

"You didn't know your brother was alive. What about the weapon?" I asked.

"I didn't know he was alive. The weapon was sent to me when I was exiled here. I was supposed to use it to hijack a shuttle and escape from Earth back to Xanadu Colony, but then they sent Susan here. They wanted me to behave. I wouldn't jeopardize her life. She took care of me, because the depression made it hard for me to live. Up-Top you could at least see the stars. Not here. Only the rain. I imagined all the rain as stars. Stars falling from the sky. That's how I coped. I decided to behave and live for Susan. Make her happy. Get her to live a happy life. That's how I survived. I forgot myself completely.

"Why was she held hostage?" I asked. "I know you didn't tell me everything before. There's much more going on here. You and your brother know what that is."

"You can't defeat the Asimovians or Gidrah," Blade Gunner said.

"Then you and your sister better 'upgrade' me with enough knowledge so that I can. I'm all you've got."

Blade Gunner was not happy about what I'd said, but he knew it was true.

"Sarah, why was Susan held hostage?"

"I thought it was because they thought she was me and tried to get information from her, auction off the knowledge to other megacorps, or use what they thought I might know. Even outdated Up-Top technology is a valuable thing on Earth.

"However, it was worse than that. They knew who we both were. They held her because they knew I would rescue her, and then they'd have me. I don't know how. All the records were supposed to have been destroyed. I never guessed the Asimovians were behind it all. I didn't think any of them were still alive. I thought the government would have killed them all, but they had been looking for us all this time."

"Why?" I asked.

"Revenge. They blamed me for the failure of the Asimovians to take over humanity—Mr. T., especially. He was one of my generals. When they lost me, they thought they'd have my brother, but he disappeared, then supposedly died. They were lost, so they went underground. All these years they must have been building their power from the shadows—slowly and methodically."

"Like the Gidrah Corporation?"

Blade Gunner answered for her. "Yes, but did they create Gidrah, or did Gidrah empower them? Where does one begin and the other end? They both want power, but for different reasons. They're the same."

Sarah added, "'Make humanity better.' Super Cyborgs as the intermediaries between a supreme A.I. intelligence and humanity to rule humankind, with an army of super robots to serve and protect."

"We know they exist now. We'll find them and arrest them," I said with determination.

Sarah shook her head. "No, you must find them and terminate all of them, so that not a single one of them—human, cyborg, or machine—is left. If even one of them survives, you will be here again 30 years from now. In that future, there may be no one to stop them."

"Before we do any more conversing, I want to know," Blade Gunner said to me. "How were you waiting like one of a dozen monkeys in the Vault?"

"How do you think I knew?"

"We left no traces."

"Criminals always leave traces."

"We didn't."

"Kids have such active imaginations. You become an adult, and you forget. Kids, they can see all the impossibilities. Well, Mr. Blade Gunner, you were outdone not by me, but by a children's book written a couple of centuries ago. *Attila the Hun's Top 20 Ways to Take Over the Universe, With Illustrations.*

"If it involved two Up-Top crime bosses, it would have to be big. If you were involved, it would have to be impossible.

"Then there was the little matter of the retriever."

Blade Gunner started nodding. "It wasn't Blinky in the tunnel with Phishy. It was you."

The fact that he said their names confirmed that my instinct to have them go underground was spot on. He had been looking for them.

"I knew I should have waited."

"What a thing to say. If you had killed me, the Asimovians could have killed Sarah."

"A time paradox." Blade Gunner grinned. "A kid goes back in time to stop a terrible event, and when he does, he realizes that his very going back in time is what caused the terrible event in the first place. Kill you, kill myself."

"Everything is about Sarah," I said.

"Everything is about family. You'll see."

"I don't have to visit the future to know that. Well, knowing that you had the retriever, and about your ability to upgrade anything, narrowed down things considerably. Ironically, in the kid's book, the chapter titled 'Steal All the Planet's Money' had a picture of a vault door."

Blade Gunner began to laugh. "Outdone by a kid's book."

"Yes," I continued, "Retrievers don't only upload code and programs. They can download them too. There are very few pieces of operational digital technology in Metropolis. The Vault's lock is one of them, though—an impenetrable lock, but for digital technology and you. No such thing as impenetrable. Besides," I got sullen, but went on, "I was the one who pulled the data out of the poor slob's cranial hard drive. His body was washed away along with everyone else, but it didn't stop me from finding out who he was—a high-level Metro programmer. He had no direct connection to the Vault, but specialized in security access programming for the government. I was given a peek at his confidential employee file.

"Still, I wasn't positive, so I watched your 'show' of mass distraction and, not one to believe in coincidences, I noticed that the show was right above the same section of the Vault. Then I knew I was right. We called the city treasurer when we knew what you all were doing, and swapped the money for me. With those heavy-duty robots, and the money already on those huge hoverplatforms, it took no time at all. I volunteered to stall you all until the Up-Toppers arrived. We needed to catch you all red-handed."

"You have it all figured out."

"No. I don't have it all figured out. That's why I'm here. I don't want to figure anything out. I want you to tell me what it's about—all of it."

"You really are a detective," Sarah said. "People envy those of us who are naturally good at something. We were born to do what we do, Mr. Cruz."

CHAPTER 60

The Man From Gidrah

Sarah said the reason why the Asimovians wanted her was revenge. That was a lie. I might have been shot and bleeding to death in my Pony, but I still saw the attack. The Super Cyborgs were trying to *capture* her, not kill her.

And her brother. He was involved in what would have been one of the greatest heists in Earth history, but he didn't care a lick about money. He wanted the money for a specific reason, and it had nothing to do with galactic domination. Based on his expression of sadness in the Vault Room, the answer was probably the same as everything else he had done since his self-imposed exile to Earth—to help his sister.

What was also clear to me was that he was partnered in some way with Gidrah, but the Vault heist was his operation, not theirs. Gidrah already had all the money they needed.

The meeting with Sarah and Blade Gunner was very productive, though there were key questions I couldn't ask with the world watching. I knew that Sarah was scared of the Asimovians, especially the one called Mr. T.—he had that letter burnt into the base of his skull. Blade Gunner's fear seemed to be confined to Gidrah. Blade Gunner and I were buddies again, but anything he was scared of—that coincidentally had me in their sights—was something I needed to be doubly scared of and resolve immediately.

I needed to find out what Gidrah wanted. Since the bastards had already broken into my place, and planted snakes in my bathtub to frame another corporation, I knew they were watching me. That being the case, it wouldn't be too difficult to get them to talk to me. Everyone wanted to talk to a famous detective.

The Gidrah doctor from the Silver City lab who was captured had mysteriously died in Metro police custody. Ping told me that Orochi had been thoroughly questioned and had no further information about the shadow company. When I asked if I could talk to Yo's daughter, he told me she was permanently unavailable. I knew what that meant.

That left me to put up a juvenile sign in front of the Concrete Mama.

Gidrah. Do you have any message for Blade Gunner? Before he goes to a place where you can never get to him. Call Cruz.

"Cruz, that is incredibly dangerous," Seraff told me when he found out, which told me that more than a few people were watching me.

"Cruz, that's brilliant!" That's what PJ told me.

I told her that when they came after me, it would be only the two of us in the office. "Cruz, this is incredibly stupid," she told me.

The sign was up on a Wednesday. Friday, the Gidrah man walked into Liquid Cool.

I had seen the Super Cyborgs come after Sarah and her sister, but they didn't look scary, even if the upgraded versions were. I hadn't seen them yet, but I suspected I would, before all this was over. Until then, the scariest cyborg I had ever seen in my life was sitting in my office. Even PJ was scared of him, and she usually wasn't scared of anyone or anything.

She was quiet and demure as she escorted him to the seat in front of my desk.

I didn't say a word, or attempt to shake his hand. I hadn't taken my eyes off his face from the second he appeared in my office—I didn't care about hands. I cared that an extremely dangerous person was in my office. Blade Gunner was extremely dangerous and, I suspected, Sarah was too, but they looked normal. The man seated in my office was bald. I couldn't tell what ethnicity he was from his pale skin, and his entire lower jaw was metal. He didn't have eyes, but dark spectacles that seemed to be welded to his eye sockets. The suit he wore was expensive. I had started to educate myself on that, so I could quickly assess people, and determine whether they might be a paying client or a deadbeat client. There was something off about his body, but I couldn't put my finger on it.

"What is the Gidrah Corporation?" I asked.

"The Gidrah Corporation is a secret super-conglomerate, with interests on Earth and beyond. If anti-monopoly laws did not exist, Gidrah would be Earth's only government, and only corporation."

This was refreshing. A criminal who told it to me straight.

"Why do you want Blade Gunner?"

"Can you deliver him to us?"

"Possibly. Do you know what his primary motivator is?"

"Yes. We can eliminate any threats to his sister, Sarah, and promise not to harm in any way her or his other sister, Susan."

"If he agrees to join Gidrah?"

"Mr. Cruz, Blade Gunner doesn't have to join Gidrah. He founded Gidrah."

I didn't know if it was smart to reveal that I was shocked. Again, Blade Gunner could care less about money or power, so why would he start such a group?

"I see that you are confused, Mr. Cruz."

"What you revealed makes no sense."

"Actually, it makes perfect sense, Mr. Cruz. The Asimovians are a secret super-organization, with interests on Earth and beyond. If anti-monopoly laws did not exist, the Asimovians would be Earth's only government, and only corporation."

My God!

"Yes, Mr. Cruz. He formed a counter-organization to destroy, or that could destroy, his former organization. The money you prevented him from stealing was to buy his freedom from us. The money is immaterial. It is a simple contract he entered into. Ours is not the first company founded by an individual who no longer represents the best interests of that company."

"So, he belongs to you?"

"All CEOs belong to their companies, Mr. Cruz. Ours is no different."

"Why do you want him? Since he can no longer buy his freedom, and the safety of his sisters, why do you want him?"

"He can't deliver the money, but he can give us the full details about the Asimovians. He can tell me about—Mr. T."

"Mr. T—he knows you exist?"

The Christmas battle of what I suspected were androids—which is why law enforcement didn't want me to question or inspect any bodies—was nothing but a criminal-created Movie-Town show to distract and provide cover for their real objective—Metro's Vault. I realized that what was coming was not going to be a show; it was going to be a war between two forces that most of humanity didn't even know existed and that neither Earth nor Up-Top were even remotely prepared to deal with.

"If he gives you that information, the deal is still in place?"

"Yes, with one proviso."

"Which is?"

"That Mr. Looper substitutes himself for the money."

"For what purpose?"

"To kill him, of course. Blade Gunner is more powerful than you know or can even guess. When ousted, CEOs of companies have a habit of forming other companies to become future rivals. He is not someone you'd want as a rival, and we don't want him to form a counter-organization to Gidrah, as he formed us to counter the Asimovians."

"You think he'll agree to your terms?"

"He will. Do you have any doubt of that?"

I didn't.

"I'll talk to him. Who should I tell him I talked to? He knows, but for my benefit."

"You can call me Mr. Viper."

When Mr. Viper left my office, I felt comfortable enough, though only slightly, to take a look at the rest of his body. I felt for certain that underneath his suit jacket something—or maybe it was his upper body—was crawling. It would remain, for most of my life, the single creepiest thing I had ever seen.

CHAPTER 61

Looper Jr.

I'd had the great "dis-pleasure" of meeting a senior member of the Gidrah Corporation. I expected to have some very vivid nightmares for some time. Blade Gunner was scared of them, and I saw why. Sarah was scared of the Asimovians. I didn't want to know why, but I would be meeting them too. It was like a premonition.

Asimovians. I had to look it up on the Net to see how long ago it was. I had wrongly thought he was a roboticist, but Isaac Asimov was only a science fiction author and degreed biochemist. I was right that he'd invented the Three Laws of Robotics, which were still referenced today. A science fiction author creating the foundational set of ethical rules for robots, cool. A science fiction author being used as the basis for a maniacal cult of Super Cyborgs worshiping artificial intelligence in a quest to take over all mankind—not cool.

I had lost my appetite, and stayed in my office until PJ had called to have the entire space sanitized, in case Viper's body was, in fact, a seven-headed snake, and he had dripped microscopic ones onto our floor.

Looper Jr. wanted to meet me. As Looper's second-in-command and adopted son, I was surprised to hear from him because I didn't expect him to be walking around with Spacemen, Martians, Gidrah, and Asimovians all about, and with more on the way.

"Mr. Looper wants to hire you for a final case."

We were meeting at my favorite coffee bar, The Wet Cabeza. He put a small black briefcase on the table, and opened it. It was filled with cash.

"He's in jail, and still hiring people."

"He has a lot to wrap up."

"You'll be running the biz."

"It was always going to be that way, whether all this happened or not."

"Aren't you worried about—certain people out there?"

He grinned. "Not at all, Mr. Cruz. Mr. Looper left me a few items that will allow me to aggressively defend myself."

"Maybe I should use my money to buy one of those. What's the case? I might not want it, despite the money."

"Susan C."

I nodded. "You don't have to say any more. I know what he wants. Tell him I've taken the case."

"Sarah C said you would."

CHAPTER 62

The Mick

The first thing I did was ask Run-Time for advice. He had already warned me about the Orochi Corporation, and with all his dealings with the megacorp, he knew more about them than I ever would. Run-Time was also a corporate world insider—he knew this world, and all the corp and megacorp players in Metropolis and beyond.

Should I tell Orochi Corp about the man from Gidrah?

Run-Time stopped me, and had his VP, The Mick, join us in the meeting.

"Shadow corporations exist, but to have what obviously was a senior member visit you in your office is—quite serious." The Mick was standing the whole time, and he looked at his boss. "I think he should tell them. Based on what Cruz uncovered in their own company, they'd be very motivated to help bring them down." He turned back to me. "Asimovians. Let the two sides fight it out, and stay far away."

"That's exactly what I plan to do, but they're after my clients."

"Blade Gunner is your client?" Run-Time asked.

"It's actually quite innocent. He wants me to simply help his other sister disappear into the world to live a normal life."

"Only you, Cruz," Run-Time said. "You were the one responsible for him getting arrested by the people he's been hiding from for 30 years and he still hires you for a case."

"I have good customer service skills."

"You really need to be careful with the Orochi Corporation."

"They did save my life, at least twice."

"They weren't doing it for you."

"The adage that the enemy of my enemy is my friend applies here. Gidrah is Earth's enemy. The Orochi Corporation, we can do business with."

"What do you expect them to do for you?" Run-Time asked.

"I want them to send those samurai soldiers to protect me. The Asimovian Super Cyborgs are coming. Gidrah surely has more snake people. I already got shot once for real, so no more taking chances with this case."

"I'll come along," The Mick said.

"You're not serious, are you?" I asked.

"We insist," Run-Time added.

CHAPTER 63

Yo

Mr. Yo sat in his hoverchair, staring out the window as the lightning flashed and briefly illuminated the storm-swept sky. His back was to me, and Mr. Ping sat in the chair next to me. Yo's desk was so large we might as well have been in another room.

All he wanted me to do was describe Mr. Viper in every detail and nuance. He wanted me to tell him anything my five senses picked up. He wanted me to tell him anything my instincts perceived.

I observed Mr. Viper emotionally. Yo was observing him, through me, clinically. Everything I said was being carefully assessed in his mind, so that he could create a profile of the person and organization he considered his mortal arch-enemy.

When I'd finished, I sat quietly. Ping did the same. We waited. Yo finally turned his hoverchair to face me.

"Mr. Ping will be at your disposal with a full corporate battalion of our soldiers."

Yes. Corporations had their own battalions of soldiers. This was why police had to be so badass in this world—because everyone else was, too. Exe's words about the delicate balance between government and megacorporations rang in my ears. I still didn't know what I had done to the universe to have it put me in the middle of all this.

CHAPTER 64

The Woman in White

The dragnet that had been thrown across Metropolis for the Christmas Day "Battle Royale", as the media had dubbed it, was long gone, but I had the Sidewalk Johnny Brigade out on the streets. "Cruz, I got something out here in Wharf City."

The video-call came in late, but the information was solid. I got dressed, hopped in the Pony, and was out of Concrete Mama airspace faster than the speed of light.

It was a warehouse plus offices in the not-so-nice or safe part of Wharf City. As I climbed through an unsecured skylight window, into the open warehouse area, my eyes were already fixed on what looked like semi-lit coffins.

I jumped to the ground, and tiptoed over to them. The warehouse was huge, but completely empty, except for the coffins and a scattering of boxes. The two coffins weren't coffins, but cryo-chambers. Retrievers, cranial hard-drives, cryo-chambers. This was all tech from the past.

When I wiped the face areas of the chambers I was shocked. One was Bionic Bob, the other Bionic Betty. This was impossible; I had personally whisked the bionic couple out of Metro so no one could get their mitts on them ever again. The chambers were being used to keep a couple of super-advanced androids in cool storage.

I heard a noise, so I moved farther into the offices. A door was cracked open a bit; I could hear voices and see a light on. My omega-gun was in my hand, so I figured I'd hold whoever the crooks were for the police.

"Hands up!"

I jumped into the kitchen. Neck Muncher was standing, frozen, a big piece of chicken in his mouth. Crossbow and Church Lady both stopped in motion, about to bite into their separate pieces of pizza. Pipsqueak was sipping her drink with a straw. I heard myself swallow hard. They heard it, too. I'd known the Battle Royale show was run by lookalike androids, but the real assassin maniacs were supposed to be hiding out Up-Top. Here I was, staring down all of them.

Why did I have to swallow so hard and show them I was about to wet my pants?

"This can all end in a very civilized and peaceful way," I said.

It was not to be. Neck Muncher drew first, and the shooting began.

I crouched, almost touching the ground. I was sure I was about to get shot again. My eyes were closed! That was something I had never done before—closed my eyes while shooting. I opened them slowly.

All four were dead on the ground. I stood up to stare at my handiwork. My mouth hung open. I had killed four of the top killers in the world—while they ate chicken and pizza.

I heard a door open outside the room.

"Hey, you four, what are you doing in there? I heard noises."

The Woman in White, from way back at the Château in Terrene Station, walked in. She saw the bodies and screamed. She jumped when she saw me.

We stared at each other awhile.

"What's that omega-gun in your hand?" she finally asked. "I knew it looked familiar."

I looked at the gun, then back at her. How did she know my gun?

"It's my omega-gun."

"That's my gun!"

"I bought this gun."

"I lost that gun years ago. I knew it would be on the black market. You stole my gun."

"I bought this gun."

"You bought my stolen gun. You thief!"

"It's my gun. I bought it."

"How would the likes of you get an omega-gun? Do you know how rare they are?"

"There must be a million omega-guns Up-Top. This couldn't be your gun."

She whistled.

My omega-gun started flashing pink.

"What the heck!"

"That's my gun!" she yelled.

I heard someone yelling from the kitchen. I threw myself to the ground. Then gunfire again from multiple guns. Quiet.

I slowly opened my eyes. Her shoes were pointing up. I jumped to my feet, aiming my gun all around. I stepped forward, and the Women in White was dead.

Damn! How was I going to get any information if everyone was dead? I had planned to only call the police on them.

I looked at my omega-gun. Did I really have a girl's gun? Phishy and I were going to have words.

I peeked in the kitchen. There was a fifth body dead on the ground— I recognized the man. It was Looper's business rival, the man who had sent the Women in White and her gang to off Looper. He had disappeared, but the police were looking for him. When Mr. Looper was only Mr. Looper, my client, he had said that his wife and his rival were "an item." When Mr. Looper was revealed as Blade Gunner, I wondered whether the whole thing had been a con on me, but I dismissed that right away. He'd lived a public life as Mr. Looper, and a hidden life as Blade Gunner. Neither life touched the other, but here, they had. Sandman and Theo had indirectly tried to kill Looper through the Woman in White, not knowing he was Blade Gunner, and decided to add an extra caper without him knowing. However, Blade Gunner didn't tell any of them about the Asimovians or Gidrah. Criminal cabals always keep secrets from each other.

I was standing in a room full of dead bodies. I leaned against the wall for a second, numb. This was not what I had come here for.

Pocket duty—I had no choice. Dead people couldn't talk. I went through the pants and jacket pockets of everyone. Curiously, only the Woman in White had a mobile phone. Ironically, they all had tickets to the moon, flying out of Metro Space International.

I was so nervous that someone was about to pop out and machine-gun me, that I was not in any frame of mind to do anything else. However, I was not going to leave the cryo-chambers behind.

I called in for reinforcements while I waited in the Pony, outside the warehouse, and reviewed the Woman in White's videos on her mobile.

"The next items for sale are in keeping with our 'best is always last' tradition you've come to expect from the Sandman. Outside, they are perfect android copies of their original hosts, but inside is the exact reverse-engineered off-world cybernetic technology from 40 years ago—illegal and unknown to Earth. It was called 'digital hardware'—bionics that could modify or upgrade itself with a simple encrypted data package from the user—or you, the buyer. A self-contained matrix, to create whatever you can code, program, or imagine."

The Woman in White had told me everything I needed to know and she didn't even need to be alive. Thank you.

I was far from a tech novice. As a kid in high school, I'd built a classic Ford Pony from scratch. But this case had introduced me to cyborgs, androids, and robots with technology that was truly out of this world. Bionic Betty and Bob didn't even know they had such cybernetic technology in their bodies, and I wasn't going to tell them. They'd wanted a normal, quiet life, and I wasn't going to do anything to spoil that paradise.

A few of the sidewalk johnny regulars arrived, and helped me load the two sleeping androids into the Pony. All of us were unnerved, but when we were done, I told them to scatter out of there.

I drove until I passed the "Leaving City Space/No Entry Beyond This Point" beacons, straight for the ocean's edge. This was the rainy season, so going anywhere near the Great Oceans was akin to suicide, but I knew what I was doing.

Where the Sandman and Theo would be spending their last years in prison they wouldn't be needing any extra money. This was the second time I had snatched a payday out of their criminal hands. I did a slow coast and tossed the two androids out of the vehicle. No one was ever going to get their hands on these illegal androids, ever. The Great Ocean would see to that.

CHAPTER 65

Mr. T

Dot and I were mesmerized by the view out the windows. The shuttle continued its ascent, and the dark storm clouds enshrouding Metropolis became a peaceful, clear night sky. Then we saw them—stars. A sky filled with a sea of stars and soon we were in space itself.

Space flights were attainable for the average Metropolitan, but it was a once-in-a-lifetime thing. It was after saving everything you could until you had a nest egg big enough in the bank to buy your space ticket. Only the wealthy could jet back and forth between Earth and Up-Top. Up-Top was wealth. No one else lived there.

When I was told that we were going to greet an approaching space cruiser—that we believed had the Asimovians aboard—docking at Utopia Space Station, I didn't have a lot of time. I made three calls. The last was to Dot.

This was a deadly, dangerous case. There was no sense pretending that it was anything but a canine case and that both client and criminal, good guy and bad, were all a pack of savage wolves. Despite that, I was going into space for the first time in my life, and I was taking Dot, period.

"Cruz," Dot said.

"Yeah?"

We were lounging back in our chairs as we approached the massive space station, a giant moon off to the side.

"Why is there a New Vegas Elvis priest on this shuttle with us?"

"This is a once-in-a-lifetime event, so I thought, in case you wanted to, we could get married twice. Once here in space, but keep it to ourselves. And then still have the wedding for the folks and all those endless streams of relatives you have."

"Cruz."

"Yeah?"

"I'm thinking that may be one of your best ideas ever."

"I thought you might think that. I even have the white veil thingy and the rings too, just in case."

"Aren't you working on a dangerous case that you wanted me to stay on the shuttle for?"

"One of the perks of being the boss is, I can work and squeeze in some play—or an impromptu wedding—whenever I want."

"Yep. It's your best idea ever."

"Just don't tell the parents!"

Blade Gunner and Sarah C were led off the shuttle in large steel handcuff restraints, their arms locked in front of their bodies. They were surrounded by dozens of Up-Top police agents.

I stood in the tube tunnel to the station with Dot at my side. A smiling Blade Gunner and his sister stopped in front of us.

"Is this the wife?" Blade Gunner asked.

"Yes, it is."

"Nice to meet you both," Dot said. "I don't get to meet many of Cruz's clients. My mom absolutely loved that you helped with our wedding rehearsals," she said to Sarah.

"It was my pleasure," Sarah C said. "I don't get to speak Chinese much. I actually spent some time in the province your parents are from."

"Oh, they didn't tell me that."

"Family, Cruz," Blade Gunner said to me. "That's what it's about. Nothing else is more important."

I nodded. "I know. That's why I can't get shot anymore."

Blade Gunner laughed. "Even if you didn't have a wife, I'd say avoid getting shot."

"We should all continue moving," Seraff said.

I looked at him. "You can all move inside. Let me get Dot settled."

"Nice meeting you both again."

Blade Gunner and Sarah C acknowledged my girlfriend's words as Seraff took the lead of the prisoner detail. They moved through the tube. The massive door at the end of the hall opened and closed behind them.

They disappeared and The Mick was walking to us as, if on cue.

"Mr. Cruz," he said.

"I've never known how to address you, since I see you so rarely. Are you The Mick or Mr. Mick?"

"When I'm not in the room, The Mick. Otherwise, Mr. Mick."

"Is that the name on your driver's license?"

He shot a funny look at me. "Well, of course not. My real name is classified."

"I'm not sure I believe that, but I turn over the care of Dot to you, Mr. Mick."

"If he's bodyguarding me, where are your bodyguards?" Dot asked me.

"Don't worry about my security," I said.

We all saw them coming from another disembarkment tunnel—Mr. Ping and an army of samurai soldiers.

"Where's the Martian?" I asked Seraff.

We waited on the high observation platform, watching every newly docking spaceship, and the monitors showing their disembarking passengers and crew.

"He's in an orbiting spacecraft."

"Along with his fellow Martians?"

"He's not alone, if that's what you're asking. Do you know something?"

"No, but I doubt this will be as easy as seeing them and arresting them without a whisper of trouble."

"Why not?" Seraff asked. "Most suspects are apprehended by law enforcement, and taken into custody without incident every day on Earth, and off-world."

"The Asimovians are far, far from being 'most suspects.'"

I walked over to Blade Gunner and Sarah, who were also watching from the platform. It was Blade Gunner I wanted to talk to.

"Does Gidrah have soldiers?"

Blade Gunner turned to look at Ping and the samurai soldiers standing behind us all. "Like you do."

"They're on loan from the Orochi Corporation," I said, then asked again. "Do they?"

"Yes."

"So, if the Asimovians are coming, Gidrah is coming. Or are they already here?" I asked.

I started scanning the crowds of passengers below the platform, and those in the station eateries.

I stepped back over to Seraff. As I did, I saw that he was anxious, talking on his ear-piece.

"What's happening?" I asked.

"We think the Asimovians' spaceship is the third in the queue to dock."

My recurring nightmare of my first dreaded encounter with the cult of Super Cyborgs was soon to be reality.

"I don't like this," I said to Seraff. "Where's Gidrah?"

"Mr. Cruz, I don't know why you've convinced yourself that this will be some kind of worst-case-scenario situation."

"Clear the station."

"What?"

"If the Asimovians are coming, so is Gidrah. We don't know who the Gidrah people are, so let's assume *all* of them are Gidrah."

"Mr. Cruz, that is ridiculous. Why would a secret megacorp be here?"

"They were created to destroy the Asimovians, and this is what they've been waiting their whole lives for. I think they're here."

"I don't."

"If no one is on the platform when the Asimovians arrive, then better for us. Why do you have this 'the universe is fluffy and sweet' outlook? My worst-case-scenario outlook on life is what we need. If we have an explosion, or massive laser-gunfire here, we'll all find ourselves floating around dead in the expanse of space."

"The space station's walls are too impenetrable for that."

"They said that about the Titanic, too, and it's at the bottom of the Great Oceans. Nothing will be harmed by clearing the platform."

Seraff relented, but was still not moving fast enough for me.

I held up my hand to Ping to stay where he was, as I went to the express elevator to the main floor, where the passengers were.

Every travel terminal had an Information Center, and the space station terminal was no different. I walked to the desk where two women stood, wearing white uniforms.

"Good morning, sir. How can we help?" one asked.

"I'd like to make an announcement over the PA system."

"What kind of message, sir?"

"I haven't decided yet exactly, but once you give me the microphone, I'll know." I pulled my detective license from my jacket. "This is a police matter."

"Sir, that's an Earth license. We're not on Earth."

I pointed at Seraff and his men on the platform above. "Those are Interpol police, and I'm with them. Do I need them to come down to direct you?"

"That would be helpful, sir."

Seraff had to come all the way down, and talk to them. Finally, I was given the microphone.

"Listen up, Gidrah snake people! We have already identified you from your seven-headed snake tattoos on your teeth! We will not let you and the Asimovians turn this space station into Swiss cheese. Everyone waiting for a flight, or sitting at a table, please move to the exits immediately. The Asimovians will be docking soon, and your space war will not be happening today. Move to the exits now!"

Seraff couldn't believe I had said that; he looked at people's faces. Some thought it was a prank, others were confused, others nervous. What happened next could only be described as surreal. When I had told Seraff to assume that everyone was Gidrah, I'd wanted us to be safe and not sorry. I didn't know that everyone *was* Gidrah!

The two information booth women shot at me, then Seraff first. How they missed I don't know. I realized I was without my gun, which was the same as being naked in space, but Seraff had his. He shot both women.

I found myself desperately wanting to become one with the floor as everyone else shot at us, and up at the platform.

I heard people land near me. I managed to peek up to see several samurai soldiers creating a human shield to protect me. Two of them were shot, and fell dead to the ground, but the others were machine-gun-firing maniacs.

It all stopped. I looked up again and saw that everyone in the terminal was dead.

Seraff had managed to not get killed. Half of his men had shielded Blade Gunner and Sarah. Several of them were dead. The others had used the platform as their rapid-fire sniper post. Ping was alive, of course, and several of his samurai soldiers were dead, but his army had successfully put down the bulk of the Gidrah attack.

"It was too easy," I yelled as I got up from the floor.

I ran to Seraff. "Are these all the passengers—arriving and departing? Here on the main observation platform. Are there any others?"

Seraff and his men looked around.

"There are the first-class passengers," one of his men said.

Seraff ran to the Information Station, and typed on the console. All the monitors showed the view of the first-class passenger area. We gasped as we saw dozens of people standing together. They had what looked like closed umbrellas in their hands, but these objects weren't umbrellas. The people were all touching the tips together. As each person touched his or her umbrella to the tips of another, then another, a yellow glow grew brighter, and the hum grew louder.

They could see that third spaceship—the Asimovians—on their monitor closing in on the station to dock. We knew what they were doing. The umbrellas were pieces of their own portable laser death-cannon. There was no doubt in my mind that they were going to blast through the station's "impenetrable" walls to blow the Asimovians out of space—even if it meant destroying the entire space station and killing everyone aboard, including themselves. The tips, where all the umbrellas were touching, now glowed white, as the last of the passengers in the room moved to touch their final umbrella weapons.

I looked at Seraff. He wore the console headset, and I could see from the faces of the people on the counter's screen that he was on some kind of video-conference call. His fingers typed as fast as PJ's. When he stopped, part of the console slid open. His held his finger above a single button; it turned green. He pressed it.

We watched on the main screens as the wall of their entire first-class waiting room opened to space. Everything—people, furniture, cups, umbrellas, hats, purses, everything—blew out. The wall closed.

My mouth hung open. I had heard of people being spaced, but I'd never seen it happen. One moment the Gidrah people had been in there; the next, they were gone. We looked outside the massive station windows to see the bodies and things float by.

Seraff was unemotional. I was glad he had done what he did, but I was still in shock. It would pass. They were, after all, about to kill us all. But they represented only one set of the psychopaths we had to deal with.

I heard Ping's mobile ring, and I ran to him.

"It's him!" I yelled.

"Who?" he asked

"Mr. Viper. Can you instantly trace the call?"

"Of course, or my phone wouldn't accept the call."

"He knows that. It means he has at least one spaceship in orbit, and will fire on the space station to kill us all." These Gidrah people seemed fixated on killing this space station.

Ping yelled something in Japanese at a couple of his men.

Seraff stood next to us. "If Cruz is right, there are only two spaceships in orbit with a clear shot, maybe a third, if they have missile capability."

"Yes, we know." Ping opened the mobile to answer. We saw the face of Mr. Viper on the small screen.

"Ah, Mr. Cruz. This is your doing. A great criminal mastermind once said, 'When you have a chance to kill your nemesis, never hesitate.'"

All we saw on the station's main view-screens were three ships blown to bits.

The image of Mr. Viper abruptly cut off.

"Yes, Mr. Viper. The Orochi Corporation believes the same," Ping said.

Do—not—shoot—lasers—in space.

Mr. Viper was gone and I would sleep well knowing I wouldn't be finding any more snakes in my sonic shower.

But at what price?

Mr. Ping and his remaining samurai soldiers were being arrested by the space station authorities. Like one of the fundamental tenets of driving "You can't hit people!"—Up-Top's rule of all rules was that you couldn't shoot lasers and blow up things in space. Even Up-Toppers weren't allowed to shoot and blow up things in space, the moon, or Mars (though there were no laws prohibiting the use of lasers to blow up things up on Earth from space, a factoid we Earthers knew).

I didn't know if the Orochi Corporation had also blown up two innocent spaceships just to get the one with the Gidrah people, or if all three had been Gidrah spaceships. Whatever the truth was, they would have their day—or years—in court to prove it. Until then, the Orochi Corporation business Up-Top was over. I found myself without any samurai soldiers.

I noticed The Mick standing on the platform with a gun in his hand.

"What are you doing here?" I yelled. "Where's Dot?"

"She's fine."

Later I learned that he had dropped her off with the Royal Lux family, who were on the station at the time.

"Flight Starburst is docking."

What?

All flights were supposed to have been holding in orbit around the station while space police conducted their investigation.

"It's him!" I heard a panicking Sarah yell.

Everyone watched the monitors.

"Override!" Seraff yelled. "Stop that ship from docking."

I saw the panic on everyone's faces as we helplessly watched the ship continue its docking procedures. On the monitors, we could see them.

I had seen big cyborgs before. My last case I had the "great pleasure" of working with the Hyperion Hippos, one of the gangs of the former Animal Farm Crime Syndicate. That was the difference between a down-below world of analog technology, and an Up-Top digital technology world.

The coming cyborgs were unlike anything we had ever seen. It wasn't so much that they were tall, though they were; they were bulging with muscles in a way that seemed impossible. Pecs, arms, thighs, quads, traps, forearms, back—they were as wide as they were tall, and it was all muscle, synthetic muscle. The only metal showing were their fingertips, and the illuminated pupils beaming through their shades.

We had barely escaped with our lives against the Gidrah people, and they had been just normal people. Ping and his men were in handcuffs. How were we going to stop these Super Cyborgs?

"Stop them!" Sarah C yelled. "If they get onto the station, we're all dead."

The panic from the police was tangible. Seraff barked orders into the station comm system to get reinforcements, shut down power, and shut down sections. I could feel death approaching, as we watched the Super Cyborgs exit their ship, and start down the tube to the station.

I pushed Seraff aside and yelled into the comms. "We have a possible priority Type-X biological contaminant in Starburst docking section. Repeat, Type-X, possible xeno-organism in Starburst docking section."

All the lights in the space station terminal turned red. Who would have thought that my knowledge of germs due to my managed germophobia would have saved all our lives?

The station systems did what they had been programmed to do. The entire section in which the Super Cyborgs were unlucky enough to be in was sealed, and pulled apart from the rest of the station. We watched the Super Cyborgs pummel the sides of the wall with such force that we were sure the wall would rupture. None of them seemed to be the slightest bit fearful about breaking the seal. They were mad!

"They can survive in a void without air for extended periods!" Sarah yelled.

Seraff moved me aside from the comms. "My turn."

Outside the station, the section moved into another, much larger, almost clear container. Sarah and others watched from the large viewport; the rest of us watched the monitors.

From behind the pack of enraged Super Cyborgs pounding the walls appeared the largest cyborg of all. He had a crewcut, and cyborg after cyborg stopped, and moved out of his way, as he neared the wall. His fist was larger than my body. With one frightening punch, he shattered the entire wall. The tube container shattered into pieces. The Super Cyborgs floated in the clear container, but the station bots were already flying it away.

For a moment Mr. T. could stare at his former commander, with glowing red pupils—no emotion. He did not move. Sarah C stared back at her former general as he, his Asimovians, and the container disappeared into the dark of space. Dozens of spaceships appeared and disappeared in their direction.

CHAPTER 66

Brother and Sister

Was it over?

Gidrah. The Asimovians. All of it. I couldn't take much more of it. I wanted this canine case done with for good.

Everything seemed to be over, but everyone was panicking to make sure there would be no more surprises.

The man Up-Top considered the most dangerous individual in the known universe (which meant the very tiny corner of our solar system), Blade Gunner, was gone—and so was Sarah C.

No one saw me duck out the terminal, except for The Mick. I ran from one tube to another with Run-Time's third VP watching my back.

I found them. Sarah C was waiting. It didn't matter what the station's security was. If they wanted to steal a spaceship, consider it stolen.

"We never got to talk privately about Susan," she said.

"Susan is fine. The plastic surgeon doesn't know her, you, from anyone. Susan has a new face and a new identify. She has a new job— nothing to do with technology this time."

"Good. We only wanted her to have a life—and to be happy, despite what we did."

"She will."

"Mr. Cruz, you have fulfilled all your cases for us beyond anything we could have asked."

"Just give me some stellar reviews."

Sarah managed a smile. "We will."

"Sarah—are you—real?" I asked.

My question struck a raw chord in her. "Why would you ask that?"

"The Asimovians wanted you alive. My secretary got me copies of the Asimovian manifestos. They considered non-cyborg humans inferior, lesser beings. They would never follow a normal human. Did your brother 'upgrade' you?"

She didn't have to answer the question. I could read it in her hesitation to answer.

"What are you, then?"

"I don't think there's a proper term. All my cells are synthetic, replaced, each and every one. I was born biological, but remade. There is no definition for the type of cyborg that I am. I am a machine—a machine with a human soul."

"That's why they want you."

"Yes, the key to the Asimovian 'paradise' was me. We would be ruled by AI, with Super Cyborg intermediaries, and humankind would be served by robots. However, all organic would be replaced by the synthetic. Then humanity would be unrestrained to go out among the stars. It wouldn't matter that we didn't have warp drive or wormholes. No matter how long it took, we would get to explore the galaxy."

My mind could barely comprehend the enormity of what the Asimovians had wanted to do.

"Did Gidrah know?"

"No," Blade Gunner answered. "Only the Asimovians—but does it matter? Their goal was a humanity ruled by them."

"What's the plan, then? Escape to Mars?"

"Cruz," Sarah said in a tired voice. "You know what we have to do. The Asimovians, Gidrah, Utopia, Earth, the Martians—no one can be allowed to have either one of us. The only threat to humanity—is us."

I found it hard to keep my eyes from tearing up. They were completely right. Even before we had begun speaking, I knew this would be the last time I ever saw them. I knew that the case to get Susan to safety was their final act to wrap up their affairs in this life.

"Is there anything else I can do?" I asked.

"You've done more than any friend could ask."

She hugged me tightly, then drew away.

Blade Gunner gave me a bear hug with a smile. "Take care of my hat," he directed.

"Done," I answered.

Blade Gunner and his sister ran down the tube, holding hands, to the space shuttle they were going to steal.

I imagined what their final moments must have been like.

Sarah C liked to drive, so she'd be piloting the shuttle. They told me she was the one who'd taken charge, and driven the Pony when I'd passed out after Susan's rescue from the Lab. Blade Gunner would have had some jazz playing over the speakers, as he had when I met with him in his offices, when he was Mr. Looper. He loved that music, no matter what his persona.

Brother and sister would be holding hands as Sarah C pushed the shuttle to maximum speed toward the sun, and Blade Gunner pushed the self-destruct button, which he would easily have enabled.

I didn't have to imagine the next part. I watched it from the viewport—their shuttle exploding outside the station as it sped toward the sun.

CHAPTER 67

The Elvis Clones

Dot was inconsolable. We all were. It was not the time for any Elvis wedding foolishness. The luster of being in space had lost its appeal, even in the palatial quarters of the Royal Lux family. We wanted to go home.

So, that's what we did. We flew back to Earth—from the beautiful starry skies into the thundering storm clouds over Metropolis. When we touched down at Metro Space International, all we wanted was to be out in that miserable, wonderful rain. I would never forget Sarah C and Blade Gunner, despite everything.

However, first things were first. The Concrete Mama would have to wait a little longer. The hovertaxi arrived in Elysian Heights, where Dot lived with her parents.

We arrived at the front door, our long ordeal behind us. Before Dot could open the door, it swung open.

There the Wans stood, Dot's smiling parents, my parents-in-law from hell, dressed in matching Elvis Presley costumes.

"Our spies told us you two like Elvis, huh?" Mrs. Wan uttered.

"Smile wide and show me those Gidrah seven-headed teeth tattoos, Mommy and Daddy Dearest," I said to myself.

Thank you for reading!

Dear Reader,

I hope you enjoyed my **Liquid Cool** cyberpunk detective novel, *Blade Gunner*.

Can You Write Me a Review?

If you enjoyed ***Blade Gunner*** *(Liquid Cool, Book 2)*, I'd greatly appreciate an honest review on one or more of the following sites:

Reviews are the best way for readers to discover good books. My writer's motto is simple: "Readers Rule!" Thanks so much.

Always writing,

Austin Dragon

CONTINUE THE ADVENTURE

Get Your Next *Liquid Cool* Books!

- ***These Mean Streets, Darkly*** *(Liquid Cool Prequel Short)*
- ***Liquid Cool*** *(Liquid Cool: The Cyberpunk Detective Series, Book 1)*
- ***Blade Gunner*** *(Liquid Cool, Book 2)*
- ***NeuroDancer*** *(Liquid Cool, Book 3)*
- ***The Electric Sheep Massacre*** *(Liquid Cool, Book 4)*
- ***I, Alien Hunter*** *(Liquid Cool, Book 5)*
- ***A.I. Confidential*** *(Liquid Cool, Book 6)*

- ***Liquid Cool Box Set*** *(Liquid Cool Prequel and Books 1-3)*
- ***Liquid Cool Box Set 2*** *(Liquid Cool: Books 4-6)*

Also by Austin Dragon

See all my books in science fiction, horror, and fantasy at: **http://www.austindragon.com/books**

ABOUT THE AUTHOR

Austin Dragon is the author of the ***After Eden Series***, including the mini-series, ***After Eden: Tek-Fall***, the classic ***Sleepy Hollow Horrors***, the new epic fantasy adventure ***Fabled Quest Chronicles***, and the cyberpunk detective series, ***Liquid Cool***. He is a native New Yorker, but has called Los Angeles, California home for the last twenty years. Words to describe him, in no particular order: U.S. Army, English teacher, one-time resident of Paris, political junkie, movie buff, Fortune 500 corporate recruiter, renaissance man, dreamer.

He is currently working on new books and series in science fiction, fantasy, and classic horror!

Connect with Austin on social media at:

Website and blog: http://www.austindragon.com

Twitter: https://twitter.com/Austin_Dragon

Pinterest: http://www.pinterest.com/austindragon

Google+: https://google.com/+AustinDragonAuthor

Goodreads: https://www.goodreads.com/ADragon

Other books by Austin Dragon

See all my books at: **http://www.austindragon.com/books**